DION
A TALE OF THE HIGHWAY

BY JONATHAN MAAS

JONATHAN MAAS

Copyright © 2016 Jonathan Maas

All rights reserved.

ISBN-13: 978-1530897308

ISBN-10: 1530897300

WGAW Reg #1868010 and Library of Congress Reg # pending.

A TALE OF THE HIGHWAY

Dedication
To Tommy Munoz
Comedian, Wrestler, Spurs Fan, Friend

Acknowledgments
Too many to mention here, but you know who you are.

CONTENTS

The Dream	13
The Highway	23
The Light of Reason	35
The Thumping	49
Retjar the Damned	81
Ari	91
Running on Empty	113
Cruz's Outpost	131
The Last Party	147
The Gelkins	173
The Crows' Gethsemane	191
The Purple Planet	209
The Jarkeeper	257
The Jarkeeper's Coercions	275
The Perfect Code	295
The Garden	303
The First Party	315

The Note

After a bizarre dream a man wakes up in the middle of a deserted highway, with no clothes, and no memory of who he is. In front of him is a vehicle with keys and a note inside: *Drive this forward. Drive, or there will be consequences. The consequences will be immediate, and they will get worse with every transgression.*

The Highway

The task is straightforward, but what happens next is anything but. As he unravels the mysteries of both his past and future, he'll come to understand that there are dark truths around him, and he'll find that those who wrote the note meant every word of their threat.

But underneath the terror he'll find an inner strength, and he'll find the power that comes from reason. He'll need them both – because his decisions on this lonely night will impact this world in ways he can't even begin to imagine.

A TALE OF THE HIGHWAY

"Through me, the way is to the suffering city;
Through me, the way is to eternal pain;
Through me, the way among the people lost.

It was Justice that moved my Creator;
Divine Omnipotence created me,
The highest Wisdom and the primal Love.

Before me there were no created things,
Only eternity, and I too, last eternal.
Abandon all hope, ye who enter here!"

- Dante's Inferno, Modern English Translation

A TALE OF THE HIGHWAY

The Dream

I dream that I'm in Hell, though it's not the underworld of the modern day with fire, brimstone and winged demons pointing hooked lances at you from every corner. Instead I find myself in the Hell of old, with rain coming down on me, cold and cursed, dark and endless.

The gloomy Hel of the Norsemen (*Hel* with one *l*) was like this, and the ancient Hades that preceded it was gloomier still. Perhaps the second level of Dante's *Inferno* was like this most of all, where piglike gluttons wallowed in freezing muck, with no hope of salvation.

But this is not the Hell of old, and there are no piglike gluttons wallowing around me. It's just me, alone to face the cursed rain, coming down black, piercing my flesh and ripping into the dreamt floor beneath me.

The rain's not the worst part of this place though. Worse still, I also feel the dearth of hope, and I feel it in the profoundly terrifying way one can only feel in a dream. My world is so dark, so forgotten, and the rain falls so ceaselessly that I find myself envying the faithless, those who have no afterlife in store for them. I'd even trade places with an animal that died centuries ago as a matter of nature, never to be noted, never to be missed, its animal soul not able to experience that which I feel now in this dream, the despair of a believer fallen to a bad end.

/***/

I look around, lucid and conscious, and other than the cursed rain I see that the ground is coated with something like mud, and whatever it is, it feels a little out of place here. The substance is greyer than grey, more lifeless than non-existence itself, and I soon realize that it's the source of my dreamt despair. *Hell is bad, but this substance is somehow worse.*

This strange sludge feels like it can take anything in its grasp and drag it down, then drain it of hope in a place where there is none left to lose.

I see a mound in the distance, ominously large with two protuberances bulging upwards, one on each side. I approach it without hesitation. It's many times my size, but what could damage me further in a place such as this?

I reach the mound and I find that it's actually a creature, one that at some point must have been terrifying in and of itself. But now it's all but overpowered by the grey sludge around us both.

I recognize it though.

It's the dying remains of Cerberus, that three-headed dog whose only purpose is to separate the living from the dead, the underworld from that above.

I shake my head in disbelief. Cerberus is supposed to be a fearsome creature, and in another time would have snarled at me with its three sets of teeth, each one bigger than my body. *In another time this dog would have surely feasted upon my soul, tearing it apart again and again.*

But *this* Cerberus has been muzzled by the sludge. Its teeth are still sharp and I can see that its jaws are still the size of my outstretched body, but the grey has taken the creature, and it now breathes its last faint breaths, wheezing harmlessly by my side.

I then feel a tepid sensation on my leg, perhaps a fish somehow swimming through the mud. I quickly realize that it's not a fish, but rather the giant tongue of one of Cerberus' submerged heads licking my body. I can't tell if it's doing this out of deference or camaraderie, and I wonder if either of those words hold any meaning in this place.

Perhaps this giant dog is just cowed by the despair around us, and with its last act it's just pleading with me to not let it die alone.

/***/

I can't help but feel for this creature, even though in another time its three heads would have ripped me in two. But Cerberus is not going to do that now and I pet one of its gigantic heads, whispering soothing words as it lets off its last yelp.

The last howl is mournful, and I get an odd sense that it's grieving more than just its own death. It feels like it's lamenting the loss of Hell itself, its wail harbinging the end of one era to make way for the next. I look around at the grey sludge and wonder if this place will soon be no more.

I would normally have thought that the destruction of Hell would be a good thing, but from Cerberus' ghostly whimper I can't be completely sure of this. Whatever the case, the massive creature lets off one more defeated breath and collapses into the muck. It lies there as inert as a beached whale, its bulk a reminder that even the mightiest rulers will surely return to nothingness, even the indomitable terrors of the underworld.

/***/

I feel a crushing sense of loneliness now, so much so that I would even wish this creature back in all its fury, if only that I wouldn't have to face this grey muck alone. The rain falls even harder than before, cold and hard, hitting my body like knives. Dante said that the worst of the damned envy every other fate, and I feel that now. I'm alone, and I'd choose any other place than this.

I decide to give up right now, to dive deep into the grey mud and end it. I want the despair to be over, to get away from the cursed rain above. I'll end up like Cerberus beside me, unmoving and all but vanished, but it will be over. I steel myself for the descent, a one-way journey that might even bring me a worse fate than I have now. But I can't really think about this, I can only think about getting out of the rain, leaving this despair and escaping the ceaselessly cutting rain.

I'm about to drop down when I'm stopped by the sound of distant thunder, and a faint crying. I listen again and the thunder claps once more, overpowering and angry. And the crying? It's not exactly the wails of an infant, but rather a *bleating*. I look forward and see a barely perceptible movement through the dark rain, a middle-sized creature with a warm light on its head, walking fearlessly through the muck, its nose barely above the surface like a deer swimming through a river.

It's not a deer, however, but a goat, and it seems to be moving towards me with a purpose, though I know not what.

The thunder roars again, and I don't particularly care for it. My surroundings fill me with desolation, but the lightning—I just don't like it. It comes in terrifying and angry, as piercing as the rain around me. The rain lacerates my flesh and the lightning threatens to do the same, and I want both to stop.

The goat seems all right at least. It's got a single glowing horn right in the middle of its head, but other than that, it's just a goat. It's not of the lightning, it's not of the grey mud, and it's not Cerberus either, so I welcome it.

It seems like a friend, or at the very least a guide.

I wade forward to meet it halfway, and it bleats again, undeterred by the rain and muck surrounding it. The creature's either unafraid or unaware of its dismal environment, but whatever the case, it gives me courage. I pet its matted head and it shakes my hand off, still a goat. I take a look at its single prong, iridescent and shining with a strange, powerful light.

The light makes me feel that anything is possible, even in a despairing environment such as this.

The goat turns around and walks towards the distant thunder, and though the sounds of the lightning still terrify me, I follow. I follow the goat and follow the light of its horn, a light that tells me there is *hope*. I don't know how I might escape this dreamt place, but the glowing horn tells me that I *can*, and that's all that matters. I know that I'll be able to escape from Hell, and if I can do that I know that I'll be able to do anything when I get out—*anything*.

/***/

We come to an intersection, if you can call it that, because there's mud all around, and the four paths no longer have distinguishing edges. The roads are all gone, but the goat has led me to four ends, four fates with no more visible roads to them, but distinct paths nonetheless.

In front of me I see the formerly distant lightning, cruel and unforgiving, sent with a purpose. I sense that it's angry at me, as if I've done something wrong and a punishment awaits me there, or at the very least a scolding. To the left of me I see a place of torrential winds, and a young woman being blown about therein, helpless to the gales that buffet her without stopping.

Beside this woman I see another path leading towards an iridescently purple planet, shimmering with indescribable colors but with cracks of the grey color that now surrounds me, like a ruby beginning to rot.

To the right of me I see a room with the same light as the goat's single horn, and though it's distant, small and surrounded by the gloom of this place, it shines strongly and gives me comfort. The light gives something *stronger* than just hope.

I look at the goat to ask where I should go first, and it bleats in response. It's up to me, and I consider my options for a moment.

I feel compelled to move forward to meet the thunder, not out of some sort of self-loathing or some strange desire to inflict harm upon myself, because such desires don't have real meaning in a place such as this. My desire to move forward is one born of a strange sense of *responsibility*, an emotion that feels unsettling to me, but one that I can't ignore.

I move towards the thunder without a second thought and everything disappears, everything but the lightning in front of me, overpowering, crackling with life and anger despite its deathly surroundings.

/***/

I enter this chamber, if you can call this featureless area that, and I realize that even the lightning isn't immune to the grey sludge's influence. The bolts crackle ceaselessly, threatening to leave me as ashes each time they do so, but the electricity seems to be disheartened by the mud beneath. It explodes through the sky but seems to stop right before it hits the ground.

I sense that we're no longer alone, and the single-pronged goat beside me looks forward, calmly sniffing the air in front of him. There's a presence here, and the goat bleats as if to announce my arrival. The unseen presence in front of me grows stronger and angrier, but since the goat is still showing no fear, I also decide to have none.

The sky crackles, and I hear a deep male voice coming from the darkness:

    YOU HAVE DISAPPOINTED ME,
    SON.

I'm taken aback by the words. *Disappointed? Son?* The voice is resolute, as overpowering as the lightning that preceded it. I'm not exactly frightened, but I am a little surprised. *It called me* Son*, and I don't remember having a father. In fact I don't remember anyth—*

    YOU HAVE DISAPPOINTED ME

> FOR YOUR WHOLE EXISTENCE.
> BUT BEFORE THIS, YOU HAVE
> BEEN JUST AN ORDINARY
> WASTREL, DOING NOTHING
> AND ACCOMPLISHING THE
> SAME. BUT NOW—

I hold up my hand to quiet him, and then tell him that I don't know what he's talking about, let alone who he is. My voice doesn't quiver either, not one bit. A father's scolding might bring fear in other circumstances, but a scolding from an unremembered father brings nothing but utter incomprehension. I look down at the goat, and it doesn't lend me any insight, but seems to suggest that I listen. The voice continues:

> YOU HAVE ACTED FOR THE
> FIRST TIME IN YOUR LIFE,
> DISOBEYING ME. DOING THIS
> HAS WROUGHT UNTOLD
> DESTRUCTION UPON OUR KIND.
> DOING THIS WILL WREAK
> DESTRUCTION UPON THIS
> WORLD. LOOK AROUND YOU
> AND SEE THAT THIS WILL BE
> THE WORLD'S FATE. LOOK
> AROUND YOU AND SEE THAT IT
> IS ENTIRELY YOUR FAULT.

But how could this be my fault when I don't even know what's happening, when I don't even know my own—

> YOU WILL FIX THAT WHICH YOU
> HAVE DEFILED, THAT WHICH
> YOU HAVE RUINED. YOU WILL
> FIX THIS. I WILL MAKE SURE OF
> IT.

/***/

Before I can say another word, before I can look at the goat for further guidance, the floor drops beneath me. I descend through the grey muck, falling, falling and then falling some more. I drop further and further until I realize that I'm suspended in nothingness, and no longer in the grey sludge. I feel a profound emptiness around me, not as if everything is now gone, but as if I'm in a place where nothing ever was.

I try to turn around but find this impossible, because I have no leverage with which to push off. I then see distant stars and realize that I'm in space, and I wonder if this place is a truer eternity than the Hell from which I had just been ejected. *You can move in the underworld, and as I've just seen, even Hell can change. But space? Nothing changes here, not ever.*

I then look down and see that I'm mistaken, for I see Earth, and it's suffering much the same fate as the purple planet that I'd glimpsed in the other chamber. The earth has a grey coating upon it spreading over the land, and a few spots staining the ocean. The world is being cleaned neatly, a drop of grey starting in one place and then spreading outward, and it's growing on every continent. There's even spots on the icy poles.

/***/

I feel a presence beneath me and look down to see a gigantic, dark creature. It seems even more massive than the earth because it's much closer, and it's getting closer with every moment. I then realize that *it* is not the one getting closer, but rather I'm falling towards it, captured by the unyielding, inexorable pull of its gravity. I look down and it's difficult to see, for whatever it is, it's nearly as black as the space behind it. I squint and can barely make out an oversized narrow edge jutting out from it, and I see that this edge is split into two. It spreads it two limbs, fanning them out until its outline forms an eclipsing silhouette against the sun. It stretches its appendages further until I see feathers and—

It's a crow. A giant crow.

I'm moving too quickly to consider the inexplicable nature of the situation, and I soon realize that its jutting edge is actually a beak, and its jaws are splitting apart so that it can swallow me whole. I fall towards it, picking up speed, and see the full enormity of that which is about to prey upon me. I fall deeper into the crow's beak until the half-decayed earth disappears, then the sun, then the stars and then everything else. Just darkness, and then—

/***/

I awake from this dream.

It's odd because I rarely remember my dreams, and when I wake I almost always remember the night before, no matter what happened. But this dream I remember in its full bizarreness, and as far as my memory upon waking, when I awake in the real world I remember—

/***/

Nothing. I don't know where I am, let alone why I'm here. I remember the dream as if it were real, but I don't know who I am, not even my own name.

A TALE OF THE HIGHWAY

The Highway

Let me take a step back. I know who I am *now*, as I'm telling you this. I remember everything, or at least know enough to understand it. I'm *me* again, that's for sure.

I'll try to keep thoughts from my "fully-aware" present self to a minimum, and when I do, I'll add them as footnotes.[1]

But I want to tell you the tale as it happened, in the moment, when I woke up on that long, unnamed stretch of highway. It's a better-told tale this way, and if you've stuck with me through that strange dream, I think you've earned that much. In any case, when I wake up in the real world I remember—

/***/

Nothing. I don't know where I am, let alone why I'm here. I remember the dream as if it were real, but I don't know who I am, not even my own name. All I know is what's around me: the hard road, the cold air against my naked body, the night sky and a big car in front of me, its driver-side door wide open.

The sky is lit only by the moon and I have a blazing headache and an empty feeling in my chest. I want to vomit. The anguish is enough to convince me to close my eyes and lie back down on the asphalt. I do this, and though the headache remains the other feelings dissipate. The chyme that had been swelling up in my throat drops back down into my midsection, and I feel a little better. After a few moments I open my eyes cautiously, worrying the moonlight is going to hurt. But oddly enough, it helps. I let the moon wash over me and my headache is soothed, and I'm soon as I once was.

---

[1] No spoilers either, or at least I'll try for none. Just a few thoughts here and there that I can't let go unmentioned. But if you're the kind of person who skips footnotes, not a problem. Just extra thoughts here and there.

A TALE OF THE HIGHWAY

I can't be sure of this though, because I don't remember who I once was. Still, there's no more pain, and that's all I can think of right now. I don't know if I experienced a hangover,[2] but I feel a lot better. I look at the moon, and it stares back at me, as if to let me know that everything is going to be OK.[3]

/***/

I stand up, feeling great until I realize that I still have no idea where I am, let alone *who* I am. Or why I have no clothes on. Or why I'm in the middle of the road with nary a soul around. Or why there's a car in front of me, a big one, with its front door wide open.

/***/

I walk on bare feet to the car and it's a rather upscale, surprisingly spacious vehicle with thick round tires, and keys that are dangling from the ignition. There's also a message on the seat:

> Drive this vehicle. Drive along this road, in the direction that the vehicle is pointed now. Drive until this road ends, and then drive some more.
>
> Drive, or there will be consequences.
>
> If you do not drive, there will be

---

[2] Funny how hangovers act like this. We all expect so much from the night before: a new mate, unforgettable times, life itself. And when the wine delivers on every last promise, we want the exact opposite the next morning. We want sleep, quiet, and complete freedom from discomfort. All we want from the night before is to feel everything, and all we want the next morning is to feel absolutely nothing.

[3] It wasn't going to be OK, of course, but for the moment I feel great, and it is.

consequences. If you stop, there will be consequences. If you change directions, there will be consequences. If you drive until this road ends, but fail to drive some more, there will be consequences.

The consequences will be immediate, and they will get worse with every transgression.

I guess I should drive.

/***/

I can drive at least. I'm naked, and I don't remember anything, but I know how to drive. Turn the ignition while instinctually depressing the brake pedal with my foot.[4]

I don't feel particularly compelled to follow the note's commands, and something deep inside tells me to get out of the vehicle and *run*. I could run down the highway in the opposite direction, into the adjacent field, anywhere.

But I drive. Naked in a strange car, headed down a deserted highway in the middle of nowhere.

Drive along this road until this road ends, and then drive some more.

The instructions are straightforward, at least. I depress the gas

---

[4] My short-term memory is gone, but some of my long-term memory is intact. I don't know who I am at this point, but I know how to drive, how to breathe and how to run from trouble.

pedal, and my foot feels odd, vulnerable.[5]

Still, I look outside and see the moon watching over me. It gives me strength, like a mother watching her child play from afar. If I should fall and hurt myself the moon will be there, worrying at least.

But I know I've got to be wary of the empty world around me.

The moon watches over me, but the ground beneath is very real. And if I fall, there will be consequences.

/***/

I pass a cornfield ahead, stalks dense, impenetrable, but edges too square and too well planned to hold danger. It's not an impenetrable rain forest, alive with sounds of shrieking animals waiting to keep you there forever, nor is it a dreamt meadow filled with magic and mystery.

It's a cornfield, a place designed to nourish the world, a place I can also see is great for hiding. I'm in trouble but this dense piece of farmland is safe, and good things happen when no one is looking.[6]

Perhaps the best way to deal with vanished memories is to make new ones.

I laugh at the thought, and it sounds familiar. I don't know if it's my own aphorism, and I'm not sure it makes complete sense, but it sounds

---

[5] There are certain barriers between oneself and this world that we take for granted, like sleeping under a thin blanket even when it's hot outside. Gas pedals aren't meant to touch bare skin either, even in the wildest of times.

[6] Cornfields are great for hiding, but I don't normally think of them as designed to hide from enemies or unforeseen danger. They're great for hiding from *consequences, responsibility* and other soul-deadening words. A cornfield is where you take a few friends, and more than a few drinks, out of the sight of all those who would judge you. A cornfield conceals, protects, shares your secrets and reveals them to no one. It hides you from watchful eyes, and allows interesting things to happen.

pretty good right about now.

/***/

I pull over to the side of the road, take the keys from the ignition and get out. My soles aren't quite thick enough for the asphalt beneath, and I look forward to the soothing crackle of dirt and leaves underneath my feet. I know that I'll soon be in nature—a square-edged plot of domesticated nature, perhaps, but still more real than asphalt.

I face the cornfield. Its stalks are kissed with moonlight and swaying ever so slightly: a beautiful portrait that moves when you take your eyes away. I want to go in, but I also feel the urge to bring something to this—*event*, whatever it is. I have my health, I have the cornfield—I just need something.

I need a bottle.

/***/

I find a case in the backseat, and it's *filled* with bottles. It's hard to differentiate them in the darkness, but my long-term memory kicks in and I see them as filled with wine: some red, some white and a few rosé. There's even a perfectly clear bottle tucked in a slot. It looks like it's filled with water, but I can sense from the calligraphy on its label that it's anything but.

In any case I just need a bottle, so I take one out and it's a cabernet sauvignon, and I sense that it's a medium-grade vintage. I can't exactly say why, but I think it's a fitting start, so I decide to take it.[7]

---

[7] In retrospect, I think my affinity for this bottle came from my long-term memory, and came for two reasons. First of all, it's a cabernet sauvignon. Cabs are the can't-miss grape that make can't-miss wine, and I may have gravitated towards it during this time just to hold on to something solid. Second of all, I may have liked the fact that it was a medium-grade wine. Too cheap and there's no point – too expensive and it puts too much weight on the event. I'm

A TALE OF THE HIGHWAY

I grab the bottle's neck and head out into the cornfield, still without a reason to do so, and I'm about to reach the stalks when I realize that I don't have a corkscrew.

This is a problem, though just a small one.

There's still a lot of ways to open a bottle without one, so I look around for a knife. There's no knife around, so I look for a shoe.[8] I'm still naked, so there's not one of those either.

I don't want to smash the neck of the bottle against the ground—too much mess. Too much broken glass for someone else to clean up, and I just can't do that. I need a drink, but not at the cost of doing something that uncouth.

So I take the bottle and enter the cornfield. At the very least I can hide amongst the moonlit stalks, and there might be someone or even some*thing* to help me. You never know.

/***/

The stalks are tall and sturdy, nearly twice my height. Their stems are evenly spaced, and their leaves spread out to make a thicket.

I can hide amongst the stalks quite easily, but there's nothing here to help open this bottle, nothing that won't break immediately. Still, I don't worry about it, and keep going, and then I see someone, or perhaps some*thing*.

/***/

I soon find it's a little of both. It's a scarecrow set amongst the stalks. A stuffed effigy, arms askew with a narrow belted waist and two pant legs that spread outwards, making something between an *X* and a

---

headed out to a cornfield with a can't-miss medium-grade cabernet. Let's see what happens.

[8] My long-term memory served me well in a few cases, and I had quite a bit of long-term memory about parlor tricks such as these.

T. A hay-filled martyr, hung from the poles as a warning to all those who would deign steal the field's harvest. The scarecrow isn't too effective though, because I see a crow perched on its shoulder, all but blending in with the night sky behind it. I recognize the bird from somewhere, and when it opens its mouth to caw at my arrival, I know precisely where.

It's the crow from my dream, or at least it looks similar.

Fortunately, this bird is normal-sized and refrains from swallowing me whole. It just looks at me and then caws once more before flying away, presumably to tell its friends that I've invaded the field and that they should act accordingly.

The bird disappears quickly and quietly, pure black against the light-blue night, a shadow that flies away from the moon.

I turn my attention back to the scarecrow, and realize that it has shoes. They're worn out, bleached by the sun and containing more holes than actual shoe, but they have soles at the bottom. I take the shoe off and then find a flat rock on the ground. I place the sole on the rock and pound the bottle against the sole. The cork lifts up, then lifts up some more until I can pull it out. I hold the bottle up to the moon, and toast her.

I still don't know who I am or where I am at this point, but I realize that the moon's there for me and always has been.[9] I'm grateful for her presence, I really am.

/***/

---

[9] You should remember this too if you're ever drinking alone. You've got companions all around, perhaps none so ever-present as the moon. She helped your ancestors navigate the cold, unforgiving seas, and she was watching over you since your birth. So next time you're alone in the night, look up. She might be hiding behind a cloud, or perhaps visible only as a sliver, but she's there with you, and has been every moment of your life.

A TALE OF THE HIGHWAY

The scarecrow's shoes don't quite fit me, but the clothes do. Somewhat. They hang off me like the rags that they are, with crow-pecked holes leaving my skin exposed. It's better than naked though. I don't mind naked if it's the norm wherever I am, but my long-term memory tells me that it usually isn't, so I feel fortunate to wear something at least.

I tie the clothes around me as best as I can, shaping them until I'm just a man down on his luck, not someone deranged. If someone sees me now they might feel pity, but they won't fear me. I don't know who I am, but the thought of being feared makes me uncomfortable. Intimidation doesn't give me a thrill, it's not who I am.

I strap the shoes on as best as I can, and though they don't fit perfectly my feet hold on to them. At the very least I'll need them for the other wine bottles, because I've all but drained the cabernet in my hand.

I take the last draft straight from the bottle, savor it, and think of all the work it took to bring this to my lips. I don't know the wine process,[10] but I can think about the collective effort it took to fill the contents of this bottle, and I'm thankful for it.

I feel fortunate to be here, drinking wine, and I toast the moon again and feel good.[11] I still don't know who I am or where I am, but I

---

[10] I of course know the winemaking process *now*, from the grapes, to fermentation, to—that's about it. That's the beauty of the whole thing: its simplicity. Grow the right grapes, take their juice, let it ferment. All you need to get those three steps just right is a few centuries of accumulated knowledge, and you have it.

[11] I've always thought that the desire for a glass of wine and the need for *a drink* come from two different places. You *enjoy* a glass of wine, but an end-of-day gin and tonic? That's a punch in the face. More accurately, it's *relief that becomes routine*, the always-waiting reward that prevents a grey-faced workadaddy from quitting his job and sailing around the world. Don't get me wrong: stiff drinks hold a great place in this world's history, but they're often just there to wrap up the 9–5, the reverse of one's morning coffee. Wine might

can feel good, and that gives me the first clue to my identity.

You woke up from a hellish dream only to find your memory gone and a car with a threatening note in it. But you still find a way to feel good. You can enjoy yourself and be appreciative of this world, even in a time such as this.

/***/

I come back to the vehicle, and I realize that something isn't right. The car's still there, and I'm still alone, but something's not right. I look ahead of me and see nothing, and then nothing again on both sides of the road. I notice something behind me, though, a faint bit of movement. There's a flit in the air, a soundless quiver cutting through the night. I can't see it clearly, but I can sense it coming. I can sense *them* coming. Them, it, him.

The crow. And he's brought some friends.

They come forward like a cloud, a dark wisp of smoke barely visible in the night. The murder flies together until they coalesce, and take on two distinct shapes.

The shapes look like two men, and I see that they're both walking towards me.

/***/

One man is big and dark, a smooth chocolate brown that gives him a timeless age. Head shaved smooth, ears folded neatly backwards, nothing for an opponent to grab onto if they choose to fight dirty. A big man, too, a body that could have gone to pot, but its owner chose not to let that happen. Probably does a lot of push-ups, a lot of other things

---

hold the same relief, but it's an experience. Every bottle holds a unique flavor, a unique story—and it's an experience.

too. Ageless. He could be twenty, could be fifty, could be a thousand.

The other man (if you could call him a man, because like his partner he was a flock of birds only a few moments ago) is slightly different. Paler, thinner. Still of indeterminate age. Shaved head, in shape, but he doesn't seem to be a fan of push-ups. He looks like the kind of guy who avoids any and all vices, well past the point of being good for your health. I'd bet he doesn't even drink.

They're both well dressed, wearing matching dark suits that look like they've been custom tailored, and somehow made out of feathers.

I don't know who they are, but I take out another bottle for them. A straightforward merlot.[12] It will give us something to talk about, and if they don't like it I'll get another from the back. I have no glasses, but I'll offer them the first swig.

I place the shoe on the asphalt and give the bottle a few gentle hits. Cork goes up, then I twist it out with my hands. I don't really have a pocket, so I palm the cork, give the men my most sane, broadest smile and then offer them the bottle with the neck pointed outwards.

They don't smile in return.

As I would come to learn later, Crows rarely smile, and when they do, it's for all the wrong reasons.

/***/

The smaller one speaks. I'll call him *the Beak*. I'll learn his real name later, maybe the most frightening name I've ever heard, but at the time I just think of him as *the Beak*.

---

[12] I subconsciously play it safe here, just like I did with the cabernet. A merlot is a bit softer than a cabernet, without so much tannin. Shades of chocolate and plum, a safe peace offering for my two trailing companions. Little did I know that my companions didn't care for any sort of wine, and wanted anything but peace.

"We know you read the note," says the Beak. "And the note was clear. *Drive, or there will be consequences.* You stopped driving."

I can sense that the Beak likes to talk, so I let him talk. Unfortunately, the conversation doesn't exactly take a turn for the better.

"Now it's our turn to do things to you, and they're going to hurt," says the Beak. "A lot. But I want you to understand that what we're about to do is entirely your fault. We wouldn't be here if you hadn't stopped the car. All you needed to do was drive until this road ends, and then drive some more. That's all we asked, and you failed at that, purposefully."

I've already sensed that I'm not one for conflict, and it's pretty clear that these two men are not going to be my friends. Without a moment's hesitation I run towards the car, and I'm planning to jump in and then be on my way, well away from the Beak.

The decision to flee comes easily to me, but I don't see the Beak's friend coming to meet me at the car. The big dark one just *appears* in front of the vehicle, and I soon realize that he's supernaturally fast.

He couldn't have run, because I don't think either of them *run*, but he can sure fly. He may have turned into a crow, maybe a flock of crows, and then turned back into his old self well before I reached the car. Whatever the case he meets me there and pushes me down hard, until my skin scrapes against the asphalt. He straddles my arms with incredible weight, leaving me helpless. He gets up and I still can't move, which is somehow worse. I'm at their mercy, and it looks like they're about to begin.

/***/

I won't go into the grisly details, but know that there are plenty. They take their time, they don't relent, and they are thorough. No part of my body escapes untouched, no patch of skin remains untorn, no joint remains anywhere near its corresponding limb.

The Beak just watches, while the big one does all the work. I'll come to learn that the big one also has a name, one just as grisly as his sole purpose, but after this beating I just called him *the Claws*.

The dark man does stop striking me for a moment, though only to gather his energy for a particularly powerful blow. The Claws winds up and delivers it with perfect form, and it's enough to take me out of this world, at least temporarily.

The Light of Reason

Unconsciousness brings relief from their torment, and it also allows me to dream again. I fall down through the blackness, collapsing into my own mind until the pounding on my body can only be felt as a reverberation in the distance. I know they're still up there punishing my body, but I've now retreated within myself, and can only feel their impact secondhand.

Boom.

Boom.

Another pause and then—

Boom.

This blow is just a bit fainter, due only to the distance. The impact is just as strong as the others, but I'm farther away, falling into the cave's depths while the Claws pulverizes my corporeal form in the earth above.

/***/

I soon find myself back in Hell, and back in the grey sludge. It's been growing in my absence, an expanding decay that decomposes completely, death without the promise of rebirth. I once again see the mound of Cerberus in the distance, and though he's long since exhaled his last three breaths, I'm glad to see something familiar in this chamber.

I approach the heap, still hesitant lest one of its jaws snaps at me in some sort of postmortem spasm. But I soon realize that this won't happen, because Cerberus is dead—more than dead. The creature is now *extinct*, a relic of a past era, never to harm anyone again.

Cerberus is so far gone that it won't even survive in legend, its life so muted that it may as well have never existed in the first place. This dog is more than extinct—he's been erased.

I then see smoke coming from its body, and approach to see an ulcer on its side, an opening where the grey sludge has found a path inward. I peer into the creature's innards, black and terrifying but being overtaken by the grey mud that's now working its way through the oversized corpse, smoldering as it devours the monster's organs.

Cerberus is being dissolved by a despair greater than that which once fueled it.

I then hear a bleat and look up to see the goat, perched upon Cerberus' haunches. The goat isn't looking at me directly, though I'm sure he knows I'm here. He stands on the giant dog indifferently, and I gain strength from that. This goat hasn't succumbed to despair or fear, and might not even be aware that he should feel such things in this place. He's just here, and his single prong glows with a strange warm light.

I look around at the rooms attached to this chamber, first seeing the place where my alleged father stayed. It still crackles with electric energy, but the lightning's power feels a bit more subdued than last time. I see the room with the wind, and I see the portal to the purple planet.

I then take a look at the room with light, and the distant illumination fills me with warmth. It's glowing the same color as the goat's single prong, and I can't help but smile when I see it.

There's hope here. Somehow there's hope in this place, and it's in that room.

/***/

I walk towards the room, and the goat follows behind me at his own pace. The room is quite far away and quite high above me, an alcove tucked away into a mountain. I walk through the grey mud and then upwards, climbing towards the light. It becomes quiet as I climb, and I can once again hear the faint tremors from the darkness above, the echoes of the Claws as he continues to beat my body in the real world.

But that light ...

I understand that I'm in a dark place, and I know that dark truths await me when I return to Earth. But I can't help but feel hopeful as I climb one of Hell's mountains, and approach the light.

/***/

The light is from a room, and the room is graceful and cozy, though I can't quite put a finger on the specifics of its design. It has brilliantly painted walls and wood cabinets, and the cabinets hold an array of accoutrements, art and machinery. I see most every style of painting and sculpture imaginable, with some pieces looking ancient, and some looking modern. There are earthen bowls and elegant plates. There's a wood cask that looks like it's meant to churn butter, and it sits next to a strange translucent cube suspended in smoke.

I look in the middle of the room and see three men sitting around a marble table. The first man is pug-nosed and pot-bellied, the second man is built like a bear and the third man has a refined elegance to his form. They're not yet aware of my presence, and they're arguing.

/***/

"There have been *five* major extinction events before this," says the elegant man. "The Cretaceous-Paleogene event was caused by an asteroid, but asteroids aren't necessary to bring destruction. One extinction was caused by a climate fluctuation, and one was caused by volcanic activity. But in all cases things *die* during these events, and they don't come back. Millions of years of struggle through evolution and adaptation, and then just like *that*—three-fourths of the species on this earth are *gone*, maybe more."

"Do you think extinction events serve a purpose?" asks the snub-nosed man. "If so, what might it be?"

"I deign not venture a guess," says the elegant man. "I don't know if these catastrophes hold a purpose, let alone what it might be."

The snub-nosed man smiles.

"The wise know that they do not know," says the snub-nosed man, before looking at the bearish man. "How about you, Aristocles, do you think there might be a purpose to these events?"

"Nature is always changing," says the big man. "It flows like a river, and will always do so. One lizard born is slightly different than its parents, and even a single human body changes with every moment, growing strong and then decaying as it approaches senescence. Perhaps extinction events are simply a natural manifestation of the natural world, where everything changes, and everything erodes back into nothingness."

"Must everything erode back into nothingness like you say?" asks the snub-nosed man. "Absolutely everything?"

The bearish man smiles.

"Everything in the natural world eventually erodes," he says. "But the natural world isn't all that there is. Ideas don't erode."

"Ideas?" asks the elegant man, mock-shaking his head as if he's heard this thought countless times before.

"Yes, for though a species of lizard might go extinct," says the big man, "the *concept* of the lizard doesn't change."

The big man shakes his head.

"Perhaps a more elegant response lies in mathematics," says the big man.

"Your beloved mathematics," says the elegant man knowingly.

"Yes, my beloved mathematics," says the bearish man. "For though the concept of the lizard might require someone to be around to remember it, a triangle is still a triangle no matter what. Mathematics are unchanging, immutable even if no one is left to remember them."

"And that might very well be the case when all is said and done with this grey mud," says the elegant man.

The bearish man doesn't understand the meaning of this.

"I said we've had five major extinction events *before this*," says the elegant man. "Human growth may have abetted the sixth extinction event on the earthly plane, and it may have started this some time ago. And if you look out our window into the decaying expanse of Hell, you'll see that we may be entering the seventh—"

I hear a bleat and look down to see the goat has announced our presence. His horn glows gently, and I realize once again that it's the same color as the light that illuminates this room. The snub-nosed man turns around, surprised, and then smiles broadly.

"It appears we have a visitor," he says. "A rare sight in these times. What's your name, son?"

"I don't know," I say.

My answer hangs in the warm air for a moment, and then the goat bleats again.

"Well, that's understandable given that you're here," says the pot-bellied man. "However, we can sense that you also have a presence on the earthly plane. Would we be accurate in assuming this?"

"I believe so," I say. "But I can't say anything with certainty."

"That's understandable as well," says the man. "In any case, my name is Socrates, or at least it was. We're shades down here, spirits reflecting what we once were in life."

"Socrates."

"Yes," says the man, now pointing to the man built like a bear. "This is my star pupil, Aristocles, known commonly by his nickname, *Plato*. And beside him you'll see *his* star pupil—Aristotle."

/***/

"The point I was getting at," says Aristotle, not overly impressed by my presence, "is that there were five extinction events before humanity, and humanity *itself* is the sixth. For the last century alone the world's biodiversity has shrunk dramatically, and there's no end in sight."

"I still don't understand the problem," says Socrates, exuding a dramatic, almost comical tone of consternation. "There were five extinction events before this alleged one, and the world survived. What makes this one any different?"

"Ours is completely different," says Aristotle. "Because it's deliberate, or at the very least caused by our *choices*."

"Does that matter?" asks Socrates. "Does it matter to the species obliterated by an asteroid that at least its own dissolution wasn't deliberate?"

"Intent matters when you have *the choice*," says Aristotle. "You of all people taught us that right and wrong lies within each person, and the key is *knowing* what is right. Unlike the previous events, we *know* environmental destruction is the wrong path, and that *does* matter. There's a difference between natural cataclysm and that which comes from humanity, between the inevitable and the avoidable."

"I disagree," says Plato.

"How so?" asks Aristotle. "Look at the world above. Can there be any doubt that humanity is exacting a terrible toll upon this earth?"

"I don't disagree with that," says Plato. "Humanity comes with a great cost."

"A great cost," repeats Aristotle. "A great cost indeed."

Plato shakes his head, then winks at me.

"What I'm saying," says the bearish man, "is that humanity is *worth* the cost."

The goat bleats in agreement.

"How so?" asks Socrates.

"Let's start with your past extinctions," says Plato. "Five great waves of life arrived and left, and what came of them?"

Plato lets the question hang in the warm air for a moment.

"Absolutely nothing," says Plato. "Unless you count fossils, which of course took human innovation to find and then ascribe value to."

Plato smiles.

"But humanity is unlike any other species," says Plato. "Because our kind uncovers *ideas* that do not change. We may destroy millions of years' worth of what we've recently come to learn is called evolution, and that's not right, not by any stretch of the imagination. But at least we get the *idea* of evolution, and countless other ideas as well, which is more than any other previous species has given this world, or to this universe for that matter."

Plato gets up and ambles over to the door. He looks out back over the great expanse of Hell, and he seems to be looking at the room that contained the purple planet.

"I wrote a dialogue called *Republic* touching on the concept of a perfect society when I was on Earth," says Plato. "And though I've learned enough while down here to tweak it in countless ways, I still think humanity can reach that ideal. And part of this new ideal will include harmony with *nature*, Aristotle."

Plato ambles back over to the table, hulking over us but with kind, thoughtful eyes not meant to dominate.

A TALE OF THE HIGHWAY

"I hope humanity gets there, and brings our *ideas* beyond this earth," he says. "But even if humanity fails in this endeavor, it will surely be worth the cost, because the alternative is oblivion at the hands of another extinction event. Sooner or later fate will come for us, just as it's come for everything else. I hope we succeed, but even if we don't—at least we tried."

Aristotle thinks about this, then gets up to look out the door where Plato once stood.

"I don't know if it's worth the cost," says Aristotle.

"The dinosaurs dominated this world for over a hundred million years and nothing came of it," says Plato. "And I agree we may be in the sixth extinction, but—"

"I'm not talking about the dinosaurs," says Aristotle. "And I'm not talking about the sixth extinction either."

Aristotle points towards the grey sludge, now encroaching upon their doorframe.

"I'm talking about this," says Aristotle. "This despair all around us, the seventh extinction."

"The seventh?" asks Plato, looking at Socrates.

"I was about to ask the same question," says the pot-bellied man, shrugging. "Perhaps our visitor can lend some insight?"

The three men look at me, and I shake my head.

"I don't even know my name," I say, now looking at Aristotle. "And I don't know anything about the grey substance, other than it's stronger, and quite possible worse, than Hell. Do you know anything about it?"

"I can't say I do," says Aristotle. "But I have a sense of things, and this material that's encroaching upon our chamber is like nothing we've ever seen. Humanity's failings in the world above are manifold, but they only make Hell stronger. This sludge isn't born of environmental destruction, greed, war or lust. It's something else."

"Something strong enough to destroy Hell," I say.

"Something that *will* destroy Hell, its strength notwithstanding," says Aristotle. "In these times the word *strength* has little meaning."

Aristotle thinks for another moment and then shakes his head.

"I know this grey mud is like nothing I've ever seen in my time down here," he says. "I've tried to classify it, but it defies my desires. It's dangerous though, more dangerous than Hell itself. I feel it's going to destroy this place, and then the world above, including humanity and every perfect idea our kind have. We won't be worth the cost, because everything will be gone. Everything will be eradicated by this matter that comes nearer to us with every passing moment. That's all I know."

Socrates thinks about this and then looks at me again.

"We've been arguing like fools this whole time as if we were real and our guest the shadow," he says. "I think we should ask him what he knows."

"I know nothing," I say.

"Do you?" asks Socrates, once again taking on a dramatic mien of ignorance. "I'd just feel better if I was certain."

/***/

I tell them everything up until this moment, leaving nothing out. I tell them about waking up here amongst the grey sludge, and how the sludge overtook Cerberus. I tell them about the angry lightning. I tell them about waking up again on the road with amnesia, the vehicle and the note. I tell them about the cornfield, the wine and the Crows. I tell them about the beatings, which are still going on at this very moment.

"You may not know your name," says Socrates with a smile. "But it seems to me you know quite a bit."

The goat bleats, and his horn glows until it all but disappears into the room's warmth.

"And there's this goat here," I say. "He seems to be on our side."

Aristotle smiles at this and goes off to a far corner of the room. He opens up a clear cabinet that holds several trays filled with plants grown in a translucent liquid. He takes one of the trays out and places it on the floor before the goat, who sniffs it once before nibbling on the plant matter and slurping up the water.

"I agree—it seems that he's on our side," says Aristotle. "If there are any sides in this time."

Socrates furrows his brow.

"Plato, what do you think?" he asks. "Not what do you *know*, but what do you think?"

Plato thinks.

"I think there are dark forces up on Earth trying to protect Hell from something worse," he says. "These Crows that bring torment are demons, and are not on humanity's side, and they're fighting a battle that we don't want."

"How can I be expected to fight in a battle that I don't want?" I ask. "I don't even remember my own name."

I look out the door towards the cold expanse of the underworld.

"And even if I had my memory," I say, "if the battle's between Hell and Hell's destructor, how could I possibly pick a side?"

They consider this, and then Plato looks at Aristotle.

"What does logic tell us?" asks the big man to the elegant man beside him.

Aristotle thinks about this for a moment.

"When two armies not your own fight over *your* domain, it's best to refrain from choosing sides," he says. "For doing so will either result in ignominious defeat or an unwanted victory."

Aristotle thinks for another moment.

"Can you flee?" he asks.

I remember doing just that, and I remember how quickly the Claws flew towards me the moment after. I shake my head: *probably not*.

"Then consider picking your *own* side," says Aristotle. "The side of truth."

"What do you mean by this?" I ask.

Aristotle nods at Plato.

"Many years ago, Socrates was just a man who came to Athens," says Plato. "All he did was stand in the center of town and ask questions, and he'd ask them to anyone who came by. Man, woman, child or slave, the rich and the paupers alike. That's all he did, and it soon incurred the wrath of a few powerful people. Socrates' questions would seem mild today by comparison, but he was charged with *corrupting the youth*, and was forced to drink hemlock for his sins."

Socrates takes no pride in this tale, but Plato does and looks on his mentor admiringly.

"There was an odd clash of ideas at the time, a battle much more esoteric than the one you're experiencing," says Plato. "But Socrates picked his *own* side, the side of *truth* that Aristotle just mentioned. Socrates found his truth in the form of questioning, and *your* truth may come in another form. But my teacher chose his side, and though it led to his death, he changed the world for it. He never wrote down a single word, he just asked questions, and because of the truth found in those questions, humanity is forever uplifted."

I think about this, and the goat bleats. I look down and he's done with his water-born meal, including the translucent liquid itself. Aristotle brings another tray filled with soil-grown plants, and the goat resumes his eating.

"I suppose it's strange, waking up in a war that you don't understand," says Aristotle. "And then coming down to meet us here, in a surprisingly comfortable corner of Hell."

"Yes," I say. "I don't understand the world above, and your little den hasn't made things any clearer. You three don't look like you belong in Hell, and the comfort of this place does seem a little incongruous with all the surrounding despair."

Socrates nods at Plato to speak.

"To answer your question about how such allegedly *virtuous* souls such as we could end up in this place of damnation," he says with a laugh, "I'll tell you that we *chose* to be here. We may not be perfectly virtuous, but we have chosen the side of truth, and this entails that we must come here, to the place of darkness. What's the use of preaching reason in the vault of heaven, where perfection has already been achieved?"

Plato stands up, walks towards the door and then peers out at the bleak expanse outside.

"We *chose* to bring truth down here," he says. "For where else is truth more needed than Hell itself?"

Plato looks at me.

"As you can see, we've not been entirely successful in this endeavor," he says. "And since we are shades, our influence on the world above is even less."

Aristotle smiles.

"Perhaps *this* is the true reason why we exist down here," says the elegant man.

"What do you mean?" I ask.

"I'm talking about *this* meeting between us right now," says

Aristotle. "We've made a cozy alcove in this place, but not much else. Perhaps we came down here so long ago only so that we could meet you here today, the one who can still walk the earthly plane. Perhaps in this time our sole purpose was to impart our thoughts to you. Though we know little more than you about what's happening, we do understand the importance of truth, and perhaps *that* is the message we were meant to share."

"Perhaps," I say.

There's a tremor coming from outside, and I feel an invisible force pulling me away. It's not pulling me back towards the grey expanse of Hell, but rather *upwards*, to Earth and that desolate highway.

"Our time is short, so I'll share but one more notion with you," says Socrates. "Do you recognize the light pervasive in this room?"

I nod that I do, and then point at the goat's single prong, which glows the same hue.

"Hell does not come with such light," says Socrates. "So where do you think it comes from?"

I look around and see no apparent source of this illumination, so I shake my head to say that I don't know.

"This light comes from our reason," says Socrates. "That may sound a little abstract, but know that wherever there is *reason*, and there is the yearning for truth, there is light. Reason brings light down here to Hell, and it will bring the same to an earthly world caught in the midst of a dark battle. As long as there is reason, there will *always* be light, and you will always be able to find your way."

A TALE OF THE HIGHWAY

The Thumping

I awake with the dream fully remembered but subsiding, the three men's words making way for the pain now coursing through my earthly body. Every part of my frame screams for attention, and I can still sense the Beak kneeling down and creeping in close to my ears.

"I just want to let you know that I loved doing that, I really did," whispers the Beak, even though he never touched me once. "I really hope that you transgress once more so that I can do this again. Please, stop the car, turn around, run away. We'll be there, every time."

The Beak shakes his head.

"But I'm obligated to warn you that you really should follow the note. *Drive until this road ends, and then drive some more.* Every word of it is truth, and if you transgress again, there will be a worse punishment the next time. Break the rules again after that, and it will be worse than the second. We may have to get clever, but I assure you that we will find a way to make it even worse. That's why we're here: to peck at you until you relent."

The Beak stands up and motions the Claws back towards the darkness.

"I hope you transgress again, I really do," says the Beak, still not smiling. "But I must warn you that you shouldn't, because we're flying in the night, right behind you. We're always watching, *always* there. Everywhere you go, we're watching. Every time you transgress, we'll be there right after."

/***/

I watch them fly away, not so much disappearing into the darkness as breaking up into pieces and resuming their form as a flock of birds. They've become part of the night itself, one of the few parts that can actually hurt you.

I turn my attention back to my own self, and I'm broken beyond repair. Twisted and bruised, a shattered vessel with no hope of holding water ever again. And yet I know I've been here before. Not *here*, and not this bad, but broken after a bad twist in the night.

/***/

I pass out again, this one a dreamless sleep, and wake up hours or moments later with my legs a little tender but no longer throbbing. My back is still rubbed raw, screaming for attention, but I only hear its wails because the rest of my body has quieted down. I get up cautiously, not yet trusting my body or the world around it—but I can stand. My back is still on fire, a mesh of scratches from scraping against the asphalt with every one of the Claws' bludgeons. My front is OK however, skin once again smooth. I see that it's still gently kissed by bruises, but these contusions are on their way out. I even see one vanish before me, soft yellow disappearing into my moonlit skin.

I look behind me, back aching as I do so, and I don't find my trailing companions. I glimpse the faintest motion in the distance, and one flutter of silhouetted wings is enough to tell me that they're still there, and that I must leave. I can sense that I'm not normally one to follow the rules, but I know well by now that I don't enjoy conflict either. I avoid problems, and the Claws' talons hold problems and nothing else.

/***/

I enter the car and press my scraped back against the seat, and blood finds its way through the scarecrow's rags and into the upholstery behind. I feel bad about blemishing the vehicle, as if I'm getting in a clean bed while caked in mud. But I've been muddied against my will, so I sit back and feel myself connect to the seat. The upholstery immediately fuses with my blood and everything else that's leaked out of my wounded skin, and I remind myself to refrain from shifting around too quickly.

I turn on the ignition and drive.

I don't like the Crows, but their task is straightforward at least.

/***/

Five minutes later my back is killing me. My other aches have all but disappeared, and there's nothing to silence my back's cry. The road makes it worse. This is a modern car and I'm on a flat road, but you never know how much motion is beneath you until drive with a few patches of skin torn from your body. Every bump, dip and fissure echoes through the vehicle, and though it's surely muted by the car's shocks, it still reaches me. Again and again.

I look in the rearview mirror and don't see them, but I know the Crows are there, waiting for me to stop, waiting for me to transgress, waiting for me to do anything but drive. I can't stop, but if I continue at this pace I'm going to crash, and if I crash it'll be bad on all fronts, worse than I could possibly imagine.

I think for a moment. I can sense that logic isn't my strong suit, but my immediate predicament doesn't require Aristotle to figure itself out:

> I was beaten savagely, enough to require months of rehabilitation. Maybe so savagely I would never recover.

> I passed out for a moment and then woke up feeling fine, all but my back.

> The Claws barely even touched my back during the beating. The injuries there were secondary, when he beat me so hard that it rubbed me against the asphalt.

> There is nothing special about
> my back, at least not as far as I
> can tell.
>
> The only thing I can see about
> my back is the way I landed. My
> back touched the ground, the
> rest of me faced the sky.

The moon. The moon healed me. It healed me when I awoke for the first time, and it healed me now. I was near death, and the only thing that watched over me was the moon above, gazing upon my injured body but not my back, which was pressed against the asphalt.

I look up at the moon and she looks back at me, quiet as a stone, but not quite denying my theory either. *The moon has always been there for me, just as she's there for us all, but this time it's different.* This time she's giving more of herself.

But I can't stop and embrace her so easily, for the Crows are still behind me, waiting for the slightest excuse to bring their torment. The moon has power but they're quicker than she is,[13] so I can't stop by the side of the road and stretch out in front of her.

But my back is still screaming, and I'm losing focus. If I crash, the Crows will not be kind.

I look around the car gingerly, and the slightest movement causes me to wince. I don't find a solution around me but I look up and see exactly what I need: a *moonroof*.[14]

I open the panel and then slide another button to open the glass. I feel the rush of the air moving past, or rather the air *staying still* while

---

[13] Destruction is often quicker than the rebuild, and quite often gets the last move.
[14] I didn't know this name at the time, but it's such a fitting moniker given the circumstances I've included it in the narrative.

my vehicle cuts through it, and the noise grabs my thoughts away from the pain, giving immediate respite. I continue to drive but lean forward, eyes still on the road but back exposed to the air. The moon isn't directly above, but I open the window as well and that gives it a more complete angle.

The moonlight alleviates the pain immediately, cool water on the burn. It takes a little time, incremental in its progress, but the light is soothing—*soothing, and nothing else.* There's no sting as the wound heals, just a pure analgesic calm coming with every moment. The main burn disappears and the small scraps can finally clamor for attention, worried about being forgotten. They won't. I take off my ragged shirt and bend over further, still driving but stretching my body until all parts are covered.

My injuries soon disappear, and I am whole again. There may be a few minor, ignorable cuts left on my backside, but they can wait. I don't know when I'll be able to take care of them, but they can wait.

/***/

Now healed, I can inspect the car. I need a drink, but I'm still driving so I can't quite take out a cork with my shoe. I bet I could given enough time though, so I still take a bottle and put it in the passenger seat. *This wine looks like it's driving with me, my companion in this journey.* The moon is the distant mother, watching from afar, but the bottle is my comrade, my peer, my schoolyard chum, waiting beside me until we can find some trouble. Not the kind of trouble that's currently entangling me, mind you, the kind where crows fly behind you, waiting to peck you apart. But this wine could get me in the good type of trouble, the kind that makes memories, forges friendships and teaches you a thing or two.

But I digress. The bottle—a Gewürztraminer—stays in the front seat, either unaware of the mystery around me, or keeping its thoughts secret. I look around the front and see my area: static, clean. The empty space clears my mind and allows me to focus on the task at hand, but it doesn't give me any clues.

I open the glove compartment and find that it holds a set of audiobooks, or rather a hefty little container filled with compact discs. A square plastic brick, and the cover shows a white-eyed statue of a man. Nothing creepy, just a marble figure with a beard. Dry letters beneath it, a lot of text, academic. Intense-looking guy in a box in the lower right, whose name is *Dr. Julius Shaw*. He's wild-haired with a piercing gaze. Has an aquiline nose and a stare that sees right through you, sees all your misdeeds laid bare, but he won't chastise you for it because he sees through the folly of human frailty as well.[15]

He looks interesting, but I don't think he's going to offer any clues, at least not in the short term.

I look in the left door's lower holder—nothing. I'm hoping for a phone, to call anyone for help. It's pretty desolate out here, but it's a road, so there's bound to be a signal somewhere. All I would need is a signal, and I could dial anyone in the contact list and start asking for help. If there's no one in the contact list, I could dial 911. My long-term memory has held on to that number, at least.

That's it, find a way to call 911.

The Crows will see this as a clear transgression, but it's worth a shot. I'll call up the police, tell them strange men are following me, and they've already beaten me once. I'll try to sound as rational as possible, and lie when they ask if I've been drinking. Or maybe I'll tell the truth, that way they'll come faster. I can't see any landmarks, but maybe they'll locate my signal through triangulation of cell phone towers, or something like that. Maybe I did something before, committed a major

---

[15] He's clearly some sort of professor, but probably a loose cannon in his department, a genius type who would get tenure despite a mutual loathing between him and his dean. Not that Dr. Shaw would find any true value in tenure.

crime, and they're just waiting for my call. They'll get my message, send out an alarm to twenty other officers, and get a special handler on the phone. She'll say in a calm voice: *Listen, it is very important that you remain in the car until you reach such-and-such point. You are in a state of amnesia because you've been a victim of so and so, or maybe you're the criminal that's on his way to do this and that. Whatever the case, listen carefully because I'm going to tell you exactly who you are, and what this is all about.*

I'll see the faerie-light of flashing red and blue in the distance, and I'll stop. The Crows don't want me to stop, but they didn't say anything about police. Or better yet—

I'll tell the police that I'm out of control, and they need throw those strips that they have.[16] You know those strips with the spikes on them? I'll tell them to throw those down and then—

Drive until this road ends, and then drive some more.

It's not an airtight action, because it will only be the *end of the road* metaphorically, but it's about as close as I can get. The police might think I'm on some sort of drug, or under some sort of delusion. For all I know, they'll be right on both counts. Whatever the case, if they end up pushing my rag-clothed body into the back of a squad car, I'll go without complaint. If the Crows visit me in the holding cell, I'll surely be done for, but if the Claws and the Beak can materialize in a holding cell, I'll have been done for no matter what I did.

There's not much solace in a fatalistic outcome such as this, but there's some, and I can't think that far ahead right now. I just need a phone.

/***/

There is no phone. Not in the glove compartment, not in the door

---

[16] I don't know if I was aware of these strips at the time. I may have been. In any case, this was my general line of thinking, so I'm keeping it in.

side containers, not attached to the visor, not under the seat. I reach as far as I can into the back, even scouring the pockets behind the front seats, but nothing's there either. *There will be no special handler on the radio explaining in a calm voice precisely what happened, there won't be a squad of police cars forming a barricade in the road, waiting to arrest me.*

It isn't going to happen, because I have no phone. I check again, scouring the empty places and hoping that the phone magically appears. It's a futile task, I know, but I've got time and stranger things have happened recently, so it's worth shot.

No phone, but I do find something. The right door holder, something square and thin, and I reach over and grab it. I can't quite get ahold of it, so I press my fingers against it to pin it against the inner wall. It snags on the inner edge of the holder, but I stay patient, and finally work it out.

It's a picture of a uniquely beautiful woman with dark skin, brightly dyed green hair and lipstick to match. I can't stop staring at her. I force myself to turn the picture around, and the back side has some writing, writing that tells me my name.

I know my name at least. My name is *Dion*.

/***/

The note on the back is fairly short:

> To Dion:
>
> I'm sorry. You're Lancelot, Paolo and more, more than just a man. But I'm not more than what I am, so I brought this upon you, just so that I could have you for myself.

I'm sorry. Now I have nothing, less than nothing, and I'm sorry.

— Ari

I think about this, but can't glean any clues from her words. I'm assuming I'm Dion and she's Ari. Both names are a little gender-neutral, but I can tell it's not my handwriting, and I wouldn't send her a picture of herself, anyway. She seems familiar, though, and so does her name. *Ari.* I don't remember her, but I somehow *know* her. Perhaps I knew her before all this, and something is echoing within me. Maybe I met her in a dream, a real dream where I'm anyplace else besides Hell. Maybe I loved her for centuries, and all that remains is a faint bit of recognition.[17]

/***/

I read the rest of the note again. As far as the other names go, neither Lancelot nor Paolo ring a bell, but I make a mental note to ask her about them if I see her. *Hey Ari, I have no memory of you, and two Crows are chasing me. The Crows turn into men who beat me every time I stop, and then the moon heals me. But first, what's that reference to Lancelot and Paolo?*

I read the letter once more, and another thing jumps out at me. *She says that I'm more than just a man.* I don't know what it means, but it does check out. This might all be a hallucination, but still, regular men

---

[17] No memory, a semitragic note from a woman I don't remember—this screams *blackout*. But in retrospect I know it wasn't a blackout, at least not in the normal sense. Blackouts are intense: you can leave work at 5 p.m. on Friday and wake up Sunday morning on a beach in Spain, with no idea how you got there. But I wasn't experiencing a blackout. Blackouts are lost time, when you drink (or take) so much that your brain doesn't process short-term memories. You can't piece together your memories from the night before because there are no memories to be pieced together. It's the equivalent of waking up from surgery. It's scary, but this is different. At this point I don't know my name, and I don't know who I am. It's more than just waking up on the beach in Spain: my identity, my *self*, is gone.

don't heal themselves with a few minutes of moonlight.

I don't really feel like more than a man, though, because I can't really do anything out of the ordinary. If I could, I would have disappeared long ago, and reemerged far away from the Crows. Maybe I'd find a couple of people on a beach somewhere, and we'd have some fun.

I turn the photograph around and there she is, uniquely beautiful. Dark skin, with the radiantly green hair that matches her lipstick. It's a unique color combination but it fits, like leaves against brown bark. She has a strength to her, too, one derived from wildness. There's something about her that captures me, and though I don't know what it is, I hope to see her one day.

I think about her for some time, and it takes my mind off everything. The grey sludge, Hell and the Crows are still waiting for me, but all I can think about is this girl in the picture.

/***/

I need a drink. I feel like I'm making progress in this mystery, albeit incremental, and I need a drink. I look at my companion in the front seat, the Gewürztraminer, and it looks comfortable, so I look back in the case, hoping for a bottle with a screw-on cap. I have no such luck, so I take the seat belt off the Gewürztraminer and bring it close to my lips—so close, yet so far.

I try opening the wine bottle with my shoe, and it's a challenge. It's difficult enough to uncork a bottle with just asphalt, but the interior of a car holds less solid surface. There are some flat spaces around me, but they're slick, and they quickly curve into rounded edges and cushioned seats.

I still try, pounding the wine against the walls, the well where my feet are, and even the ceiling. Some of these might work given time, but I need to hold the shoe in place and it's hard to do this with one hand on the wheel. I eventually settle on the padded armrest between the two front seats. Its top is cushioned but there's a solid structure underneath. I can also lay the shoe on it and pound the wine bottle gradually, while keeping my foot on the gas and my eyes on the road. It might take some time, but I have time – at least I do now.

I take the shoe and place it on the surface, making a solid cushion. I place the wine bottle on the sole, and deliver a little tap. I then give it a solid *thunk*, and then another and another, hearing a little echo afterwards. I see the cork moved just a fraction above the lip of the bottle. Two more small taps, and then one more solid thump, and there's another echo. The cork works its way upwards until I can almost pull the rest out with my teeth, and I begin salivating at the thought of the first sip. I give one more toast to the moon, my constant companion, and then give one more hit to the bottle, which pushes the cork up just enough to be taken out without splitting it in half, and I hear the echo of the bottle hitting the arm rest once more.

Or so I think. I continue to drive in silence, and then place my thumb over the cork so the bottle doesn't spill all over the place. I give the shoe another solid thump with the bottle's bottom, right where the glass indents.

I hear a *thump* in response, but it's not an echo. Whatever it is, it's coming from the trunk.

/***/

I drive in silence, thinking about the sound, and then tap the midsection again with the bottle. The trunk thumps in response again. I wait and tap again, and there's another tap in return.

"Hello?" I yell.

No response.

"Hello?" I yell again. "Can you hear me?"

Silence, and then another thump.

"Are you Ari?" I ask.[18]

Silence.

"Who are you?"

Silence.

"What are you?"

More silence.

"Can you hear me?"

Silence, and then a thump. Whatever it is, it's there. Or rather *here*, with me, in the trunk.

"Are you in danger?"

Two thumps. I think for a moment.

"Listen," I say, deciding to lay it out again, all of it. "I don't know who or what you are, but my name is Dion, or at least I believe it to be. In any case, I don't know where I am, or what my identity is, or what I'm supposed to be doing."

I think for another minute.

"Well, I know what I'm *supposed* to be doing," I say.

I tell it about my task of *driving until this road ends, and then driving some more*. I tell it about Hell, and the father figure that yelled at me in the dream and said that I've ruined everything. I tell it about the Crows,

---

[18] I worry about it being Ari, though I can't quite believe she would be in my trunk at this point. That would imply that I'm some sort of serial killer, and I know I'm not that. But I also know that the Crows are killers, so I can't ignore the possibility that she might be in danger.

and I tell it about the grey sludge.

As I say this out loud, I realize that it does make a bit of sense for something to be in my trunk. The Crows, as evil as they are, couldn't be too invested in having me drive this car for its own sake. There must be something more at stake than just a vehicle, and this creature could be it.

"I still have to ask," I say, covering my bases. "Are you one of them?"

Silence. I cautiously take the thing's word for it, or rather *absence* of words—or rather absence of thumps.

"I guess if you were, you would have hurt me by now," I say. "Or something else. And yeah, I can't see anyone even remotely associated with the Beak being silent like you are."

A solid thump of agreement. I think some more.

"Maybe the Crows want to hurt you, even worse than they want to hurt me," I say. "Maybe they already have."

Silence, and then an emphatic thump, this one sadder than the rest. I tap the wine bottle twice in solidarity, and then pull the cork out with my teeth. I toast the moon again, and then Ari, and then the thing in the trunk. I might have no memory, but I'm no longer alone.

/***/

Whatever is in my trunk, it won't let me stop and let it out. I believe it wants to escape the trunk, but I propose stopping, and through a series of panicked thumpings it tells me that this isn't a good idea.

I take a sip of the wine and it's spicy, with a great aroma. It's a white and should be chilled, of course, but the slight warmth allows the full flavor of the Gewürztraminer to come out.[19]

"You're worried about me getting beaten by the Crows again," I say.

The creature thumps in the affirmative. I figure this could be a trick to keep me driving, but there's something genuine about the creature's thumps. I can't explain it, but it's there.

/***/

We drive on in silence awhile, and I realize my companion isn't the most loquacious of creatures. Whatever it is, it's quiet, even for an entity that only thumps.

"So we should keep driving?" I ask.

Silence, and then a reluctant thump.

"So we should keep driving," I say. "Until we think of something better, a way out of this. And then we stop."

A solid thump. We're on the same side and we're getting somewhere, or at least it appears that way.

"Then let's think, and maybe have some wine," I say, before realizing my passenger can't drink right now. "I'm sorry, I shouldn't have offered that."

The creature thumps that this is OK.

"Do you need anything at all?" I ask. "To eat? How about water?"

---

[19] You like that Teutonic name? Gewürztraminer was developed by the Italians, in a German-speaking area of the country. It's a cold-climate grape, and the chill brings a sweetness to the wine. That's what I love about this wine: even in the cold, grey skies where it's grown—British Columbia, Southern Chile, and of course Deutschland and South Tyrol in Italy—there's some sweetness, a distinct flavor you can't even find in the tropics.

Silence. I guess my cohort can do without. Still, I've got to offer something.

"Some music?"

The creature thumps in the affirmative.

I turn on the radio and there's no music. I press *seek* and the numbers go up and around the bend with no sign of slowing down. Not even a crackle from a half-received signal, just quiet, consistent static. It figures. I look around and see that though the world around me isn't as empty as the Hell I'd just escaped, it's still pretty empty. There's a road, there's some land, and that's about it. There's nothing particularly distinctive around, and definitely no radio towers.

"All right, no music," I tell the creature. "But there's got to be something else here. Something to help us both think."

There's a quick thump of affirmation, and I realize that whatever this thing is, it's got a great attitude.

I take another sip of the Gewürztraminer and then look around the vehicle. I think about what I've seen here—the photo of Ari, the case of wine, the square plastic brick of discs—*that's it*. I recork the wine loosely and put it in the middle holder. The bottle fits perfectly, a vehicle to suit me.

I pull out the CDs from the glove compartment, the lectures by the wild-haired Dr. Shaw. *It's not exactly the party I had in mind, but it might be fun.*

"This might give us an idea of how to get you out of here," I say, to an affirmative thump in response.

If not that, it might help us think. Whatever the case, I sense this intense-looking academic with a piercing gaze lives out of my comfort zone, and I know that this is where most of the interesting things in this world reside.

A TALE OF THE HIGHWAY

/***/

I read the title on the front: *On the Importance of Philosophy*. Take out the first CD and put it in. A symphonic melody plays as an introduction, and I use it to gauge the best volume for my comrade in the trunk. The creature thumps when the volume is just right, and I take my fingers off the dial.

The music ends and I hear: *Ordered Home Audio presents: "The Importance of Philosophy," by Dr. Julius Shaw. Unabridged and read by the author himself.* The music stops, and it gets to it.

Let the party begin.

/***/

The Importance of Philosophy

Chapter 1: The First Philosopher

A long time ago, thousands of years before the Common Era, there was a Mesopotamian settlement called *Qut*. At the time, the village of Qut was transitioning from nomadic pastoralism to agriculture, and though they still depended primarily on sheep and goats to sustain the population as a whole, a few intrepid farmers started growing grains on the banks of their river, a tributary of the Euphrates.

Qut began to flourish with this newfound reliance on crop cultivation, because the farmers no longer had to pick up and move as soon as the sheep had taken all the grass in a certain area. They began to rely on the regularity of the grains, and Qut as a whole soon subsisted on the grain in the warm months, and the livestock in the cold months. After several generations they began to rely on grain in the cold months as well, and livestock became a delicacy, while the grain kept them alive.

This newfound agriculture not only let them to stay in one place, it allowed them to *build*. Generations passed down land to each other, traded, and formed the feuds and alliances that permitted history to begin.

But though the grown food was more reliable than the itinerant goats and sheep, the citizens of Qut weren't entirely independent of the vagaries of the natural world, of time, and of chance. The crops didn't always go well because they were dependent upon the rain, and when the rain didn't come, the harvest would be scant. Sometimes too much rain came and the river flooded the fields, ruining the crops. Sometimes the rain would be perfect, but pests would come too. Sometimes a fungus would destroy their stores of grains, sometimes the crops would fail without any explanation whatsoever.

Whatever the case, these citizens still lived on a razor's edge. Though their situation was much improved than when they lived on goats and sheep alone, their populations had also increased, and so had their needs. Most anything could tip them over this *edge* and into the starvation of a long winter, when each farmer knew that some of his children wouldn't survive to see the following spring.

But this sedentary lifestyle had afforded them one more luxury, however: an advanced and complex religion. Because the community shared resources, some amongst the village could spend their time studying the gods around them. There was even one man who was able to dedicate most *all* of his time auguring the voices of the deities, and this man was named *High Priest Sargon*.

During one particularly bad drought, High Priest Sargon spent two weeks divining the reasoning behind the gods' wrath. Sargon took long walks in the hinterland, and spent time in the night consuming bitter herbs, herbs that made him see the world in a different light. He fasted and he prayed, and he imbibed substances that would ensure his sleep was filled with strange dreams, dreams that gave him direct access to the gods. He could talk to them quite clearly, and ask just what it was that made them want to starve the people of Qut.

It wasn't that easy for Sargon though. He could talk to the gods in these dreams, but they didn't always talk back.

After a fortnight of augury, and one particularly messy day spent examining the insides of a sheep, the truth visited Sargon as he wandered in the desert, and the truth came in the form of a talking lion.

The lion told Sargon that the gods were upset that humanity was becoming too proud, and that they had forgotten their place in this world. The lion told Sargon that *Ashnan*, the goddess of the grain, was particularly bothered that humanity had forgotten about *her*. She was planning to return to her former role as attendant to the *Anunnaki*, which were the deities that Ashnan was originally born to serve.

The talking lion warned Sargon that Ashnan's brother *Lahar*, the god of cattle, was also becoming angry, and would soon follow Ashnan's lead and go back to serving

> the Anunnaki.
>
> Sargon asked the lion what the people of Qut must do to get back in the good graces of the gods. A falling star appeared behind the lion, and after this the lion gave Sargon very clear instructions.
>
> He told Sargon that there was a path back to the gods' good graces, or at least out of their direct contempt. Sargon listened to this message and became overjoyed with the wisdom he received, despite the fact that the lion told him that he would need to perform some bad, bad things.

There's a pause in the recording, and I uncork the Gewürztraminer and take another sip. I ask the creature in the trunk if it's enjoying Dr. Shaw's story, and it thumps in the affirmative.

Dr. Shaw continues:

> Sargon went home and slept for nearly a full day. He had slept little the previous night, partially because of his concern for the future of Qut, and partially because of the concoction of strange herbs that he had consumed. But still, the sleep deprivation, stress and herbs had been worth it, because the talking lion had given him a message, a message which he was overjoyed to share with his fellow citizens the next morning.
>
> *We have angered the gods*, said High Priest Sargon, wearing his holiest of robes, *and we must appease them with sacrifice.*
>
> The people listened but didn't quite understand, because they already made sacrifices on a regular basis. Goats, sheep and the occasional cow made its way to

the blood-soaked stones at the center of the settlement quite frequently, and not just before the seeds were sown. If one wanted to settle a feud with one's neighbor, or a couple wanted to conceive a child, or if the people were worried about an attack from ever-present hordes on the horizon, a hoofed mammal would most always be presented to the gods.

I'm not talking about sacrificing livestock, said Sargon in response.

The people took these dark words in and then looked to the left at the man they'd appointed to be in charge of their makeshift militia, and he shrugged in return. There were neither foreign soldiers nor wandering vagrants in their holding pens at the moment, and the people reasoned that Sargon must have been speaking of something else.

He was. *We need to sacrifice one of our own daughters*, said Sargon. *The daughter must be virginal, and untouched. Ashnan will take this pure blood and turn it into rain, which will in turn bring our land to life.*

The people of Qut were shocked at first, but they immediately began to see the reasoning behind Sargon's plan. Who were they to question Ashnan's wrath? They'd been diligent in their prayers and burnt offerings, but the parched earth showed an unyielding truth: that if they didn't appease the powers in the sky and make up for whatever oversight they'd levied against Ashnan and her brother Lahar, the entire town of Qut would be dust within a generation. Sargon's request was reasonable and fair, for what was the value of a single girl's life when compared to the welfare of the entire settlement of Qut? And when placed against

> the feelings of the gods, her life was utterly inconsequential.
>
> A farmer immediately volunteered his daughter to be the first at the altar. This farmer's larder had been particularly hard hit by the drought, and he had six other daughters anyway. He wouldn't miss one that much.
>
> That night the farmer told the one he selected that she would be helping her family, and warned her not to scream when she saw Sargon's blade, because her father and mother would be very upset if she cried out.

I take another sip of the Gewürztraminer, and its strong flavor can't suppress a shudder at these words. Dr. Shaw continues:

> The rain following the first sacrifice was mild, but it came and the people of Qut subsisted to the next season. The goats didn't quite fatten but they lived, and the sheep bore tiny lambs that might one day grow large if the season thereafter brought rain.
>
> Whatever the case, Sargon's annual virginal sacrifice became embedded in the culture of Qut, and soon Ashnan became accustomed to seeing a young woman led to the altar before each and every rainy season.
>
> Over the next four generations these sacrifices began to take on a momentum of their own, and soon they became steeped in tradition, mystery, and of course an unquestionable importance. It became part of what the people of Qut did to start the harvest, as essential to the season as the actual sowing of seeds.
>
> The sacrificial temple grew, and became ornate. The blade used to kill the young woman grew sharper and

gained etchings of Ashnan, among other things. The ceremony grew in length too, and soon took up the better part of two weeks.

The people soon recognized the importance of the girl who was to be sacrificed, and recognized that their entire livelihood depended on her blood as it poured onto the stone beneath. Soon a mythos developed around the girl, and it became a great honor to be selected for the sacrifice. The people of Qut developed a ceremony in which she was treated exceptionally well during the days before her slaughter. The logic was that she should be treated as a living goddess before her death, because Ashnan deserved nothing less.

The people of Qut still experienced drought of course, and still experienced a number of other problems.

Sometimes too much rain came, and their river flooded the fields, ruining the crops. Sometimes the rain would be perfect, but pests would come too. Sometimes a fungus would destroy their stores of grains, sometimes the crops would fail without any explanation whatsoever.

One farmer noticed this and brought it up before the ceremony one year. The farmer noted that he didn't believe they should sacrifice the girl they had chosen, because although it wasn't the farmer's daughter—it was his neighbor's—the farmer had grown quite fond of the lass, and had even thought that she would grow up to marry one of his sons.

The farmer then said that he had visited a neighboring settlement, and that these villagers had some interesting methods of irrigation that the people of Qut should explore. The farmer stated that his people should do this, and that first and foremost they should consider sparing this young woman's life.

The people were aghast at this affront and became angry, perhaps no one so much as the current high priest, who had spent his entire life in the pursuit of Sargon's dream.

The high priest immediately declared the farmer a heretic, and accused him of being out to starve the people of Qut. The priest then demanded that the farmer be put on the altar next to the girl, though there would be no such godlike treatment for the farmer in the days before the sacrifice.

The people listened to these words, then swarmed over the farmer and held him back as he writhed, begging for mercy. The farmer didn't apologize for his suggestions about sparing the girl's life, but said that he had a family to support, and that they would be destitute without him.

The high priest listened to these words carefully and sent forth the command that the farmer's family should be placed beside him at the altar. The farmer screamed and begged even more, pleading with the high priest to spare his family's life, stating that he would now go to the altar willingly, but the farmer's words fell on deaf ears.

Days later, when the high priest was rinsing the blood off his hands, with the screams of the farmer and the farmer's family still echoing through his own ears, he thought about the farmer's words. The high priest knew that the farmer was foolish of course, but part of him couldn't help but *admire* the farmer's conviction. The high priest reminded himself that if the farmer had had his way the people of Qut would have surely starved – still, the high priest couldn't help but think of the farmer's unyielding opinion. The farmer's thoughts were both heretical and foolish, and would surely have led to Qut's ruin, but the word were worthy of memory at least.

The high priest rinsed the last drops of blood off his hands, and soon thought of other things. The oracle had found a bad sign while examining the entrails of a sheep, and it portended an invasion. The oracle didn't indicate from where or by whom, let alone *when*, but the high priest knew that he had to examine the oracle's words closely, and wanted to speak with her about what she had found in the sheep's intestines.

I recognize that it's something of an unsettling tale, so I press *pause* and ask the creature in the back if it wants to continue. It thumps in the affirmative, so I press *play* again. Dr. Shaw continues, now with a somewhat lighter voice:

What I told you is of course not entirely true. High Priest Sargon is a fictional character, and there is no such place as a Mesopotamian settlement named *Qut*. But I won't say it's *completely* false, because this fictional tale does hold some truth. In fact it holds a tremendous amount of it.

There was no High Priest Sargon, but there have been countless examples of him throughout history, the vast majority of which have gone unrecorded.

Here's what happens in early history: someone sees the great power of nature around them, and is frightened by it, and it's a human instinct to *focus* that fright into something that they can control, or at the very least *understand*. The vagaries of rainfall become the whimsy of gods, and the harsh realities of a drought become the god's wrath.

These crude feelings aren't eliminated with the first steps of human development either, and in fact they are *amplified*. An intrepid citizen might learn to circumnavigate the gods' wrath through irrigation, but this remarkably effective technique will soon lead to a surplus population. This extra citizenry needs ever more sustenance, and a future drought will lead to suffering on a grander scale. In addition to this, the aforementioned innovation can support a class of holy men, who have naught else to do but spend their days indoors, thinking of all the ways that they can get back in the gods' good graces.

These priests will instinctively see that pre-emptive *suffering* will appease the gods, and it's a base human instinct to see truth in this. It's an even baser human instinct to see truth in having *another* suffer on one's own behalf, and have that person pay the ultimate price for the welfare of society.

The First Philosopher

That Qut farmer who spoke up for the innocent victim was of course not *the* first philosopher, because though humanity's primal instinct is to follow without questioning, the aptitude for reason is also born within us all, even those like High Priest Sargon.

But for the intents and purposes of Qut, and the world of High Priest Sargon, that farmer was the first philosopher. The *first*.

Let's take a step back though, and ask a precursory question: *What is a philosopher?* There are many definitions, but for now let's say that a philosopher is anyone who truly *questions* the world, anyone who refuses to take the surrounding universe at face value, anyone who at least *attempts* to get to the root of the matter.

The intellectual and philosopher Jostein Gaarder likened human existence to being born as a microbe on a single strand of a rabbit's fur, a rabbit that has somehow been pulled out of a hat by a magician. That rabbit is the universe, and we lowly microbes can't hope to see the rabbit that holds us as a whole, let alone truly understand the rabbit. Above all else, we may never be able to understand *the magician*, how he made the rabbit appear, nor for what reason the magician chose to bring the rabbit into being.

But we bacteria have two options: first, to retreat inwards to the rabbit, where we can see less, but where it is *warm* and there is less to see that might frighten us. We can also pick the path of the philosopher, and find the furthermost tip of the fur, and do our best to see as much of the rabbit as possible and at the very least *contemplate* this extraordinary creature that encompasses all known existence.

Those of us in the modern era have the added benefit of those who came before us, who spent their lives

> building a philosophical scaffolding so that we might have an incrementally better view.
>
> The farmer had no such luxury, and though he helped bring the scaffolding into being, or at least suggested the possibility, he paid the ultimate price for simply questioning the world as a philosopher, for simply asking *why* an innocent young woman must die a horrible death, when the human invention of irrigation would obviate the need for such a thing, perhaps ten times over.

Dr. Shaw pauses in his speech, and I use the time to take another sip of the wine and then take a look back at the trunk. The creature in there is silent, but I can sense that it's listening. Dr. Shaw continues, with a calm, clear tone:

> If you ever want to appreciate philosophy, just take a moment wherever you are, look around you and then think about your life. Think of your schooling, the hospital you were born in, and the vaccines that were administered as you grew up in this world. Think about the fact that you can walk alone in a city, see a group of strangers on the horizon and not for *the slightest instant* worry that they might kill you and take everything you own, just because they can.
>
> Think of your ability to vote, to choose those who would lead you. Think of the fact that if you're falsely accused of a crime, you have legal recourse to state that you are innocent.
>
> Hopefully, you live in a society where all these things are truth. But whatever the case, *whatever* freedoms you so enjoy were most likely birthed by philosophy, and quite often the case by someone like the farmer

who simply asked *why*, a question that would only yield truth a myriad of generations after he was slaughtered for it.

So feel grateful for your current freedoms, but know that you do not owe them to High Priest Sargon, Ashnan, Lahar, the Anunnaki or the talking lion. You owe them to philosophers, but not just to the ones you know, like Socrates, Galileo and all the rest, who by providence fell into the immortal annals of history. You should also thank the farmer and his family, who died namelessly so that a fraction of a truth might be revealed. You should be grateful for the teacher who whispered into the ears of a young Galileo Galilei's ears that there was more to learn than the dogma he had been told. You should thank the nameless woman who argued vociferously with a young Socrates while he worked as a stonemason, who excited his burgeoning mind before he left his workshop once and for all.

I take another sip of wine. Dr. Shaw continues:

History seems to be dominated by one theme: endless war. This recurrent theme suggests that humanity's primal instinct is to *follow without questioning*, but once again this isn't humanity's whole story. Our first instinct might be to pick up the sword, but on a deeper level humanity values reason above all else.

In the moment, we place great value on the warriors who defend our city gates and take the arrows that would have otherwise pierced our own flesh, but over time, we value reason. Over time we come to appreciate those who speak not of what is at face value, but what is underneath. Over time we find tremendous value in those who question, even when those thinkers come from a tribe not our own, and even when those thinkers come from the tribe currently launching arrows at our city gates.

For though we are grateful for those heroes who stand in the line of fire against the pointed missiles, we realize that there is a deeper solution to this, which involves questioning everything. That questioning might not protect us from a mortar headed our way, but it may hold the key to preventing another mortar from ever being launched again.

The aptitude for reason and the desire for truth is also born within us all, even those like High Priest Sargon. It may be buried underneath anger, ignorance and fear, and it might take a philosopher like the farmer to pull it upwards, if only slightly.

Unfortunately, our first instinct is often to appease the forces around us with blood, ideally another's, be it the farmer via the high priest's blade, or another man's son sent to the city wall. But deep inside, we know that though the path of another's blood might be easier to understand, it's ultimately the incorrect path. Deep inside even Sargon knew that the power of irrigation might serve Qut's needs more effectively than the plan from the talking lion. Deep inside we all know that sending another's sons towards the incoming arrows might feel like the right decision, but that it's not the ideal one.

Deep inside we are *all* philosophers, every single one of us. Some in this world might suppress that instinct (if you turn on the news you'll see that many suppress it quite well), but once shown the *full light of reason*, even the most dogmatic, myopic, xenophobic person will not go back to the dark.

I think about that phrase, the *full light of reason*, and harken back to my time in Hell with Socrates, Plato and Aristotle. Dr. Shaw continues:

> Philosophy brings us the light of reason, and that light shows us *truth*. Upon the frame of *truth*, everything we hold dear is built. Everything.
>
> At the very least, philosophy keeps our necks away from Sargon's sacrificial blade, and it might be the only thing that can keep it away.
>
> It's an important discipline — perhaps the most important. But keep in mind that this crucial role is not merely meant to be limited to a professor, one whose thoughts are wrapped in esoteric language and then printed in an academic journal.
>
> Philosophy is within us all, and it is *all of our* responsibility. That means you too, so crawl to the farthest edge of the rabbit's fur as you can. You can do this by reading, listening, debating and *thinking* at every opportunity. As soon as the light of reason shows you truth, grab hold of it and climb ever outward. You might not see the rabbit, let alone the magician, but you will see *something*, and you will do your part to ensure that the farmer and the countless others who have died for truth, who have died for basic *reason*, will not have died in vain.

/***/

The chapter ends, and I turn off the player before it gets to the next track. I think of Shaw's words in silence, and realize that even if it only involves yes or no questions to the creature in the trunk, I have to question my situation a little further.

"Who put you in the trunk in the first place?" I ask. "Was it the Crows?"

Silence.

"Someone else did?" I ask.

There's a thump.

"Was it Ari?"

Silence.

"Was it me?"

Thump.

Hmmm.

"Am I the bad guy?"

Silence.

"I locked you in the trunk," I say. "But we're on the same side."

Thump.

"I kidnapped you, but in a good way," I say. "I freed you from something, and I am taking you somewhere."

A strong thump.

"But the Crows want me to take you somewhere else," I say. "A bad place, at the end of this road and just a little more."

A solid thump.

"But you don't want me to stop the car and try to release you," I say. "Because the time isn't right. The Crows will beat me again, and you won't get out."

Thump. I think for a moment.

"Let's just say I could release you right now," I say. "I stop the car and open the trunk before the Crows get to me. Would that be a good thing?"

A reluctant thump, and I get its meaning: *good idea, but it's not that easy.*

I think of Shaw's words, and think of the farmer and High Priest Sargon. If I had to assign roles in this tale, I'd be the farmer, and the Crows would be High Priest Sargon. I'd say my cohort in the trunk would be *the truth.*

"I need to stop the car and let you out," I say. "Or at least try."

Silence, and I do see its point. I might fit the part of the noble farmer, but *the first philosopher's* story didn't exactly end well. Still, I can't just keep driving like this. I've got to question my surroundings, keep trying to find a way out. There's a truth here, and it's up to me to release it to the world. If I end up like the farmer, so be it.

I'm going to open this trunk, no matter the consequences.

Retjar the Damned

I stop the car, pull the trunk-release lever under the steering wheel, and get out. It's still the same moon above, and it's still the same breathless night. The wind picks up a little, enough to let me know that the world isn't on my side, and the clouds start peeking over the moon to let me know that time might not be either. I scurry to the back of the car and find a strange apparatus on the trunk's door with a beautiful engraving of an anvil and a hammer on it. There's no slot for a key, only a pad with four digits, set at 0000. I knock on the door, and my comrade inside knocks back hurriedly.

I turn around and see a flicker in the sky, and it's enough to let me know that the Crows are coming. I tug on the trunk and it won't open, and I turn it to 0001 and tug it again. It's still shut, so I enter 0002, nothing on that. I look back and see the Crows have descended and are beginning to take their somewhat human forms, the outlines of my nemeses just barely visible. I start from the other end, 9999. Nothing. I can feel them behind me, a biting cold wind coming from their wings to tell me what's to come. I panic, enter 7453, and then 4958, and before I can even try to open the trunk I'm yanked back by clawed hands. I'm pulled down to the ground, a weight on my body leaving me prostrate, completely helpless. For a moment I revel in the fact that I got a few numbers in, and it's technically now a matter of time before I solve this. But the small victory is pushed away by a brutal punch to my midsection. I can't think of anything now, save for thoughts of the Beak's admonition that each time I stop, these sessions are only going to get worse.

/***/

"I'm really glad we get to do this again," says the Beak moments later, now standing above me. "There are certain rules that our kind must abide by, rules that *you* seem to abandon every time you come to Earth and take human form."

The Beak ruffles his body ever so slightly, perhaps still adjusting to his transition from bird to the aforementioned human form.

"But *we* follow the rules," says the Beak. "And in this world, in *this* plane of existence, we can't simply stop you every moment we please, because *you* have a task at hand. We'd love to take you from that party-wagon of yours and have our way with you, just because. I'd even ask Chronos to slow time down after each transgression, maybe even *stop it* outright, just so I could make these sessions count a little more, but I didn't bother to do this. We follow the rules because we know what's at stake, and we don't bother to ask Chronos for a favor, because he doesn't take sides in these things. If he understood the full gravity of the drastic and final consequences of your mistake, he might change his mind, but we can't bother with that right now. Your father has told us that we must punish you every time you stop moving forward, and that is precisely what we'll do."

The Claws are on top of me with the weight of a thousand marble slabs, and the Beak kneels down and whispers into my ear.

"But we'll make this one count, make no mistake about that," he says, his breath smelling of dead flesh. "We'll do such things that time will slow for you all by itself."

/***/

The Claws slugs me in the stomach once again, and it hurts, but I'm still present.

"I want to tell you what's at stake, I truly do," says the Beak. "And I'm not giving this speech to play the part of the dastardly villain announcing his plans right before the hero is rescued, for I assure you, there will be no rescue and you are *no* hero. I'm telling you so that you'll know why you're wrong in doing what you did, so when you ultimately get sent to the underworld for punishment, *real* punishment, you'll understand that you have no one to blame but yourself."

The Beak looks at my vehicle, particularly the trunk.

"And I want you to understand that no one tricked you into abetting the Titan's escape," says the Beak. "You acted on your own volition, with no one else. So when you find yourself in Hell, the *real* Hell from which there will be no waking, understand that you arrived there by yourself. You dug yourself through the earth until it was too late, and I take great joy knowing that this notion might be your worst torment of all."

The Beak gets up. I try to speak, to ask him what I've done, but I can't open my mouth. The weight of the Claws has compressed me into utter helplessness. The Beak signals the Claws to begin his work, and the brown-skinned man clenches his thick fists. He's about to deliver his first punch when the Beak grabs it and places it back by the big man's side.

"Not yet," says the Beak. "There will be time for this later, but for now, let's fill him in on the *big picture*. Perhaps that will convince him to complete his task. After all, that's what we were sent here to ensure."

/***/

"The *big picture*," says the Beak. "I'll start my explanation with a question. Let *me* ask *you*, what's the purpose of Hell?"

I don't have an answer, and I can't speak anyway. The Beak seems to realize this, but lets the silence hang in the air nonetheless.

"It's known many names," he continues. "It was *Tartarus* back in our day, and it was a rare fate indeed. To arrive in Tartarus you really had to do something atrocious. Only a few unfortunate souls fell down to that punishment, those who committed regicide or those who betrayed their countries, leading their own nation to its destruction. But whatever the case, you had to do something *big* to end up in Tartarus. You had to die on the wrong end of a legend and end up as a cautionary tale to scare young children."

The Beak looks around at the emptiness around us. Other than the road beneath, this land is unoccupied, seemingly untouched by humanity. *I wonder if this place looked like this when people were sent to Tartarus.*

"But Hell nowadays?" asks the Beak. "*Anyone* can get in. Murderers go first of course, followed by thieves and adulterers. But the underworld's acceptance doesn't stop there, not even close. Worship the wrong god, or even nothing, and you're in. Set up a hundred schools and save a million lives, but die with a soul uncommitted, and you're in."

The Beak shakes his head.

"So Hell not only exists, but it's growing, expanding exponentially to match the pace of a burgeoning populace on this earthly plane," says the Beak. "And you can't exist and grow without having a definitive *purpose*, right?"

I have no answer, and the Beak doesn't wait for one. Instead, he looks towards the dark horizon with disgust.

"These humans, they've been shedding gods with every passing millennium. From a thousand, to a hundred, to one, and the way things are going, one day to *zero*."

The Beak pauses and squints his eyes.

"With every passing day these mortals get one step closer to permanent apostasy, and to make things worse, they have the gall to call it *progress*."

The Beak doesn't quite smile, but he does affect a smug look of self-satisfaction.

"But whether you're a believer or heretic, worshipper or *anti*theist, Hell still exists, that's for sure," says the Beak. "And you still haven't answered me *why*, why does it exist? *Why* would an infinitely compassionate deity allow a place with such agony to *be* in the first place? Our Creator *creating* His children just so some can end up in the dark terror? It doesn't make sense. Fathers care for their children for their whole life, not merely up to the point where they leave the house!"

If I could talk, I'd poke so many holes in this incoherent reasoning that it would rival the scarecrow's rags that I'm currently wearing. But the Claws is pressing down on my chest with an ever-increasing fury and I can't speak, so instead I think of my own apparent *father*, the one who scolded me in the dream and apparently brought the Crows in the first place.

The Beak nods at the Claws, and he strikes me in the face. My jaw loosens, but only slightly.

"I'll allow you to speak just this once," says the Beak. "Tell me why *you* think Hell exists."

The Beak lets me ponder upon this, and then I force a smile to let him know that I have the perfect answer to his question. My mouth can barely push the words out, so he leans in closely. I gather up my strength and whisper in a clear voice that he should go fuck himself.

The Beak stands back as if I'd just spit in his dead little eyes, and I wish desperately that I'd been able to do just that.

"Bold, strong words," says the Beak. "Before all this you wouldn't have dared say such a thing. Even in one of your inebriated ramblings, you wouldn't have said that."

The Beak looks at the horizon once more, and once again affects an air of utter disgust.

"But you found a way to don a mortal form, a true mortal form where other humans could see you as one of their own," says the Beak. "And you began to cavort with these *humans*, these glorified apes that we formerly had no problems controlling. You couldn't see their kind as a whole because you were in a constant state of intemperance, but they were growing at a rapid pace, and we had to do something about it. We had to do something to control them."

Control. That's it. Perhaps Hell is the beating stick that keeps humanity in line, or at the very least the thorned center of existence that makes humanity's self-consumption unpalatable. The Beak's reasoning is still flawed, and if I had the words I'd still tell him to go fuck himself, but I see where he's going with this.

"Hell was made to control humanity's direction," says the Beak. "But as humanity's power expanded, Hell had to grow to accommodate, perhaps exponentially so."

/***/

The Claws strike me once, and then twice, and then until I lose count. The Beak eventually holds him back, if only for a moment.

"Now let me tell you about these *humans* whom you so love, from whom you so inexplicably seek acceptance," says the Beak. "If you recall I referred to them as *glorified apes*, and I didn't say that merely to be pejorative."

I don't quite believe him when he says that.

"Humans still share the traits with their wilder cousins," says the Beak. "But *which* cousin is their closest relative in spirit? Some might say the chimpanzee, some might say the bonobo. Are you familiar with either of them?"

I'm not, at least not in my current state.

"Then let's start with bonobos," says the Beak. "They *look* like chimps, just a little darker in the face. And they deal with stress in an interesting way: by having an orgy. Quarrels, a meeting of strangers, an argument over access to a watering hole, all problems are resolved by having a massive binge of procreative indulgence. They aren't often seen in zoos, because your human friends find sexual excess distasteful."

The Beak kneels down beside me and brings his voice to a coarse whisper.

"But chimps? Chimps are a different story," he says. "Cute in zoos, but they're a pack of killers in the wild. Sit around, patrol their territory and then attack another group in coordinated assaults."

The Beak shakes his head at me.

"You love your fellow humans because you think you're with a bunch of bonobos," he says. "You'll drink with them, any random group of mortals passing you by, it doesn't matter who. One big celebration, one big orgy, over and over again, because this is what humanity is all about, right?"

I don't have an answer for this, but if there's an expert on what humanity is all about, it's not the scowling Crow above me.

"This isn't the essence of what they are, for if humanity's existence was merely the lifelong party you think it is, there would be no need for Hell," says the Beak. "Humans aren't bonobos. They're chimps—hungry, insatiable, violent chimps. They'll drink your wine, but only to take respite from their endless strife, to recoup for the next day's battle. They'll ostensibly form friendships at your parties, but these are really just the forging of *alliances*, groups meant to outcompete or destroy something else. You might think your environment of unending intoxication helps couples find love, but all you're doing is helping them *breed*, to make way for a larger generation to consume, kill and destroy."

His logic is flawed, and I wonder if he's ever been to a party in his life. But again, I see the general direction his argument is headed.

"But to merely compare your friends to chimpanzees would be *incomplete*," says the Beak. "For humanity is far worse. In every human heart lies a terrifying power, and if left to their own path they'll do things to this world that make even the gods shudder."

His point made, the Beak signals the Claws to resume. The big man starts beating and tearing at my flesh. After a few moments he stops abruptly, and I feel relief at the cessation. I take a look at his dead eyes, however, and I can tell that it's merely a taste of what's yet to come.

"And we were sent here for a specific reason," says the Beak. "You freed the Titan, to help it unleash our fire, to bring it to the humans. But we know that this fire will ultimately burn the whole world down, so your father sent us to ensure that *you* are the one to stop this from happening."

The Beak gets up, and looks over the stalks of grass waving in the moonlight. The grass sways hypnotically and I hear the faint sound of animals shrieking at each other, to find a mate or to stake their territory. I can't help but think they've fallen neatly into an equilibrium, like less-prideful versions of the Beak's much-loathed humans.

"You see, human potential transcends even destruction," says the Beak. "If humanity is unleashed as you and your comrade have wished, *all* of this will one day be gone, and I mean *gone*. I'm not saying that this earth will be ravaged by war or decimated by overpopulation, but everything you see here will be *gone, eradicated*. If your goal is met, this world will meet a bad end under the grey substance, and the fate will be a final one."

I try to start piecing together his message about the grey substance, the fire burning the whole world down, and a fate that will eradicate the world. I think about how Cerberus was so completely *eradicated* in Hell, so thoroughly extinguished that the monster might as well never have existed in the first place. I'm beginning to put these things together when the Beak nods at the Claws, and the coal-eyed man compresses his talons into a tight ball, and then bludgeons me with a brick of a fist. He does this twice more, I cough up some blood, and then the Beak resumes speaking.

"You purport to love humanity, and you wanted to make them more powerful than the gods, to free them from the *control* of Hell. But you fail to realize just how dangerous your fellow partygoers are, not only to themselves, but to the world. Nothing around us will remain alive," he says, "and I mean *nothing*."

He kneels down to whisper into my ear, which is now covered in dried blood.

"You might not remember me, Dion, but my name is *Retjar*," says the Beak. "Before all this you called me *Retjar the Damned*. But all you need to know right now is that we will ensure that you keep driving this vehicle forward, and that we come from a very, very dark place."

Retjar the Damned. His full name causes me to shudder, and this somehow allows me the energy to spit right between his dead little eyes. Retjar stands up in response, then shakes his head to ruffle himself off.

"Very well," he says. "I guess it's time to begin."

A TALE OF THE HIGHWAY

Ari

Once again I won't go into the grisly details, but please know that there are plenty, even more than the first session. They take more time, and they're more relentless, and much more thorough. No part of my body had gone untouched the first time they had pulverized it, but they still find more parts to break, parts that I'd have never thought existed. The Claws reigns his fists down on me without remorse, and I sense that he's even more unreasoning than Retjar, if such a thing is possible.[20]

/***/

This session does end though, at least to my conscious mind, and it ends with a final decisive blow. My amnesiac self leaves this earthly plane, bludgeoned down into the asphalt by the force of the Crows, and is then pushed down even further, and perhaps also *pulled* to the world beneath.

I find myself falling through the familiar darkness of the underworld's upper atmosphere, and it's too empty to be cold, too pointless to hold despair. *This is a place between existences that's remained undrawn, where nothing ever was and nothing ever will be.*

But the cold soon arrives, and the despair comes shortly thereafter. The realm of Hell shows itself beneath, and I'm either falling towards it or it's coming towards me, waiting to swallow me whole. It approaches with such speed that I believe it to be the latter, a consuming *active*

---

[20] Perhaps such a thing is possible. Retjar is abominable beyond description, but the Claws is somehow worse in his own way. Retjar is surely evil, but he's bound by his task and will eventually tell the Claws to stop. The Claws holds no limits, I don't even think he's aware of the concept of a *limit*. Perhaps my moniker for him is somewhat prescient, and he's indeed like the talons of a raptor. The bird of prey will only eat until it's full, but its talons do whatever they're told. If he's told to beat without stopping, the Claws will do that, and won't stop. This is the reality I face while smothered by this coal-eyed man, this terror with the weight of an Erymanthian Boar.

Hell, anticipating my arrival and coming to take me in its unforgiving jaws, waiting to punish me for whatever it is I've done to it.

/***/

I land in the same place I'd dreamt before, and I see that the grey sludge has completely enveloped Cerberus, leaving nary a whisker. I still see a faint mound where he had once been, but it's only a matter of time before the once-fearsome monster vanishes completely.

Perhaps it's for the best, because the three-headed dog may have outlived his purpose. This grey sludge is so pervasive that punishment is no longer a part of this place. *Absolute oblivion renders terror obsolete.*

The goat is still there of course, as indifferent and as calm as a goat should be. He's on Cerberus' faint mound, sniffing the dead air for something to eat. He's finding nothing of course, but he sniffs on regardless.

I decide to talk to him.

How do I get out of here? I ask.

The goat stares at me, as if to say that this is not the question with which I should concern myself.

How do I escape the Crows in the world above?

The goat continues to stare at me. I need a more specific question.

How do I open the trunk?

The goat makes a bleating sound in response, and I can somehow understand its meaning: *perfection.*

Perfection? I ask.

The goat bleats again, and I hear the same thing once more. I'm glad he's talking to me, but it still doesn't make sense. I understand that

I'm in Hell while my body currently lies broken in the world above, but I'd still like a better answer. Something like *6342* or even *There's another way through the back seat*, but right now the goat is telling me that *perfection* is the key to opening the trunk. *Perfection* is the way to free the creature that I've apparently already freed.

Freed or kidnapped, I don't know for sure. A lot of things don't make perfect sense right now, but this goat's single glowing horn lets me know that he's on my side. And in this place, with a world waiting above that's not much better, it's good enough for now.

I give the goat time to mention something else, but that's all he has to say. I still feel grateful that he gave me a word though, because after all, he is a goat. I remember that there are two places not yet visited, and I look to the left of me and see the woman being buffeted by winds, and in another chamber the purple planet. The latter holds an iridescent allure that entices me, but the former holds a different kind of beauty, one more powerful. I squint with my dreamt eyes and recognize her bright green hair at once.

Ari.

It's the girl in the photo. She's being thrown to and fro by a tempest blowing furiously within her chamber, and her body is limp, as if she'd been suspended in a lake. I focus on her eyes and see them filled with heavy, shameful tears, and when she sees my gaze she looks away. I look at the goat and he looks back with a flat-toothed smile.

Well, that's it, he seems to say. *I guess you have to go in.*

/***/

We wade into Ari's chamber, and it's a large, hollow cave, with rocks and wind, darkness and despair. The despair isn't that born of the grey mud, though I can see that the substance has already begun consuming this place, but rather a *human* despair. There's a poetry here, a sadness, something reflecting a great loss, and—somehow—it makes me feel alive.

This place is largely empty, but it still holds emotions. Perhaps that's what defines humanity: emotions.

The rocky walls are crumbling due to the grey mud, and I can see the adjacent chambers peeking in through growing cracks. This chamber still holds its own power though: the power of wind. There's a strong, never-ending gale blowing through the place, and I see Ari airborne, being thrown about like a doll.

She sees me on my ledge and turns away again, suspended in the air but still shamed by my presence. I wave again until she has no recourse but to come to me, and she eventually does. The winds toss her forward, but she can't grab hold of my outstretched hands. She's pulled back and then tries again, and again. She manages to twist her momentum towards my ledge, and soon hits an outcropping with an enormous impact.

She's able to hold on, and I reach out to bring her close to me. She waves me away, still ashamed.

"Hello, Ari," I say. "It's me, Dion. I think."

Silence from her.

"I really need to talk with you," I say.

Ari hides her head behind the rock.

"Please, Ari," I say. "I really need to speak with you."

I wait for her to talk, and she does.

"I'll speak with you," she says, her eyes still hidden behind the rock. "But I won't look at you."

I shake my head and laugh at this.

"I'd really like you to come here, or at least look at me," I say. "The only beings that I've seen since I lost my memory are two men. Two *bad* men, who come from crows. One talks and the other one beats me until I come here."

I see Ari thinking about this behind her rock.

"I understand,"[21] she says. "But I can't bear to face you, at least not yet."

"All right," I say. "But you will talk?"

I see her nodding behind her rock, and that's good enough for me.

"Then let's talk," I say. "Tell me everything."

/***/

She's a bit reticent at first, and I don't blame her. This place isn't the worst place I can imagine,[22] but it's not exactly a place to encourage soul-baring conversations either. I know I'd make it happen if I'd had but a single bottle of wine, but I don't. So I have no recourse but to wait her out. She tells me the background of her plight, how *she* did something bad to me, and how she fell to this end as a result.

---

[21] Ari was probably a little crazy back on Earth, but the great thing about crazy girls is that when strange things happen to you, they don't brush it off. Here I am complaining about two men who come from crows and then beat me until I meet her in Hell, and she accepts my predicament without a second thought. She might have been a crazy green-haired girl on Earth, but my world is pretty crazy, especially now.

[22] In Dante's conception of Hell, sins of incontinence, wrongdoings that didn't really hurt anyone but the sinner—gluttony, lust, adultery and the like—weren't considered as bad as sins of violence, heresy and other misdeeds that were truly malevolent. So those like Ari, who had succumbed to personal weaknesses, fell to a comparatively better fate than the others. It's still Hell, but Ari's fate isn't as bad as it could be. Oh, and spoiler alert—Ari might have committed suicide, which would seemingly send her to a different fate if you take a look at Dante's *Inferno*. But as you'll see in a later footnote with Cleopatra, there are no hard-and-fast rules when you're in Hell.

She speaks of Francesca da Rimini, a 13th-century woman forced into a marriage she did not want, who then fell in love with a young man, named Paolo, who loved her back. Like their legendary counterparts Lancelot and Guinevere, the love was real but delivered most all parties to a bad end.

I quickly gather her meaning: that her love for me was real but it delivered us both here, and though her chamber of Hell is bad, the shame she carries is worse.

I can't be angry at her, and it's not because I don't have memory to feel such a thing. I don't, of course, but there's something more.

Ari may have played a part in this, but it must have been an unwitting one. She's not like the Crows. She claims to have done bad things, but I don't think that's the whole story.

I ask her to tell me what she did.

She hides her head in shame behind the rock again, and I have no recourse but to wait her out once more. She eventually comes out, and says that she wants to tell me her story, all of it. She also tells me that her story begins with me.

"Me?"

"Yes," she says. "Sometimes you meet someone and their presence is so immediately *strong* that you can't imagine your life before them, an existence where they held no place. That's how it was with you, so that's where my story begins—with *you*."

I hear the cracking of rock in the distance, and look down to see that her chamber is falling apart. The walls are decaying on one side to reveal a burning city in the depths, and the other has broken open to show a giant, blindfolded creature that appears to be in utter dismay.

We don't have much time here, but this is important. So I've just got to let her tell me what she feels she must.

"All right," I say. "Tell me the story, our story. And start at the beginning."

/***/

Ari creeps around the rock, and her hair is windswept but still brilliant to see, with the same unnaturally bright green from her picture. *Perhaps the unnatural colors are the last to go here, the last to be taken by the grey mud.*

"It began when I was alive, back on Earth," she says. "I first saw you at night. There was a campfire."

She shakes her head at this, and then sheds another tear that's quickly blown away by the wind. She's sad, but her tone is wistful and holds tinges of joy around its edges. *Whatever happened to her, she's recalling a time when she was happy. It all went disastrously wrong, and she ended up in Hell, but part of our time has stayed with her.*

"It was a campfire on the beach," she says. "I was walking alone and saw it, and came near, and was welcome. Others were there too, and I soon came to understand that before you started the campfire, we had all been strangers to one another."

Sounds like a good time.

"It was your party, but you were pretty quiet,"[23] she says. "You were just there in the background, keeping things going and making sure everyone was welcome. Just there, present."

She smiles.

---

[23] Men who tell "the best" stories at parties are often indirectly vying for dominance when it comes to gaining female attention. They're laterally demonstrating their life experience, and thus fitness as a mate, to any listening female ears. It often leads to a great time for all, but it's not my style.

"But I noticed you," she says. "Everyone did. You were something of a legend."

"How so?"

"This wasn't the first party you'd brought. One of the revelers mentioned that you had spent a lifetime traversing the world's beaches," she says. "Setting up parties just like this. No reason for celebration other than just being alive."

I think of the Crows, and their senseless violence. Perhaps there's such a thing as *senseless joy*, and this was my way of bringing it to the world.

No, that's not entirely it. The Crows' violence, as depraved as it might be, has a purpose behind it. Everything I did before I lost my memory, from throwing these parties to freeing the creature that's in my trunk, must have had a purpose behind it as well.

I ask her if she knows why I was walking the world's beaches like this.

"You told me that you were preparing to do something big," she says. "And you wanted to party with every last human before you made your move."

She shakes her head and smiles.

"You said it wasn't possible to party with *every* last human," she says. "So you settled on walking the world's beaches, having a moment with *most* everyone. You said these campfires were building up to something you called *the Last Party*."

I ask her to tell me more about the party where we had met, and she does.

"I still remember us all there in the soft light of the campfire," she says. "The darkness hid most of our physical flaws, and the chill coming from the ocean ensured that we covered up the rest. Age, looks, money—it didn't matter there. We were all equal at this time, but not equal in a bad sense, as if we'd been stripped of our individuality. In fact, our identities, our *selves*, had never been so fully realized in that moment, at that party. And none of us had any previous connection to one another, but that arrangement somehow made us feel *more* alive, and more real."

She thinks for a moment.

"I believe what you brought us at that party was a break from the rigors of real life," she says. "Where the world always wants something out of you, and you want something out of it in return.[24] But we didn't want anything out of one another there, and we were all truly listening. Do you understand what I mean by *truly listening*?"

I might, but I gesture that I'd like to hear more.

"It's simply understanding someone, and wanting the best for them without wanting anything from them in return. And them hopefully doing the same to you. People hear you all the time, but how much of a day are we truly *listened* to?"

I think back to the Crows, who definitely want something out of me, and are so disinterested in my thoughts that they seal my mouth every time they come near.

"I'm listening to you now," I say. "We might be in Hell, but I'm listening."

Ari smiles, and it brings another windswept tear to her cheek.

"You do listen, and that's why I fell for you," she says. "It made me

---

[24] This feeling is unfortunately pervasive throughout modern life. Most people spend the majority of their days at a job where their presence is only tolerated if they perform in a certain way. This earns them the right to go to a restaurant afterwards, where they only tolerate a waiter's company provided the waiter brings them precisely what they ask for.

feel young again."[25]

She smiles at the thought, her green lipstick revealing soft white teeth. Despite the chamber's constant wind her dark skin glows with a strong vitality, and her eyes have remained unhardened by the Hell around her.

"Tell me about that *big thing* that I was preparing to do," I say. "Did I tell you anything about it?"

She shakes her head.

"I didn't think about it too much at first, because I was too consumed by you," she says. "After that party I quit everything I had to walk along the world's beaches by your side, to try to recreate what I felt that night."

She smiles again.

"And I did just that, every single party thereafter," she says. "We traveled the world, town by town, city by city, beach by beach, and every night held something new, something irreplaceable. And one day—I made a little joke about how your celebrations could bring world peace. You told me that your ambition was to do more than just that."

"More? More than world peace?"

Ari laughs.

"That's exactly what I thought," she says. "But as we traveled on, it began to dawn on me that you could do incredible things, and that you weren't exactly human."

---

[25] Young people listen to each other quite a bit. A schoolgirl tells her best friend that her favorite color is blue, and a week later her best friend draws her a blue flower. It seems trivial at the time, but the friend listened, and that matters. Unfortunately, the pressures of modern life drown out sentiments such as these, and friends eventually stop listening to one another, and perhaps stop listening to anyone.

More than just a man.

"A few nights later I asked you about it," she says. "And you told me. You told me that you were taking *human form*, but you weren't exactly one of us."

/***/

There's a rumbling, and I see large rocks shearing from the upper part of her chamber before plummeting into the chasm below. One falls onto the burning city, taking out one of its outer walls. I see a handful of souls trickle out after the blast, and a few start making their way towards the blindfolded creature. The blindfolded creature is too chagrined to notice this, and I see that some of his former captives are in a panic, and begin making their way towards the burning city.

Two sets of the condemned, trading prison cells while their world falls apart.

"What was I?" I ask. "What *am* I?"

"Something more than a human, that's all I know," she says. "But you did tell me that you were *acting* for the first time in your existence, and what you were trying to achieve would bring humanity to *the next level*."

"The next level?"

"Yes," says Ari. "You were throwing all these parties as a last hurrah before the new world came. You'd have one last party, change the world, and then have another party when the world began again."

The Last Party and the First Party. Sounds good to me.

I think of the creature in my trunk, and it still doesn't quite add up. I look at the goat to see if he understands this, and he just bleats in response.

"*How* was I going to change the world?" I ask. "What was I going to do to bring humanity to the next level?"

"I don't know," she says. "I was too consumed with love for you that I didn't even think to ask. But I saw your effect on all those around you, and I had no doubt that you would achieve all that you set out to do."

I consider this for another moment, and she seems genuine in her sentiments. But I hear the walls continue to crack, and I know that I've got to get the whole story before this place crumbles into dust.

"How did you end up here?" I ask.

Ari averts her eyes.

"I did something very bad," she says. "Very bad."

"Tell me what you did."

She can't quite tell me just yet, but I remain silent and she slowly gathers her courage.

"I erased your memory," she says.

"You?" I say, incredulous. "You erased my memory?"

"Yes," she says. "And this prevented you from doing what you were hoping to achieve. You are as you are right now because of me."

/***/

Her words sound truthful, but something tells me that this isn't the whole story. Ari may have had her problems on Earth, but she's not a schemer. She may have erased my memory, she may have been the reason why I was set upon this path, but she couldn't have done it on purpose. She's many things, but she's not malevolent. She wouldn't have hurt me on purpose.

She must have been some sort of pawn. Because she was blinded by her love for me, the Crows probably forced her to do bad things.

We talk and figure out that this is indeed the case, at least partially. I tell her about the Beak and the Claws, and she shakes her head.

"It was another," she says. "I sensed she was a being like yourself, but she was not one of the Crows of which you speak."

I ask her who this was.

"It was woman with pale skin, and eyes that were rimmed with blood," says Ari. "She was carrying a strange jar, and she visited me in my dreams."

/***/

The winds pick up and Ari creeps towards my ledge, clutching onto the rocks. The chamber has decayed further – I see the burning city below, and its outer walls have all collapsed, soon to be consumed by the grey mud beneath. The giant, blindfolded creature is now mired in the substance as well, his loosed prisoners stepping over him to make their way towards the burning city.[26]

"My name's not Ari," she says. "At least not my birth name. You said I reminded you of your first love, someone a long time ago, and you gave me her nickname. I actually love to hear you say it, but I wonder if that's how the first pangs of envy were born within me."

"Envy?" I ask. "You don't seem the type."

"I'm not, and perhaps that's why it snuck up on me so insidiously," she says. "The bleeding-eyed woman visited me in a dream, and showed

---

[26] I believe the burning city to be that of *Dis*, the city of Hell that's meant to house those who sinned with malevolent intent—murderers, panderers and the like. I believe the blindfolded creature in the adjacent chamber is Plutus, the blind god of wealth. A lot doesn't make sense here: what purpose a city in Hell would serve, and what purpose would Plutus serve in general—a demon meant to punish both spendthrifts and hoarders in equal measure.

me things that hurt me in ways I'd not thought possible."

"Anything's possible in a dream," I say, looking around at my possibly dreamt surroundings. "Tell me what she showed you."

Ari grimaces, her memories of Earth finding a way to follow her down to Hell and hurt her further.

"My dreams were dark," says Ari. "It wasn't the darkness of what's around me now, but dark and *alone*, as if the world had died and left me behind. Then she came, the woman with eyes that were rimmed with blood. She came out of the darkness and spoke to me, and her voice was so soft, and her message was so clear that I had no recourse but to listen."

"What did she say?"

"She didn't say too much at first," says Ari. "But she *showed* me quite a bit. She showed you throughout history, from early civilizations to the middle ages, to now. You've lived a long time, you know."

I feel like I have. As far as I know this could be my first day on Earth, but part of me feels like I've had a thousand lifetimes.

"I'm *more than just a man*, I guess."

"You are, and she showed me your existence in all its splendor," says Ari. "Dancing in both Greece and Rome, celebrating the autumn equinox with the ancient druids, and then traveling beyond Europe to live with the world's aboriginals, to become part of their legends just through your very presence."

It sounds like a good time.

"How did I do all this?"

"You would come down from the heavens and take human form," says Ari. "I saw you do this in my dreams, and it brought joy to my heart.

You'd come down to this earth and everyone you met would love you, time and time again. But then—"

Ari shakes her head.

"The woman opened her jar, just a crack," says Ari. "And envy came out."

This bleeding-eyed woman might not have the Crows' force, but she seems to have her methods.

"I saw all the loves you've had throughout the centuries," says Ari. "Starting with my namesake, and stretching on for what seemed like forever, until it got to me. It hurt knowing that I was so small within the context of your life, just a grain of sand compared to the ocean of your existence."

I want to tell Ari that this probably wasn't the case, and it definitely isn't the case now. *I'm sure I felt for you then—and my existence no longer fills an ocean.*

She continues.

"The bleeding-eyed woman then asked if I wanted to be your only love, and of course I said *yes*. That's when she gave me her plan."

A plan. All right, now we're getting somewhere.

"She told me that I needed to gather materials," says Ari. "Various tinctures from around the world, including a rare chemical that just got back on the market because the factory that made it had just reopened, and she then had me mix them in a certain way. She said if I put it in your wine it would make you mine, and mine alone."

It's interesting. This woman and the Crows are so powerful, yet they rely on others to do their tasks—

"I put the chemicals in your wine, just like she instructed me," says

Ari. "But you drank it, and then started convulsing on the floor and then—"

I can see that Ari wants to avert her eyes again, but she wills herself not to.

"And when I saw what it was doing to you, I knew that I had made a horrible mistake," she says. "I think about that moment quite a bit now, and in fact I think of little else. I wasn't killing you, because I don't think your kind can be killed. But I was *destroying* you. I'd wanted you for myself, and I was willing to destroy you to do it."

It's starting to make some sense now. I'm not quite human, but I can take human form. The Crows can't obtain such a real presence on this earthly plane, or at least not enough to drive a vehicle. But they can influence *me*, so they do their work on my human body so that I'll drive the car for them. *Why* they want me to drive this vehicle and *where* they want me to go is still a mystery, but I can tell that this bleeding-eyed woman in Ari's dreams works in a similarly indirect fashion. In fact, she acts even more indirectly than the Crows. *She had Ari do her earthly bidding not through force, but through emotion.*

"She tricked you," I say. "Those chemicals destroyed my memory, at least my memory in this earthly body. That's how she claimed I would be yours, and yours alone. I'd forget every other woman, and you'd be my only one."

A blast of wind blows Ari's green hair violently. I see that the condemned below are no longer fleeing towards their opposite chambers. Those that can still move are now trying to crawl up the walls, in a desperate attempt to escape Hell itself. *It's a futile endeavor: Hell's walls are not made for escaping. In any case the grey mud will soon liquefy these chambers, and leave these souls with nothing left to climb.*

I take solace in the fact that at least the souls below will no longer suffer any torment from their former fates. The burning city is now extinguished, and the blindfolded creature is currently writhing on the ground in vexation, just as helpless as those who'd escaped him.[27]

"But I knew that wasn't going to be the case," says Ari. "I realized that I'd destroyed you, and that I'd destroyed your plan to abet humanity's elevation as well. So I did the only thing I could think of."

"You took the remainder of the potion yourself," I say. "It killed you, and you wound up here."[28]

Ari shakes her head in chagrin.

"I did, and as I was falling to this place, the woman may have sent me one more dream," says Ari. "I saw two shadows, and they were doing vicious, abominable things to you."

"Two shadows?"

"Yes," she says. "Now that I think about it, they looked like crows."

/***/

I crawl out on the ledge as much as my footing will allow, then reach out and bring her close to me.

---

[27] I'd previously stated that this dynamic between Dis, Plutus and the captive souls doesn't make sense, and it still doesn't, but there's a cold truth cutting through everything now. This truth is the grey mud, which somehow brings order to this world. It's obliterating everything, but that makes sense at least. There were questions and hypocrisies surrounding both Dis and Plutus' existence, but as these strange parts of Hell dissolve, so do their ambiguities. In the shadow of the grey mud's devastation, both demon and the damned are equally helpless. That at least is understandable.

[28] I don't know precisely why Ari was sent to Hell. Some say suicide is a mortal sin, but that's not always the case. In Dante's *Inferno* Cleopatra was sent to Hell, but not because she allowed herself to be bitten by an asp. She was sent to the level reserved for adulterers, because in her time, suicide was not a sin. The rules of Hell change with the mores of the time, and for the record I just saw the *completely virtuous* shades of Socrates, Plato and Aristotle. They reside in Hell not because of sin, but because they choose to. Perhaps Hell is not so much a punishment, but rather a state of mind.

"Ari," I say, wiping another tear from her cheek. "You have no reason to feel bad."

"I *destroyed* you!" she yells. "I wanted you all to myself, and I destroyed *you*, the one that I *loved*! And with this act, I put my desires over *you*, and over the rest of the world. I couldn't see past—"

I interrupt these words by kissing her. The wind picks up even more, and her hair seems impossibly long as it wraps around me, driven by the gale to envelop us both. I then pull myself away from her green lips, but still hold her closely.

"I can't feel any bad sentiments towards you, not even a single one," I say. "I don't remember enough to feel anything bad at all,[29] but even if I did—"

I look up, and through the heavy winds I hear a faint rumbling. I wonder if it's the Claws still working over my unmoving body.

"I don't quite know who we're dealing with, but I can assure you, Ari, they're more powerful than they seem. They might not be able to walk on the earthly plane, but they know how to get their way."

I embrace Ari once more and whisper softly in her ear.

"They tricked you, and they're currently tricking me, or rather— *forcing my hand*. You did as they wish, and I'm doing the exact same thing."

---

[29] Even if I could feel anger at her, amnesia erases all sins. The darkest secrets go unremembered, and if brought up again become stories stripped of emotion. I think there's a positive message in this, in that this allows societies to move on from war and other atrocities wrought by history. There's a kind of *amnesia* that comes with the passing of generations. A war might create a million blood enemies, but those soldiers' grandchildren won't really care that much, and when indifference comes, forgiveness is an afterthought. Perhaps mortality is the key to human progress: the persistent source of amnesia that allows societies to forgive and move forward.

Ari pushes me off, unconvinced.

"I know what they did to me," she says. "And I can only imagine what they're doing to you. But regardless of my intentions, their plan leads to a bad end as well, one not too far removed from the fate you see around us."

"What do you mean?"

"I've had dreams down here as well," says Ari. "And I've seen shadows of the world that *they'll* abet."

"What's it like?"

"If they have their way, this grey substance will be avoided," she says. "But the world above will still somehow be incomplete, somehow *limited*."

This makes a little sense to me. If my plan involving the creature in the trunk was to take humanity to the next level, the world would somehow be limited if that plan were to be thwarted.

And besides, any world abetted by the Crows and this bleeding-eyed woman won't be that great.

I look below to see that the extinguished city has all but disappeared, sinking slowly into the mud. The blindfolded creature is now a faint, unmoving mound, and most of the souls have given up any notion of escape. *Their agony is muted by despair, their anguish is giving way to a resignation.* I see a few still moving but most are passively letting the grey substance take them. Some are even actively submerging themselves in the mud, just as I would have once done were it not for the bleat of the single-horned goat now beside me on this rocky ledge.

"The Crows told me that if I release the creature in my trunk, everything will be destroyed," I say. "Including Hell."

"If Hell disappears, so be it," she says. "Perhaps the universe is better off without this place."

"But they also told me that the world above would be eradicated," I say. "More than an extinction event, an *eradication*—an erasure. Maybe the grey sludge will come there as well."

"Have you seen this grey substance during your time on Earth?" she asks.

"No."

"Not one bit?"

"No," I say. "Not one bit."

Ari considers this, and then her eyes flash a brilliant color for a moment. If I had to describe the color, I'd say that it would be that of the goat's single horn and the light coming from the philosopher's room.

"Then who's to say that your plan would abet it?" she says. "Who's to say that your plan to elevate humanity, a plan that you'd laid out and thought about *for centuries*, would somehow do the precise opposite of what you intended?"

Ari comes close and kisses me once more.

"I didn't fall for you just because you're *more than human*," she says. "I fell for you because you're more—*you're more than whatever it is that you are*. I don't know your plan, but I believe in it because of you, Dion. I *listened* to you and heard something that I don't quite understand, but I know that it *matters*."

Ari looks up, and we listen to the distant rumbling.

"And those above have ill intent," she says. "That matters as well."

I believe her when she says this. *I might be forced to listen to*

Retjar's hissed warnings, but I'll listen to Ari's words a little more closely.

"Maybe this is why I chose to do what I did after my mistake," says Ari. "Maybe this is why I chose to send myself to Hell, so that I could be here to tell you to continue. Whatever path it is that you were on, you need to continue."

I feel myself being pulled away from this crumbling chamber, back up to the world above. I don't particularly care for this place, but I don't want to leave just yet. *I want to stay with Ari just a little longer, even if it means remaining in Hell.*

I hold on to her as tight as I can, but she's pulled back by the wind just as I'm being pulled upwards. I think of Francesca and Paolo as I'm ascending, of Lancelot and Guinevere.

She likens us to star-crossed lovers, and I'm still not sure what that means. But she also says that I'm more than whatever it is that I am, and that means we need not share their fates. I need not share any fate. If I'm more than just a man, it means I can make my own path.

A TALE OF THE HIGHWAY

Running on Empty

I wake up with my face on the highway, feeling like I've been buried facedown.[30] But I'm not dead and I'm not yet buried, so I pool my energy and peel myself off the road, leaving some of my flesh stuck neatly in the cracks of the asphalt. I lie on my back, itself already healed while I had that strange dream, and I let the moonlight heal the rest of me.

Left for dead with my face in the dirt like a forgotten witch. Maybe that's precisely what I am.

Ari said I was *more than just a man*, but I don't think I'm a witch. I don't even feel like a man now. I feel less, like something that's been smashed under a boot. The moon heals me, and I stop feeling like complete roadkill, but I don't yet feel superhuman.

I can't feel superhuman, because those types do what they want. They control their own destiny, or at least die trying to do just that.

I know I can make my own path, but if anything I feel like a *pawn* of the supernatural at this moment, menaced into serving another's agenda, one that I don't fully understand.[31]

Maybe I came from the supernatural, and I'm just trapped in this human form.

Maybe I'm *somewhat* human.

---

[30] Many cultures did this, to their enemies at least. They'd bury someone facedown so that the soul couldn't escape to heaven. At the very least the act would humiliate the victim in their life's final moment.

[31] I've come to learn, however, that pawns play a crucial role in history. Imagine the Trojan Horse without the soldiers hiding inside it, keeping quiet until nightfall. Without these soldiers doing as they're told, Troy would not have fallen to the Greeks. Pawns might not control their own fate, but history wouldn't happen without them.

That makes sense. I'm *more than just a man*, yet still just a man at this moment. The Crows can still beat me because I walk both this plane and theirs, and I can be healed from their anguish because of my original, supernatural self.

But your former self chose to do something big, a superhuman task, and you have to see it through.

I've got to find the code to this trunk. This will allow me to be in control again.

Control.

As I get into the car and restart the engine, I realize that control is something of which I am completely and utterly bereft.

/***/

I say hello to my friend in the trunk, and it (he? she?) thumps in response, still taciturn, but here at least. I pull another wine bottle out of the back, a straightforward Syrah, and then thump it on my shoe and the armrest until the cork rises up. I work the rest out with my teeth and spit it onto the passenger-side floor, too far to reach while driving, but it doesn't matter because I'm having the whole bottle. I take a swig immediately, and it's just what I need: firm, a bit tannic, peppery with a little bit of burnt rubber in its flavor.[32]

The wine's flavor takes over my whole mouth (and then some, because my right cheek even begins to sting), but still, I can't help

---

[32] Syrahs can have a little bit of rubber in their taste, but it's not a bad thing. Hard to explain, but if you ever get hold of a Syrah with a bit of burnt rubber in its bouquet, drink it and you'll understand. In any case, it's a firm wine, and that's what I need at this point. I don't need to savor the memories of Hell with a white zinfandel, I don't need to wax nostalgic on Ari's fate with a soft pinot noir. I need a firm wine to take over my senses and leave the past in the past, and if it tastes of rubber, all the better.

mulling over the fate of this world, and I can't help bringing it up with my friend in the trunk. I ask the creature if it can listen, and it thumps an emphatic *yes*. I feel grateful to have it here, quiet but unequivocally on my side.[33]

"Retjar seems to think that if I release you, *nothing* around us will remain alive. Just nothing."

I shake my head.

"Do you believe this?"

A silent *no*.

"Do you at least understand where he's coming from?"

A reluctant thump.

"But you're good, right?" I ask. "I know we've gone over this before, but I need some assurance. You're unequivocally on my side, and on the side of humanity, right?"

An emphatic thump, one so strong it shakes the car. I wonder if I ask this creature another question like this if it will break out of the trunk by itself.

"Here's to you, then," I say, holding the bottle up. "Here's to *us*, still trying to figure a way out of our predicament."

The creature thumps, and I tip my bottle to the rearview mirror before taking another drink. I think about Ari's sadness, Retjar's cynicism, and a decaying Hell as the highway rolls beneath us. I think more about Retjar's words, and figure that they're either untrue, or at least woefully myopic.

"Retjar owes his *existence* to humanity," I say. "I don't know what

---

[33] If I knew this creature's favorite color, I'd draw it a flower in that color to say "thank you for listening."

he is, but I gather that if his much-loathed humans disappeared, he would too. Hell probably would as well, for that matter. Some things need someone to torment to give them purpose."

The creature taps the trunk in agreement.

"That's right," I say. "And if Retjar's so confident in his argument, why doesn't he tell the Claws to get off my chest so that I can speak?"

The creature thumps in solidarity, and I toast us again. *Ari said I need to do the right thing, and so did the three philosophers.* I feel like I'm going to do the right thing and let this creature out, but still, I can't shake the last part that Retjar said.

Nothing around us will remain alive. Just nothing.

I look at the road beneath the vehicle, and the endless stretch of land around me, passing silently through my closed windows. It's empty, but it's not *really* empty, and it's anything but dead. There's still farmland, and if I pass a plot that's fallow, there's still grass. Underneath that grass are the insects of the earth, and underneath the insects are the microbes. Every bit of this world contains a nation of life, an unseen microcosm living, dying, feeding off each other, and being fed back to those they'd once consumed.

I'd understand Retjar's words if he'd given a more limited admonition, like *Humanity needs to stop war—or pollution or overpopulation, or just tone it down a bit.* I get that humanity as a whole might need some tweaking. I understand this even in my amnesiac state. But *nothing*? Even in the worst case, something survives. Something always survives.

/***/

The Syrah does what it needs to do, and erases the Crows and the grey sludge of Hell from my mind, leaving just Ari, the creature in the trunk, and the mystery of how to free it. I'm ruminating on the goat's bleated clue *perfection* and how that could be translated into four digits, when I feel a drop on my shoulder. I look down to see blood, though it feels strangely cool on my skin. It's not crusted over, and I look again and realize that it's not blood, but wine. I glance at the mirror to see that the right side of my face is still scraped in places, and there's a hole in my cheek that leaked some Syrah out onto my shoulder.[34] The mirror reveals my body to be largely healed, but still holding a patchwork of sinews, and glistening dark red. I turn my cheek to the moon, but give pause.

Maybe if I let the hole remain, there will be one less thing for the Crows to pierce in our next session. Maybe if I stay eviscerated, there will be less of me to destroy.

I turn to the moon and chide my own wishful thinking. Those like Retjar will never want for things to destroy.

/***/

The moon heals me completely, and soon the memory of the second beating is washed away, and I'm again left alone with my thoughts. I begin to think about how much it would take to open the trunk. I figure even if they recognize my pattern of attempts I could get four choices in before the Crows get me, and 9999 divided by four is around 2,500. That's quite a bit, and probably more when you factor in the harsh realities of my situation. Each beating has gotten progressively worse, and I've been sent down to Hell every time afterwards, at least so far. That's a heavy price to pay for a few shots each time, no matter what the payoff is. And suppose the Crows catch on? They probably will, and I wouldn't put it past them to erase my memory again. Maybe they'll send Ari back from the dead to slip something into my next bottle of wine, or maybe they'll just beat me so badly I won't remember where I left off.

---

[34] It figures, in retrospect. The Syrah's tannin bit me, but even the most astringent red shouldn't have bitten like this.

I might even get it right and then mess up, enter the right number but pull on the door a little too quickly for fear of the distress to come. I'd miss the number and start the cycle anew with another 2,500 beatings.

Or there could be no number: *the key to the trunk was in your heart all along, you just needed to find true love*, or something like that. A tale that includes the Crows as characters doesn't seem too likely to hold a narrative convention like this, but you never know.

Maybe there's no way to open the door. Maybe this is all just an illusion in my head, and I'll awake in a hospital gurney as a normal human, with Dr. Thumper telling me I overdosed in a car by the side of the road, and if it weren't for my wife Ari finding me and calling an ambulance (where two paramedics named Ritjar and Klaus covered me with grey antibiotics and took me to *St. Crow* hospital), I'd surely be dead by now. It was all just a dream that took place while my heart stopped, and they've never seen such a miraculous recovery, and I should really cut back on my drinking.

That would be a great ending and I'd love it to be true, but I just don't think it's the case. Everything's too lucid, and something tells me you can't feel pain in a dream. You can feel emotions, but you can't feel what the Claws delivers in a dream.

Still, this might all be a hallucination. I've got to keep up hope for that ending.

But all I can act upon is the world around me, so I've got to recognize what I *do* have. I've got to recognize that in *this* world, I've got a few characters on my side: I've got the philosophers and Ari in Hell, and the creature in my trunk on Earth. I've also got Dr. Shaw and his words, if I can count them.

And I have the goat.

I saw that one-horned goat in Hell, but he follows me around and doesn't seem too concerned about anything, including the grey mud. I've got to count him as an ally. And he gave me a clue: *perfection*.

Unfortunately, that doesn't make too much sense now, because I haven't seen anything close to that lately. I've seen strength and anger, love and fury, screaming enemies and silent friends. I might save the world or destroy it, but I haven't seen anything that's *perfect*. There's no perfection in my world right now, not even close.

/***/

I drive on for what seems like another hour, and then I notice that I have a fourth of a tank left. This could be a problem, though it's not an unexpected one. Even if there's magic all around, I believe I'm in a real car, and cars use real gas. Nothing mystical about that.

I think back to the wording on the note: *Drive until this road ends, and then drive some more*. Unfortunately, the wording doesn't preclude me from any punishment if I run out fuel. If it had read *drive until you can't* I'd have an out, not that Retjar would care, but at least I'd have an excuse. Now I have a dilemma, and considering I haven't yet seen a single building, let alone a gas station, it's not going to be an easy one to solve.

I can't help but take a little bit of solace in the soft fatalism that *there's nothing I can do about it*.

"Listen," I say to the thing in the trunk, resisting the urge to call it *Dr. Thumper*, "we're going to be in a little fuel situation here pretty soon, one way or another. But I want to let you know that I'm going to do everything in my power to make sure nothing happens to you, at least."

Silence from the trunk. I don't blame Dr. Thumper[35] for not

---

[35] I can call it by this nickname in this internal monologue, at least for the time being. I'll find out its real name soon enough though, and it will change just about everything.

responding, because from what I've ascertained, I sense this creature is the powerful and noble type. Whatever it is, it isn't accustomed to being protected. *It does the protecting, it* does everything in its power to prevent the Crows from hurting guys like me.

It's probably accustomed to protecting more than just a near-naked amnesiac like myself. Dr. Thumper probably wants to be out of the trunk and guarding humanity's future, that kind of thing.

"All right," I say. "Whatever the case, we have a fuel problem coming up, and we're in it together. Can you give me that much?"

Without hesitation, a solid, definitive *thump*.

"Good," I say. "So I'll keep an eye out for a gas station, and in the meantime—"

I don't know what either of us can do beyond that.

"Let's think," I say. "Let's relax a bit and think, because that's just about all we can do right now."

A solid thump. We drive in silence for a few moments, and I realize that we need something more.

"Let's relax *while* we think," I say. "Do you mind if we have some wine, maybe some music? It'll take the edge off."

Another thump, this one as solid as the last. I know I can't share the wine with my cohort, but I'll find a way to relax—to *party* with this creature. I owe it that much, and I can tell I'm good at partying. That's what I do best, and I'll find a way to have a good time, even while being chased by two sociopaths, on a near-empty tank.

I may have done something big by freeing this Titan in my trunk, but that's not who I am necessarily.

I'm not a savior, I'm not a fighter, and, as I've seen so far, I'm not exactly a detective. I'm good at *having a good time*, that's my strength, and I'm going to show Dr. Thumper just what I can do.

/***/

Still no music on the radio dial, and I feel bad for having even brought it up.

"Let's listen to Dr. Shaw again," I say, and the creature thumps in the affirmative before I can get to my second point. "I wish I could share a drink with you, but I can't. So I tell you what, I'll save that drink for later, and you pick the track."

The creature remains silent, and I think I get its meaning.

"All right, I'll have a drink," I say, to the creature's immediate thump. "But you're picking the track again."

My cohort agrees and I read a list of names of the CD's sections, and since the Syrah is drained I do this while reaching back for another bottle. None of the track names seem to be taking my cohort's fancy, so I take a break from this and examine the bottle I picked out: it's a clear liquid named *grappa*, and after I take out its cork, it tastes a bit strong, but right.[36]

I continue with the list of titles covering everything from democracy to Hegel, and I finally get to a track my cohort likes. It's called "Human Origins and Our Philosophical Base," and the creature seems pretty certain that we should be playing this.

---

[36] Grappa isn't wine per se, but rather a brandy made from grapes. It can be up to 60 percent alcohol by volume, so I don't suggest drinking grappa all night. Regardless, it's great now, and I take back any previous aspersions I may have cast upon gin and tonic and the grey-faced workadaddies who drink them. Grappa packs a punch, and I recognize its value at this point. Wine is a great thing, but it's not the only thing. Sometimes you need something stronger, and in my current situation—hanging out with a mysterious entity in my trunk while awaiting a beating at the hands of two birdmen—I need just that.

"All right," I say, looking at the gas tank, now dipped below the quarter mark. "Let the party begin."

/***/

Human Origins and Our Philosophical Base
Stone Age in the Modern Day

Humanity's disparate societies tend to have an inexorable directive of normalizing towards a more global culture, from the domination of the Romans to today's world caught between the overpowering pushes and pulls of Western and Eastern influences. But still, there are some peoples on islands and deep in rain forests who live much as they did before the modern era.

These cultures are scarce, and their scarcity means that these peoples should be protected and treasured, and not just for their own sake. For these far-flung and extremely vulnerable tribes are windows to humanity's collective past, and within their worlds lie human truths that could not be found otherwise.

The Yanomami

The Yanomami are a culture of indigenous people who live in about 250 villages in the remote forests of Venezuela and Brazil. Early accounts of these people painted a stone-age idyll, because their daily life seems rather idyllic. Each tribesman only needs three hours per day to gather enough food, because armadillos and mouse-sized grubs run rampant through the forest, and their agriculture is developed enough to grow plantains for most every meal.

During their leisure time the men take hallucinogenic

drugs taken from the forest, and while in a trance communicate with ghosts while reciting their people's myths.

But this idyllic world was shattered when an anthropologist studied these people over the decades, and then reported back all that he had seen.

He found that roughly a third of all males will meet their end through homicide, and more than half of all Yanomami over the age of forty had lost at least two relatives through violent means.

Inter-village coalitions come together for ritual feasts, but these alliances are inevitably a mesh of byzantine intrigue. Villages will assemble to discuss trade alliances, to bolster their defense against a rival group, or even to make plans to attack one of their neighbors. But these feasts themselves can be dangerous, and are occasionally setups that lead to all invited guests being massacred at the hands of their hosts.

Meetings aside, bands of men are constantly raiding the other villages whenever they can, and woe unto a woman of the losing party if she is to survive the attack. A defenseless woman is systematically raped by all members of the invading party, then brought back home and raped by anyone else who desires to do so. If she survives the ordeal, she's given to one of the winning tribe's men as a wife.

The Yanomami men have a veneration for killing, and it is rewarded in terms of status and of reproduction. Killing an enemy warrants that the killer performs a ceremony called an *unokaimou* to avert retaliation from his victim's soul. The aforementioned anthropologist found that men who have gone through an *unokaimou* have two and a half times as many wives, and over three times as many children as the men who have not.

I stop and ask my cohort if it likes the story, and I hear a medium-level thump in the affirmative. I share that I *somewhat* like the story, for though it might hold an even darker tone than the one with High Priest Sargon, it's lending some insight at least. I tell the creature that I unequivocally love the grappa, however, and I hear an unequivocal thump of *yes* in return.

I like the story and love the drink. At the very least they both allow me to ignore the fact that our fuel tank is now only an eighth full, and dropping.

Dr. Shaw continues:

A Reflection on the Human Soul

Though the Yanomami idyll might be shattered, this is not to say that their societal morality is somehow shattered as well, or that they are *bad* people, reflecting crude notions of the primitive, hostile savage of early pulp fiction.

The Yanomami aren't bad. One could argue that their behavior of murder and rape is a function of their own genes keeping themselves happy, forming dominion over one another yet encouraging (forceful) gene flow across villages to lessen inbreeding.

One could argue this, and one can most definitely argue that their behavior is reflective of most human history. Look at the Celts, the American Indians, the Germanic tribes plundering each other, the Romans conquering the world because they could, or tribal Africans. No matter your ancestry, go back far enough and you'll find behavior analogous to the Yanomami. You may be alive today because millennia ago one of your ancestors' husbands was killed before she was raped and started your bloodline. Keep in mind that this means you were the product of both a victim and an aggressor, for the rapist and murderer is in your blood as well.

But let's not dwell on the dark truths of the human heart, and the harsh realities of gene flow. Let's realize that *this* is the raw material that philosophers had to work with, a vicious, aggressive species contemplating its own existence.[37]

This makes the miracle of philosophy doubly precious, doubly important, and unfortunately rather fragile. For

---

[37] I have this pet theory that alcohol actually helps *quell* this aggression, on a societal level at least. I'm not deigning it inhibits *individual* violence: I've seen too many bar fights to insinuate that. I'm talking about curbing the human impulse to be violent as a state, a *country*. Think of Japan and Germany. They tried to conquer the world for years by force, and then lost World War II. They renounced violence shortly thereafter, and now own half the world through economic means. Half-baked history, I know, but let's take this half-baked assumption to its fullest extent, and we can start by noting how much they drink, which is quite a bit. They work like fiends every day, *efficient* fiends, but reward themselves with the carrot of endless sake or beer at the end of each night. No more societal aggression, only a nightly party, and these relatively resource-poor countries hold sustainable wealth. The conclusion of this half-baked theory? Good things happen when you put down your guns and pick up a glass, just like Japan and Germany did. If you don't buy this, and I won't hold it against you if you don't, at the very least please recognize that there are plenty of alcohol-free countries who fight all the time. I won't name names, but there are entire *nations* of teetotalers mired in unending civil wars, their hangover-free minds able to fully process the horror around them every morning, and their party-less evenings devoid of anything to do but plot revenge. All right, I've made my case, and I know, these are *profoundly* untested hypotheses with sweeping historical assumptions. Reiterate them during a dinner party at your own risk.

not only must the philosopher overcome the stresses of the natural world to consider truth, but the philosopher must overcome one's own nature as well.

So be thankful for everything born of philosophy that you see around you, from the food you might eat due to irrigation, to the court system that will exonerate you if you are innocent, to the woman currently working on a cure for the disease that threatens to end your life three decades hence. Be thankful, but also recognize how fragile these things are, for it is not in our base nature to do these things.

/***/

Shaw's words end and I can't help discussing their meaning with the creature. It's something of a one-sided conversation, but we do talk about everything we just heard: rape and murder, war and empires, right and wrong. We talk about birth and death and the *harsh realities of gene flow* that Shaw brought up, and I ask my cohort if it understands this. The creature reluctantly thumps that it does, and we discuss this some more as I continue to sip the grappa. It's a difficult thing to talk about, but I realize that maybe its *difficulty* is precisely why we should talk about it. It's not right for a Yanomamo woman to be the victim of sexual violence, but what's the solution? Have the modern world annex their villages, and then implement its laws? Absorb them into a city where they become a semipermanent underclass, because we find their way of life distasteful?

My cohort in the trunk doesn't seem to have a quick answer to this, and I don't expect one. There probably isn't an answer, and I begin to wonder if such a concept as *right and wrong* exists at all.

There's a wrong at least, and it's taken the shape of two Crows flying behind me. Even if their motives are somehow right, they're still *wrong about something. I know this.*

I talk more with my cohort in the trunk, and we come to a small resolution of Shaw's words: that there's a base truth in all of humanity's past, and we are all both complicit and victims at once.

"Perhaps you can say the same for every living creature," I say. "It's a world of competition, where growth depends on consuming, or at least *outcompeting*, your neighbor. And humans have minds that allow them to do this on a grander scale than anything else."

The creature thumps reluctantly.

"But I think Shaw also knows that the base philosophy of kill or be killed, dominate or be dominated, is in our *past*," I say, considering myself part of humanity. "What defines us as humans is not how much grander a scale we can showcase that base nature found everywhere else, but how far we can get away from it. We don't think of the dark secrets of our past because we all yearn to distance ourselves from it, to do something greater than kill or be killed, dominate or be dominated."

The creature thumps in a solid agreement. Maybe Shaw meant what I just stated, maybe not. Regardless, despite the dark truth of that chapter I feel hopeful, and I'm happy that we found some sort of end to this. I'm happy until I look at the gas tank, and realize that we're currently running on empty.

/***/

I drain the bottle, savoring the last bit of the grappa,[38] and then slow the vehicle, thinking that it will somehow preserve fuel.

---

[38] I drank the whole bottle all right. At this point I believe I also felt an overpowering desire for something savory, perhaps an espresso. I was still worried about another beating at the hands of the Crows, another trip to Hell, and of course the question of my purpose in this strange task, but more than anything I felt at this moment that an espresso would really match this grappa's intensity.

A TALE OF THE HIGHWAY

I can't help but think about the fatalism of this situation, and I place the blame on Retjar and his partner, for whatever that's worth. It was *they* who put me in this situation, it was *they* who set me on this road, and it was *they* who gave the vehicle only one tank of gas. They can't possibly expect me to—

I then wonder if the Crows understand the basic laws of automation, and the fact that cars require fuel to move forward.

Even if they don't, bad things will happen anyway.

I look in the rearview mirror and see the flutter of wings behind me, and know that whatever my situation, it's doubtful that the Crows care. Retjar won't pass up another chance to kneel down and whisper a few more twisted half-truths into my bleeding ear, and the Claws will just do what he's told.

But still, here it is. They wanted me to *drive until this road ends, and then drive some more*. In a few minutes, I won't be able to drive, and then I'll be stuck.

/***/

I explain the situation to the creature in the trunk, who listens patiently.

"All right, I'm running out of time soon, and I need a way out of this," I say. "At the very least, I need an option, something to do."

My cohort pauses to think, and I let it. The gas gauge is less than zero now, scraping the bottom of the tank.

A moment later the creature hits the trunk again twice, and it sounds different this time. I ask it to *tell me once more*, and my comrade does so, two thuds sounding different because they're coming from the *left* of the vehicle. That's where I look. I see a light off to the left, made faint by the distance and then made strong again by the dearth of anything around it.

It's a gas station, and it's a stretch to get there—just a bit too far away to be sure I'll make it. I have no other options though, so I continue my pace. I don't turn on my left turn signal, but I figure the Crows have to know where I'm going.

They know exactly where I'm going. They've planned every bit of this out, leaving me with but one option at all times. I inevitably take it, and it inevitably leads to a bad end.

The car sputters and I give the gas pedal one more push, to keep my momentum. I look in the rearview mirror to see that the murder is coming, a flock of black wings taking the shape of two men. My vehicle slows down even further but they keep up their pace, their wings morphing into human likenesses while still maintaining their airborne pace.

The station is closer but still so far away, a lighthouse behind a mass of cold, dark waves. My vehicle slows more, the crows behind me get nearer, and I can just *feel* Retjar smiling behind me in anticipation, delighted at the depravity that's yet to come. I begin to yell and I pound the steering wheel, as if my blows will somehow push the car forward. But the vehicle still slows by half, and then by another half, and another half again. I might make it to the turn off, but there's no way I'll make it inland.

I look forward in the hopes that the road might *end* here, which would at least bring a solid resolution.

No such luck: the road stretches endlessly beyond the station, further into nothingness. There's only the lights in front of me and the approaching beings, gaining ground while my speed decreases by half once more. The men behind me have fully materialized now, and I can see Retjar's red eyes glowing, and can somehow even see the eyes of the Claws, still the lifeless color of dull coal.

I switch it into neutral, and see how far I can coast. I creep up on the station turn off, and slow to a stop just when I reach it. I see the

Crows slow as well, waiting for me to get out, to meet me at the next step of my fate. I prepare to press the brake so that I can meet them, to get it over with, to levy a volley of questions at the Crows, to maybe proffer an explanation that they didn't give me enough gas. *I'll do this, and see how far I can get before they seal my mouth shut and begin the next iteration of their gruesome work.*

I take a breath, place my foot over the brake pedal and say a few words of solidarity to the creature in the trunk, and in response it thumps in a panic to the left of the car again. I then look that way and see what this creature wants me to see, a slight depression in the path that leads to the gas station, just below the road. I immediately angle towards it, and then the car comes to a stop right at the lid of the hill. I hit the steering wheel and yell once more, and the car just tips over the downturn, gaining fresh momentum.

We start moving again.

I laugh, because we just might make it to the gas pump. It's going to be a close call, but I aim towards the closest one. I tell the creature what I'm doing and it sends a small flurry of panicked thumps in return, from the right side of the vehicle. I look to the right and don't see anything out of the ordinary, but its continued thumping leads me to the correct conclusion: the gas tank is on the other side of where I'm headed. I angle the car so the *right* side is facing the pump and my momentum comes to a stop right in front of the nozzle, and no further. I throw it in park and remove the keys.

I turn around and the Crows are nowhere to be seen. It's just me and the creature in my trunk, safe for now in this lighthouse of a gas station, with the cold, dark waves still around us.

Cruz's Outpost

I gather the courage to exit the vehicle and inspect my surroundings. It's a gas station all right, desolated but functional, with an attendant inside, in no particular state of agitation. *There's actually another human being here. It's not another mysterious creature with untold powers, and it's not someone who has died and gone to Hell. It's a real living human being, and though I'm in the middle of nowhere, I'm somehow less alone.*

I turn around again, hoping that I see no signs of the Crows. I hope that this is the conclusion to the story, an imagined hallucination revealed. I'd love a quick end to this, where the attendant tells me that I've been on drugs the whole time[39] and that I should get some help.

If this is this case, I'll get help in a heartbeat.

But I see them on my second pass around: Retjar and the Claws, right where the gas station's light ends. They're dancing on the edge of this place, cloaking themselves in darkness, but clear and real. Unfortunately, my mind is too lucid for this to be a hallucination, or even a nightmare. They're *there*, waiting amongst the shadows like sharks circling under the waves, harmless for the moment but waiting, waiting, waiting, and getting hungrier with every passing minute.

They're there, but not coming any closer. I wonder if they're scared of the attendant. Maybe Retjar detests humans more than he enjoys beating me, so he stays out of their sight.

In any case, I'm safe.

---

[39] This would be akin to waking from a blackout on the coast of Spain. It would be a little frightening, but at least it would a punchy resolution to my tale of inebriation: *it was then that I realized the men chasing me weren't real, and it was then that I realized this whole thing was just in my head.*

A TALE OF THE HIGHWAY

I decide to work on the trunk. *Four digits, ten thousand numbers. It'll take me some time, but I'll get there. They'll become enraged, especially since I'm doing this the very moment I escape their purview. I'll be safe in the lighthouse, taunting the sharks with my own blood.*

But I've got to do it, no question. If they're so upset, let them come into the light. Let them come into full view of the attendant, let them prove themselves real, and not just the figment of my own imagination that I so desperately want them to be.

Failing that, let me open the trunk and find out what all this is about. Let me look at what I've kidnapped, let me see what I've freed. I've got to find out what this thing really means to the Crows, and what it really means to the world.

/***/

I get another three numbers in before I lose control of my body: 4444, 1024 and 2337. The first two I put in because they seem perfect to me somehow, and I enter the last one just as my body loses control of itself, and I just start pressing whatever I can.

I fall on my back, prepared for yet another session with Retjar, but I realize that he's still nowhere to be seen. All I see is a single crow land on the vehicle and stare at me with cold eyes, warning me of the terror yet to come if I enter any more numbers. It stares, stares, stares and stares some more, and then caws before flying away. I gradually regain movement in my body and get up hesitantly, looking for the Crows—the ones who have taken human form, not their flying entourage.

I find them just where they were, Retjar scowling and the Claws just as dead-eyed as ever, waiting to do what's needed to be done. Retjar gives me a look that says *this is a warning, and you won't get another*. I got three shots at the trunk that time, maybe three more if I decide to go again, but they'll be here if I do with another session, and I'll still need a few thousand more chances to go if I want to open this by brute force.

I'm still in the lighthouse though, and the sharks are still in the water. I've still got time, and I might still have options.

"Listen," I say to the creature in the trunk. "I guess I can't open this from the outside, at least now."

It thumps against the hatch from the inside, and I'm only somewhat glad to hear it. I'm happy that it understands, but part of me was still hoping for an unchanging silence that suggests that none of this is real. It's still real, at least to me, and I still don't have any other plan besides doing what they want me to do. If I open the trunk they'll beat me mercilessly, and I can't think of anything to do except—

"Except *fuck them*," I say to the creature. "Fuck Retjar, and fuck his silent friend. That's my plan, and that's our plan. *Fuck them.*"

The creature in the trunk thumps twice in response to echo my words: *fuck them*. The thumps are somewhat muted now, and I realize that it's not knocking on the hatch. It's knocking on the other side of the trunk, and that gives me an idea, one that I can't believe I hadn't thought of before.

/***/

I crawl in the back and get to work on the backseat, right where my cohort was knocking. This vehicle's got one of those plush armrests that folds down for some unknowable necessity, though unfortunately it doesn't fold down to reveal one of those sliding panels meant for holding things too long for the trunk. Still, I knock on the material behind the armrest and the creature thumps back, and the barrier between us doesn't seem too impregnable. I scoot back into the front, lay the passenger seat down, and then return to the backseat and get to work. My hands can't poke through the sturdy backing material, nor can I get a hold around the edges, not even a fingernail. I pull and prod, nudge and peel, but nothing comes out. I ask the creature in the trunk to push from the other edge, but that doesn't seem to help either.

A TALE OF THE HIGHWAY

I wonder again if this creature is a figment of my imagination, and then my heart shudders at the cruel possibility of the Crows being real and this creature not. I swallow my worry and remind myself that *either this creature's real or none of this is real*, because this entity has been here with me every step of the way. *Besides, even if it's not real, something in there is. If I poke through to reveal an empty trunk there will still be something in there, a clue or at least one of Dr. Shaw's beloved truths that will allow all of this to make sense. It might even make all of this worth it.*

I feel the material sealing off the trunk. It's solid, and impervious to my fingers, but it's not impenetrable. I just need a single sliver, and I can pull open the rest. I look around for materials, but the vehicle is clean, other than a few empty wine bottles of course.

That's it.

I take a wine bottle out, the cabernet I'd first drunk. I realize a clear wine bottle will be better, so that I might get a better view of my blade, so I take the grappa that I was just drinking. I kiss the bottle, feeling the momentary melancholy before the destruction of something beautiful, the moment before an act that cannot be undone. I take the base of the bottle and smash the neck against the ground outside, causing the sound of crushed glass to echo in the night. It's a small sound, but it's amplified by the fact that there is nothing to smother it in this empty place, not even the winds of the surrounding steppe, which should be here but are conspicuously absent.

The gas station clerk takes notice of the sound and we lock eyes. I give him a smile to let him know that everything's OK, and though he doesn't smile in return, I can sense that he understands I must have my reasons. *He's a young man but I can tell his eyes have seen quite a bit in his life, even from this distant, quick glance that we share. This gives him an underlying empathy.* I wave to him, compelled by the awkward situation to look as sane as I possibly can, and he waves back. He's a hard young man who's seen much worse, and he soon turns his attention back to his empty store, pristine and untouched by any customers' hands.

I clean up all the glass that I can, and then look for a good piece. I find one with a broad base and a single point, a shard fated for just this moment. I take it into the back seat and then poke the trunk's material, and it scratches, and then scuffs, and then hooks onto a groove. I then push forward, and the tip goes in before the base gets caught. That's all I need though, and I pull the glass out to reveal a strange light coming out of the hole. I poke my index finger in, and then push some more until it reaches through. I pull down, and it rips vertically. I tear the two pieces on top, and they come away as well, letting more of the light out.

It's the light of my dreams. The philosopher's room had it, and the goat's single prong had it. Now it's here, and it fills me with hope.

/***/

The creature's forearm comes through the light, and it's one of the most beautiful things I've ever seen. The arm is black as night and completely hairless, with long, articulated fingers that exude dexterity. I figure from the arm's length that this creature must be at least twice the size of an ordinary man, and then chide myself for assuming that it's a male. Other than its oversized structure, nothing about the limb suggests *either* gender, let alone a male one. *Whatever it is, there's something extraordinarily elegant about its arm, something superior to both human and god. Maybe this creature represents the potential of the former and a replacement for the latter.*

I feel like I'm witnessing a birth. Joyful, holy, something beyond me and everything I know.

It's a birth not yet delivered, I correct myself. *The result can go either way, glory or disaster. Whatever the case, if this is to be seen through, it's up to me.*

/***/

I can't get anything besides its arm out, so I spend the next ten minutes attempting communication with this silent creature. I speak with it and though it seems to understand, it doesn't speak in return. I try to see what else is in the trunk, to see anything but its forearm, but the light that surrounds the creature is too bright. It's soothing but it's too radiant, and it's also too hot. I still want to be near it though. I want to bathe in it, I want to sleep and live in it, but the light overpowers me when I get too close. So I can see the forearm, I can see the light, but not much else.

We develop a crude language of signing, and the creature is quick to pick things up. We get *yes, no, maybe, I don't know* down quickly, and then begin to work on the rest. We don't get too far, though it's no fault of the creature's. I quickly come to realize that there's a limitation in all things between us, and that limitation is myself. This entity starts signing quickly, performing rapidly, preternaturally agile things with its fingers that I couldn't hope to understand, let alone respond in kind.

The creature picks up on this though, and we settle on the standard *yes, no, maybe* and *I don't know*, though my comrade doesn't use the last one too much. Whatever this thing is, it's got an intellect to match its elegant forearm, and can at least understand every word I say.

"I'm going inside" I say. "I guess I need some gas now."

The creature's hand reaches out to feel the clothes on my upper body, just a few leftover scarecrow's rags. It then makes a sign that my appearance is bizarre, and I laugh at the notion in return. I then realize that I'm dressed like a derelict, and that I don't have any money in my torn pockets. I think of what to do, and I take another look at the Crows on the edge of the darkness. I see Retjar stewing silently, gleefully tallying the moments that I spend here so that he may add them to my torment later.

I look down and see that my friend is pointing, not at the Crows but at the gas station. I follow its long black fingers and realize that it's not pointing at the store either, but at the attendant, the one with the hard yet understanding eyes. The creature's fingers exude trust, and tell me that this clerk is someone whom I can also trust.

My cohort's direction compels me to go and I step out to meet a lonely shopkeeper in a long-abandoned station, to be his first customer of the night, one who will wander into his store dressed in nothing but cloth. One who will beg for unpaid fuel, and then plead for everything else that he can.

You don't need to beg, I think, looking at the wine in my backseat. *You have something you can offer. In fact, you have quite a bit.*

/***/

I bring in two bottles of wine, what seems to be a higher-end Malbec and a Polish ice wine. I figure I could barter the malbec and share the ice wine—over ice of course[40]—while doing so. The doors to the gas station open automatically, and the sight is absolutely heavenly. The floors are pristine, and I see row upon row of candies, chips and not-yet-refrigerated dip laid out before me. The refrigerated back holds a solid variety of endless beer, and the beer soon makes way for a section of unnaturally iridescent drinks. I also notice a shelf of chilled wine, and I see some chardonnay, sauvignon blanc and white zinfandel—and they're all calling my name. I know these bottles might not be as good as the one in the car, but they're chilled, and that's what I'm after. *Just a nice bit of relaxation looking over the nighttime horizon, a glass of rosé in my hand, even a plastic glass would be OK. Drinking it straight from the bottle has its own charms of course, but having a glass*

---

[40] Ice wine is not iced wine, but rather wine grown from grapes that have been frozen while still on the vine. It ends up with a natural sweetness. It's a difficult, risky winemaking process—you need a region of vineyards that freezes, and you need a labor force that can pick the entire crop quickly, and do so at a moment's notice. Subsequently, ice wines are rare, but like their sweet cousin, Gewürztraminer, they're worth the effort.

is dignified. Having a pair of wine glasses would be even better.[41]

I look around to see that this station has more than just wine, chips and dip: it has *everything*.[42] Toiletries and medicine, magazines and music. Beside the music is a bin with enough audio books to fill a library, and I'd love to take a few if I didn't have so many of Dr. Shaw's chapters remaining. There are oversized keg-shaped cups, and racks of T-shirts printed with everything from wolves to offensive phrases. There are hats and magnets, souvenirs and postcards. Things you never knew you'd need too, like mugs that plug into a car's cigarette lighter to heat beverages.

And then there's the hard-looking attendant, charged with making sense of this strange outpost. He's here keeping the order, ensuring that this pristine assemblage of goods doesn't dissolve out here in the hinterland, in this place that society might not have completely forgotten, but definitely takes for granted.

/***/

The attendant's name is *Cruz*, or at least his nametag suggests so. He's young but holds the look of a rough upbringing, with a shaved head, a thick neck, and a dark goatee framing a mouth that hasn't smiled in a long time. His skin is brown and hairy, but relatively unblemished save for a wavy tattoo peeking above his shirtline.

I notice that his eyes aren't quite as *completely* hard as the rest of him though, and still retain the underlying empathy that I saw when I

---

[41] Drinking from the bottle also implies drinking alone, and since at this point I was no longer alone, I wanted a glass, or rather two of them. Glasses are like fences between two houses: they separate at first, but allow for so many more things later.

[42] Oftentimes these stores set amidst barren land are better supplied than a store situated in a densely populated area. The surrounding desolation necessitates the shelves be stocked with anything a human can need, and more.

smashed my bottle. He doesn't look at me like a wary clerk should, with suspicion and even anger that a man dressed in rags is wandering around his store in the wee hours of the night. Cruz seems to understand that I must have my reasons for coming in here, and I give him a knowing smile to let him see *that I certainly do*. I do my best to look sane, but I see in his eyes that even this might not be necessary. If I was indeed insane, or even had the temporary self-inflicted insanity wrought by drugs (and I'm not ruling either of these out just yet), Cruz wouldn't slap me and push me out of his store and out into the dark steppe where I can do no more harm. He's seen too much in his young life to do that to another person, even one in far worse shape than I. He'd talk me down from whatever ledge I was on, and then call the appropriate people to pick me up.

I can see it all in his eyes. I see Cruz's whole hard life, and I see the softness behind his tough looks. I feel the pain he's experienced, and I feel the kindness and understanding that he could still push out to the world if given the opportunity.

I don't know him completely though. I feel there's still a mystery to him, something fundamental that I'm missing. Whatever it is, I can't think of it now. There's more at stake at this moment than the enigma of Cruz's compassion.

/***/

I tell Cruz my situation, changing the details so that I don't appear completely deranged. I tell him that everything I own was taken, and that I'm being blackmailed by two very powerful men. I tell Cruz that I need to drive down the road in front of me, but I have no gas. I tell him that I have no money either, and he nods in understanding at my words, all of them strange, and all of them true.

I tell him that I can't beg him for gas (though I know he'd probably find a way to say *yes*), so I offer to barter my malbec. I tell him about this bottle of wine, and my long-term memory kicks in enough to tell him the details: that this bottle from Argentina is a bit softer on the palate than its cohorts.[43] I don't have a price of course, but I assure him that it holds value, and that I have another case in the vehicle for further negotiations.

Cruz doesn't seem to be interested in negotiations though, but he is engaged in my words, not for the value of the wine, but for the story behind them. Cruz doesn't quite smile, but I pick up on this and tell him another tale from my long-term memory, about pinot noir grapes and how troublesome they can be to grow, and how their enigmatic nature can yield such a great flavor. I tell him that a vine's struggle often produces great wines, and that a vineyard's soil shouldn't be particularly fertile to begin with. I tell him that great wines can come from soil consisting of pebbles.[44]

He doesn't smile at these aphoristic tales either, and I'm not sure he'll ever smile at anything,[45] but he likes the story. He likes my words, and he likes the fact that I value him enough to share them. I see his lip quivering, thinking about a tale he could give in response, and then I see him stop, for fear of embarrassing himself. He's not used to being valued, to being listened to, to being seen as anything but the custodian of this forlorn outpost.

I tell him I'd like to hear what he has to say, even if it's just a small

---

[43] Argentinian malbecs don't have the robust tannic structure of French malbecs.
[44] For example, the Châteauneuf-du-Pape district in France's Rhône valley, whose stones produce great wines.
[45] Every human child is born with a smile, and Cruz, like so many adults, lost that smile at some point in his life. But let's think of the positive, and ask ourselves why most all children smile. Evolutionary explanations aside, I think it's because children are natural-born philosophers. Their smiles come from their constant amazement at the universe around them, and they're right to be amazed. So if you want to be a philosopher, think like a child, and be amazed like a child. You might just end up smiling like one too.

tale.

/***/

Cruz tells me more than just a small tale. He tells me of his upbringing, his youth spent in a cramped apartment shared with three older brothers, two of them psychotic, the eldest violently so. He tells me of the things they would say to him, how they would belittle him, locking him inside when they were playing, and shutting him outside when they were not. His mother was too busy working, too busy ensuring survival for her offspring to consider giving them any sort of life. His father was nonexistent, too absent to be even worthy of rage.

I think of my own semi-existent, incorporeal father, the one who yelled at me in the dreamt Hell, and wonder if he holds value for at least presenting himself to me. I might not remember him, and he might have sent me down this path of torment, but he is *here* in some shape or form.

I turn my attention back to Cruz, and the recollection of his life. It's not snappy like my vigneron's advice, full of meaningful lessons about grapes and life, but Cruz's story is real, and that gives it weight.

I interrupt Cruz to ask him why *he* didn't end up as debased as the environment from which he was spawned, why *he's* not psychotic. I ask him why *he* doesn't take all the torment placed inside of him and then project it outward.

I ask him why he didn't give *me* all his wrath when I dared enter his store as a penniless vagrant, why he refrained from pushing me down so that he might stand a little higher.

He doesn't understand that last question, so I ask it again: *How could he avoid treating me like shit when that's all the world has ever given him?*

He still doesn't quite understand my question, but it's not because he's dull. I sense that Cruz isn't accustomed to the concept of introspection, of looking deep within himself to examine the weakness within.[46]

/***/

I spend the next half hour talking to Cruz, and we discuss Plato's notion that *humanity comes with a great cost, but may be worth it*. Then we take a step back by speaking of existence, and what exactly it means to be *human*. We then discuss Cruz's own story, and though I'm doing the vast majority of the talking, we figure out that there are three pillars most every human seeks in life. The first would be security, which is shelter, food and the modern-day corollaries of rent money and a job that pays a little more than that. Cruz tells me that he has that. We then figure out that the second pillar is love, which at its base is *sex*, Cruz shakes his head shamefully at this one, and I don't press this any further.

I think about the third pillar for a moment, and I tell him I believe this final pillar is *value*, and that it can take many forms. I tell Cruz that humans need the first two pillars, but I think humans might *seek* the third after the first two are satiated. I tell Cruz that this *seeking* can lead to odd ends.

Cruz asks me what I mean by this.

"Well, in the worst case, the seeking of value can lead to violence," I say. "Give a young person no education, no job, and no place in society, and they might one day point a weapon at you and ask for your money. They're not so much asking for your money as they're asking to be

---

[46] Sigmund Freud had the somewhat supercilious view that religion is based on the childlike need for a strong father figure to help us restrain our aggressive impulses. He felt that as human society *grows up*, we should set divine fables aside in favor of reason, arts and the sciences. I don't believe Cruz has any of these things: no art, no science, and no powers of introspection that allow reason to come into being. Cruz doesn't even have religion. Whether Freud has a point or not, Cruz has nothing at this point, absolutely nothing.

valued, to be recognized as a human being."

Cruz laughs at this and tells me that his store has been held up a few times, and he definitely remembers each thief that entered. He didn't know who they were before, but certainly does now.

"But it's more than just petty crime," I say. "In more stressful times, that need for value could lead to war. Someone could find a kid in need of value, put a rifle in his hand and then tell him that *'only you can defend our homeland against the invaders.'* That kid will pick up the rifle most every time, and eventually fire it at another kid who's probably been told the exact same thing."

Cruz asks me if the seeking of value could end up doing something good. I think about this.

"It can definitely do that," I say. "Let's consider a girl that grew up in more fortunate circumstances: her youth is rich in support, time and aptitude. She might feel a longing to be valued by *making her mark*, and might do it by inventing a new kind of medical device, or by making a program that helps us explore space. The seeking of value can be a good thing."[47]

Cruz nods at this.

He thinks for a moment and then pulls down his shirt to show me his half-covered tattoo, which resembles a crudely drawn stream. It looks incomplete, and Cruz quickly tells me that it is. He tells me it's supposed to represent the river of forgetfulness, so that he can *forget the things he had to do*. I ask him about these things that he did, and he

---

[47] Most of the time it's a little of both. The Pyramids are glorious, and they were built because pharaohs needed to make their mark, to have a value that extended beyond their natural lives. These pharaohs enslaved countless others to build these structures, so now humanity gets to marvel at these achievements while innumerable souls spent their entire existences building them against their will.

tells me they happened when he was entering a set.

I ask what a *set* is, and he says it's kind of like a gang. He says he doesn't truly understand why he entered the gang, and I let him think for a moment. He then wonders aloud if he attempted to join the gang because he was seeking value. I tell him that he probably was, and ask him if he joined the set, or gang, or whatever it was called.

He tells me that he didn't go through with the whole initiation, and that's why he didn't go through with the tattoo.

I ask him what the other half would have represented, and he tells me that it would have been the river of memory, so that he'd never forget who he was. Cruz tells me that this was part of his set's culture: they'd have to quickly forget the bad things they needed to do to survive, but once they were in they could never forget who they were.

He then tells me that an incident halfway through his initiation made him choose another path, one that allowed him to keep the river of forgetfulness, and nothing else.

I tell him that I might have drunk from the same river, but he appears too shaken by his own story to hear my words, so I don't press him for any more details on his past.

Cruz then asks me what gives *me* value, what *my* purpose is. I think of the Crows, the creature in the trunk and this strange task that I've been given.

I think about them all for a few moments, and Cruz lets me.

"I'm currently on a strange quest and I've met a lot of strange beings, both friend and foe," I say. "They're elements of my current circumstances, but they're not a part of who I am."

Cruz asks me who I am, and I put my two bottles on the counter.

"I don't quite know for sure, but I'll show you my value, my *purpose*," I tell him. "All I need is a corkscrew."

/***/

Cruz takes me back to the shop and shows me a whole box of corkscrews, more than I need. They're returned items, but they're as good as new, and definitely better than a shoe.[48] They've got a *wing corkscrew*, a *waiter's friend*, and a *twin-prong cork puller*. I instinctively take out the waiter's friend[49] and open up the malbec. Cruz goes into another box and brings out a few returned mugs and two stacks of plastic cups, one clear and one red.

The returned mugs tend to have vaguely hostile messages about Mondays and coworkers on them, so I pour my malbec in a clear plastic cup and swirl it around before taking a sniff. I enjoy the complex aroma of chocolate, pepper and fruit, more than I could possibly describe here, but I decide to save the display for Cruz, because I want him involved. More than anything else, I want him to have a good time.

I look around to find him gone, but he soon emerges from an oversized closet with a jumpsuit. He tells me that one of the mechanics left it, and if it doesn't fit there's more in the back. I strip off my scarecrow's clothes right in front of him and put on the jumpsuit, and it fits well. Cruz then points back to the store and tells me to get a pair of shoes in my size. I mutter gratefully that I can't possibly take a gift like that and he shushes me in return, lets me know that the shoes are on him, and that he gets an employee discount.

---

[48] I call this *the sudden luxury of a reclaimed object*. When you don't have something for a while, and then you have it, you appreciate it in a new way. I also feel a little grateful to my shoe for allowing me to open wine in a corkscrew's absence, though I have no name for this feeling.

[49] The can't-miss wing corkscrew is the most popular for the average consumer, but once you get used to a waiter's friend, also known as a *wine key*, it's hard to go back. I don't know why it feels so right. Maybe it's akin to a car-lover choosing to change their own oil: you just get a little closer to the bottle this way.

"Thank you, Cruz," I say. "I don't know if I can ever repay you for this kindness, but I'm going to try."

Cruz smiles and says that it's not necessary, but I know what I'll do for him. Cruz picks up on the fact that I have a plan, and he asks me what I'm going to do. I take one more look around my surroundings at the back of the store and realize that they're perfect, and that I should start immediately. *This place is like a cornfield, but better. It's hidden by its desolation, so we can get as loud as we want. It's the only thing for miles around, so no one will be able to miss it once we get it going. We've got space, we've got time, and we've got me.*

"I'm going to throw you a party, Cruz," I say. "Right now I'm caught up in a tough situation, but my nightmare outside is going to have to wait. Because no matter what my task is, *your* life, right here and right now, is too important to think about anything else at this moment. I hope I can help you find your value, your true purpose, but whatever the case I'm about to show you mine. My purpose is to have a good time, and to make sure everyone else has a good time. And you're going to have a good time, Cruz. You're going to have the best time of your fucking life."

The Last Party

We set up shop right there in the back of the store, just Cruz and me for now. We unfold a table, and then get our drinks ready. I tell Cruz that this celebration might get a little wild later on, but for now we'll get things going with only a handful of people (if that), so I suggest starting it off with a wine tasting. He agrees. He gets a few bottles from the front, an even number of reds, whites, and even a few rosés.[50]

I pour a little of the malbec and get the party going with just Cruz and myself. I show him the basics of wine, from the aroma to the bouquet, to savoring the flavor so you can sense the undertones, aerating the wine and then swirling it to see the wine's legs.[51] I talk to him about the red, white and rosé wines, and I tell him about how they come from both dark and white grapes. I tell him about the skin of the grape being the deciding factor in the hue, taste and feel of these wines, and that he should try them all, but not overly so. I tell him that some stomachs don't react well to the acid in the white, and some get

---

[50] If you ever find yourself throwing a quick party like this, serve both red and white at the very least, and a few rosés if you can. When you have a small party with seemingly *too much* wine, it subtly suggests to the guests that the party could get bigger. They might invite friends, and even if they don't they'll be more likely to stick around, because the party *could* get bigger.

[51] I'm loathe to use the pejorative term *wine snobbery*, but if I may, I can assure you that we're not engaging in such a thing. Casual drinkers employ the terms *aroma* and *bouquet* interchangeably, and more experienced drinkers understand that aroma refers to the scent unique to the grape itself, and bouquet refers to the complex scents associated with a wine's aging process. But still, this process from my long-term memory that I'm sharing with Cruz isn't born of snobbery, if there is such a thing. We're attempting to enjoy the wine to its fullest extent, and that's a journey unto itself. Oh—and "wine legs" are just a phenomenon that indicates alcohol content. It doesn't really reflect the quality of wine, especially when you're drinking from plastic cups.

headaches from red wine.[52]

I then take a look at the white and the rosé, and though they're decent—a sauvignon blanc and a white zinfandel—they're warm, and that simply will not do. Cruz offers to get some from the refrigerated wall in the front, but I have a better idea. If all goes as planned tonight, I might have to take him up on that offer later, but we have time, so I decide to quick-chill the wine that we have. We put our wine in a bucket and drop ice and water around it, then sip the room-temperature malbec while it chills.[53]

All right, one more thing to consider before we start this party.

"Before we start inviting people, are the security cameras on?" I ask. "This will be fun, but we can't have it on tape."

Cruz tells me that the owners never check, so he can just turn the cameras off and no one will notice. He tells me he's got to leave the front pump cameras on though, just in case anyone tries to steal gas.

"That's fine," I say. "It's all going to happen here in the back anyway."

---

[52] A few unfortunate souls definitely get a headache from even a single glass of red wine, but the jury is still out on the root cause. Sulfites probably aren't the culprit, but some experts think naturally occurring histamines in red wine cause an allergic reaction, and some think tannins cause it. There are a few other theories of course, but if you experience a headache with red, I'd advise you to experiment—take an antihistamine before you drink, or choose a low-tannin red like a Beaujolais or a Tempranillo. And if you experience a stomachache with white, I'd take an antacid before you drink, or at the very least a meal. Do what it takes, because if you dismiss either reds or whites out of hand, you're missing out.

[53] There's a lot of ways to quickly chill a white. You can add salt to the ice bath, and then spin the bottle inside the bucket to cool it evenly. Frozen grapes work as ice cubes as well, and if you're in a jam, so does ice. But still, I just prefer to get a bunch of white and soak it in a half-melted bucket of ice. You're ideally taking the white from the refrigerator anyway, but even if you aren't, a half-chilled white never hurt anyone. Better to pour more than to wait. Oh, and don't try that bottle-spinning technique with champagne. It leads to a bad end.

Cruz goes to turn the cameras off, and I can't help but marvel at how perfect this place is. Secluded but open, well-lit enough for all to find it, yet dark enough to hide our insecurities. *This is the beach and the cornfield, all in one.*

But I still know that this evening only has potential as of now, and I've got to be proactive. It's going to need a push.

"Cruz," I ask when he returns. "Do you have any friends?"

He shakes his head that he doesn't, quickly and without sadness. *I aim to change this tonight, but right now this is his life, this is who he is.*

"Do you have anyone you *know*?"

We talk about it and realize that, in fact, Cruz knows quite a few people. *He works at a gas station in the middle of nowhere and this leads him to know most everyone, as counterintuitive as that notion might seem.*

But I know we can't just invite anyone over for the first guest. It has to be the right person.

"We don't need the big, over-the-top person, at least not yet," I say. "The party igniter will come later. Right now we need someone to hang out with us, that's it. Someone who's friendly and above all else *nice*. Someone who'll come here and won't leave if it stays quiet for a while. Do you know anyone like that?"

Cruz thinks about this and then nods. He knows just the person.

/***/

His name is Danny, and he arrives with a beer helmet. He's a really cool guy all right. Just the guy we need for this party, the third guy that will break the plane of inhibition. *One guy is just a guy drinking alone. Two people drinking are two friends, exclusive. But three? It starts to be a party, and all are welcome.*

A TALE OF THE HIGHWAY

He's a little crazy too, crazy enough hang with Cruz and a stranger in the middle of the night, and learn the subtleties of our wine and then laugh at all my old jokes.[54] It still sounds a little quiet because Cruz doesn't laugh, though he's clearly enjoying our company.

I ask Danny to show us his beer helmet. He pounds the wine we'd poured him straight up, and then pops two lagers from the case that he brought and puts them in the sides of his helmet. He puts in the straw and then sips to pull the amber liquid through, giving an exaggerated *aaaaah* after the drink, and I laugh. Cruz doesn't laugh at this, but he recognizes the warmth of the spectacle, and then takes another sip of his red. Danny takes out a straw from his pocket that's shaped like a pair of glasses, and puts them on before opening a third lager and placing one end of the straw in that. He takes another sip through his glasses and then talks about the beer he brought, a craft lager with a smooth, balanced taste.

Danny says he likes lagers because they're less bitter than ales, though he enjoys the punch of a strong ale every now and then.

I understand where he's coming from, but I'm not ready to forgo my malbec and the waiting sauvignon blanc and white zinfandel just yet. *In another time I could drink beer with Danny though. In another time I could drink beer with him and Cruz all night.*

/***/

Danny has a lot of friends, many of them female. I tell him to start inviting anyone he can find, and he does. He invites an ex of his named Dany (a female with one *n* in her name, and pronounced *Donny*), and she comes with her boyfriend, Will, whom Danny is also friends with.

When they arrive I ask them about this dynamic because I can't help

---

[54] My jokes are somewhat dated, I admit. I didn't know it at the time, but many were centuries old, often translated from bawdy Middle English tales. Still, I do my best to sell each joke through gesticulation, and Danny meets me halfway by laughing at just the right moments.

it, and Danny informs me that he was Will's friend originally and actually *introduced* Will to Dany, so that answers that. They're all cool with it.

I break open the rosé and we all take a sip. It's not quite perfectly cold yet, but it's cold enough, and no one is forced to put an ice cube from the bucket in their glass.

Dany is a mountain climber—Dany with one *n* and no beer helmet. While sipping her wine she tells us about her latest adventure, where she was hit with a storm and had to make a quick shelter. But the storm passed, and she was able to reach the summit at 3 a.m. with the moonlight to guide her. She tells us how she was glad the storm happened, because the moonlight reflected beautifully off of the snow, and she wouldn't have had that experience otherwise.

I note that every part of the story is filled with joy, even the specifics about the storm's wrath, and I ask her why mountain climbing makes her so happy.

Will interjects to tell us about this theory he heard about how rock and mountain climbers are generally happy because, among other things, their love is always just a weekend away. There's no winning or losing, and they aren't competing against anyone but themselves. They can always *get in the zone*. I recognize this on a deep level, and so does Cruz, who nods in understanding.

"Make no mistake though, we have our problems," says Will with a smile. "The real good climbers are addicts. Not addicted to drugs, mind you, but to the mountain. That means they're often narcissists too, raving ones."

I tell them that they don't seem particularly narcissistic, and in fact seem precisely the opposite.

"That's because we're just pretty good climbers, the happy kind, and not the insane ones," says Dany with one *n*. "We know a few really hardcore climbers, the ones that set records and push the human limit.

Their routes take months to do, and they involve enormous personal risk. You're going to be miserable for the better part of a year, and you're going to miss a few of your kids' birthdays. One misstep and you might miss all of them."

Danny with two *n*s takes another sip from his helmet, and shakes his head at this.

"I don't know," he says. "There's something different about what you say, even the craziest climber. I mean—"

Danny thinks for a moment, sipping beer through his glasses while he does so.

"When I think of self-centered people, I think of people I don't like," he says. "But some crazy climber who wants to summit some peak that's never been summited before, I like that person, and I'm rooting for them."

"We all do," says Will. "I always get a thrill when I hear another climber did something previously thought impossible. I think it's because though they climb for themselves, they're also climbing for the rest of us, pushing the limits of what we can all do. They're climbing for humanity."

I smile at this and raise my glass.

"To humanity," I say.

They all echo my words, and then cheer. Cruz doesn't smile, but he toasts with the rest of us and seems to be enjoying himself.

/***/

Dany with one *n* asks Cruz if he has any music and he shakes his head, a resolute *no* filled with meaning on multiple levels. Will asks if he can invite his friend, Clark, who knows quite a few DJs, and Danny laughs at the mention. Beer-helmeted Danny tells me that Clark owns a big bar in a nearby town, and brings a lot of excitement wherever he goes.

We've got Danny, and we've got Danny's friends. Now the party igniter is coming, the one who will break this whole thing wide open. And he's bringing music.

Cruz has heard of Clark as well, and he's overjoyed at the idea. He's still not smiling, but I can sense the warm emotions swelling inside of him. I can sense him feeling that *this is the way nights are supposed to be. This is youth, this is life, this is freedom.*

/***/

A guy named Howe gets wind that Clark is going to a party at the station, and calls Cruz to tell him that he is coming as well. Cruz tells me that Howe supplies the store with much of its goods, and after they talk on the phone Cruz walks to an area of the wall with an oversized black plastic bag tied around something large. The whole thing resembles a chunk of granite, but Cruz unties the string and removes the bag to reveal a pallet of bottled beer and boxed wine.

Cruz tells me that Howe's company had written these off as *damaged* or *stale* product and that Howe was scheduled to pick them up and dispose of them. I tell Cruz that I don't understand why someone would consider this product as a loss, and Cruz points out stains on the beer labels and the wine boxes themselves.

Cruz tells me that they had stacked a row of olive oil on top of the product, but somewhere along the way the bottles had cracked. They'd leaked out overnight, rendering everything beneath unsellable. He tells me they have a few other cases a few days past their expiration date, and they're considered stale—just as unsellable as the damaged products.

Cruz tells me that the products themselves are still good, and that Howe is bringing some more of the same.

A TALE OF THE HIGHWAY

Outside of a few blemished labels, this is all pretty fresh. We'll soak the beer in the ice bucket, and those stains will go away. For the boxed wine, it still won't be a problem. We'll put the most untouched box of red and white on a table, put the rest of the boxes beneath, and then keep replacing the bladders.[55]

On second thought, I might be overthinking it. It's dark, and drinks are drinks. Free drinks are even better. Whatever the case, we've got a lot of them, and more are one the way.

/***/

Howe is still a few counties away when Clark arrives with his truck and a caravan of friends in tow. Clark's truck is something to behold, much bigger than my car, and loaded with every extra you can imagine. The suspension sets the vehicle higher than I'd thought possible, and its frame is a mesh of elegantly constructed right angles. It has a winch in front, lights on top and an apparatus on the side that appears to be made for dispensing some sort of beverage.[56]

There are also six people in the back of Clark's vehicle, and they come out soaking wet. Beer-helmeted Danny tells me that Clark put in a Jacuzzi in the truck's bed, complete with a plastic top that allows guests to sit in without the water spilling every time the truck moves.

"It's even got little underwater seatbelts," says Danny.

---

[55] Boxed wine gets occasional grief from oenophiles, but it offers a few things that bottles do not. Sometimes you just want a single glass of wine, and as counterintuitive as it might seem, a box can be better for delivering that—*more is less* with a box. Wine bladders usually hold from four to seven bottles, but their internal mechanisms seal it up after each pour, limiting exposure to oxygen. So a large box can last you a month if you have a single glass every night, two months if you stretch it out. Boxed wine is great for parties like this as well. Sometimes you just have a lot of people coming over, and you need an answer.

[56] In retrospect, I believe it was an espresso machine. If only I'd had some grappa left.

Clark doesn't look too happy though. He's clearly comfortable directing his entourage towards the party, and Cruz tells the group to park in the back. He shows them a path out of the front camera's eye, so no one gets in trouble. I notice that Clark isn't having as good a time as those he brought. *He holds the mien of a father taking his children to a playdate—he wants to enjoy himself, but the weight of the world is still on his shoulders.*

I also see more cars coming up the highway, distant lights coming from both directions.

"Clark sure is popular," I say.

"He is," says Danny, pointing to two men coming out of the caravan, one goateed and wild, the other sharp-looking, with a mouthful of straight white teeth. "But everyone's really coming to see these guys."

Danny explains that the two men are a morning-radio DJ team who call themselves *Whitecotton and the Gooch*. They're pretty popular in these parts, and I can see they've brought a few assistants who are carrying real sound equipment.

"Before they got into radio they started out as real DJs—you know, the party kind," says Danny. "They're friends of Clark, and they bring their own fan base. In any case, the word's out, and we've got some music all right."

/***/

Whitecotton and the Gooch and their assistants set up their audio equipment a lot faster than I'd thought possible. Danny tells me they're used to doing their radio shows from areas like these: store openings, car lots and other far-flung locales that promise a great bargain and a whole bunch of prizes if you just *come on down to some address, repeated over and over again.*

Danny tells me that they aren't promoting anything here tonight,

A TALE OF THE HIGHWAY

they're just bringing music, and that's about it. In any case, they soon start the first song, a modern country tune about getting together and partying. It fits the scene of what we're doing, and even those who don't care for country music can't help but dance.

Clark comes over, says hello to Danny, and then says hello to Cruz.

"It's funny," says Clark to Cruz. "I've seen you before a hundred times, whenever I stopped here for gas. Never thought to say hi, so I guess now's as good a time as any."

Cruz says hi back, and though he doesn't quite smile I can tell that he's thrilled to finally be acknowledged by Clark.

/***/

"I started my career with these guys," says Clark, pouring himself some seltzer water into a red plastic cup, then pointing at Whitecotton and the Gooch.

We're in the back of the station, a little far off into the field behind. We can hear the music, but we're still far enough away to hold a conversation.

"I hated even calling it *a career* when we began," says Clark. "I mean, when we were young we'd just do this for fun, setting up parties for friends, and then friends of friends."

Clark tells us about how a friend of a friend paid them for a party, and how that was the start of things.

"People honestly feel more comfortable when they're paying you," he says. "They'd rather pay money than owe a favor. So we started charging, and started using that money to buy more equipment."

That equipment led them to better parties, and led them to charge higher rates, which led them to even better equipment, equipment that demanded an office, and pretty soon they had a full-fledged business.

Clark then tells about how their status grew over the years, and how his two partners found that their patter between songs got a rise out of the crowd, and soon worked their way into the radio business. Shortly after that they became radio DJs and then *morning* DJs, because the real heavy hitters worked in the morning.

Clark was the promoter, so after he left he got into the bar business. He bought one and then built it up through promotion, promotion, promotion, and then party after party after party. He still owns the bar, called *The V*, and Clark tells us that it's got multiple rooms and a minimum of two bands playing at all times. It does extremely well.

"I'm looking to sell," says Clark.

Cruz asks him why.

"First and foremost, the *liability*," says Clark. "Pack the bar with a hundred customers? Great, but first of all, some of them are jackasses every night. Someone's going to fight, someone's going to have too much and slip on something, every night. No matter what, something is going to happen, and even if it doesn't, of those hundred, about forty are driving home. You think they're all sober?"

Cruz and I both shake our heads at this, though I'm not exactly sacrosanct when it comes to that last part.

"Secondly, it's the pure financial aspect," continues Clark. "My bars are hot right now, but that can change quickly, and next thing you know I have to mortgage everything I own just to keep the doors open. And third—it's the personal toll. No weekends, impossible hours, everyone wanting free drinks off of you, and you only seeing your old friends when they're drunk, often at their worst."

Clark smiles.

"But it wasn't always this way," he says, shaking his head.

Clark tells us that he used to love running his bar, but lost that love for it over the course of a hundred nights, or maybe a few thousand. He tells us that he still manages it but can do the job in his sleep, and a glowing set of top-shelf liquor or a wad of tips means little to him. He tells us that he's tired of greeting the sunrise with overworked eyes, and *beyond* tired of the stories he accumulates: of the famous person who got drunk and hit on a waitress before pissing himself, or of the nonfamous person who drank too much and then had to be restrained.

Clark says he's tired of dreading each and every weekend, and can no longer remember a time when he looked forward to it.

"So if anyone wants to take on all this," he says, "I'll sell, and throw in the liquor license for free."

Danny thinks about this, then takes a sip from his helmet.

"But you're here now," says Danny. "You like this, at least a little, right?"

"I like it *more* than a little," says Clark, looking around at the gathering crowd of people and thinking about why this is so.

"This is how I made it happen back when I first started with my friends over there," says Clark, pointing to Whitecotton and the Gooch, who just transitioned the country song to a rap tune, and did it seamlessly. "I mean we never did anything *this* big back then, but we just had the time of our lives, you know? Doing it just to do it," he says with a smile.

"There's something more here though," he continues. "Maybe I like it because it's not my job, and I don't have to worry about customers leaving without paying. Maybe it's because the drink of choice here is wine, and not vodka pulled from the bar's well. In any case, there's just something about this party you're throwing, Cruz, and it makes me feel *alive*."

Cruz beams at the compliment, or perhaps at the validation that

Clark is calling him by his actual name.

"Maybe you're not tired of partying," asks Danny. "Maybe you're just tired of having the *same* party, every night."

"Maybe," says Clark. "Maybe it doesn't matter why. I'm going to have a good time tonight, and that's all that matters."

Clark squints and looks back towards the party.

"I'll have a good time tonight," says Clark, again with a smile. "But not as good as *that* guy."

I follow Clark's pointed finger to see a man on a couch in a goat mask. The masked man is surrounded by women, and next to them is a young man wearing a strange hat and playing guitar. The goat-masked man is partaking in a deep glass of red, right through his elongated snout. The costume bears a striking resemblance to the goat in my dreams, and the mask is really good. It doesn't even look like a mask, actually. It looks *real*.

/***/

A filmmaker named Kim arrives, and he's brought a few films. Cruz gets a projector from the front, taking it from a shelf of extraordinarily innovative electronic devices.[57] Cruz also gets a set of wireless speakers, though Kim tells him not to. He says that he can't compete with the music from Whitecotton and the Gooch, and perhaps more surprisingly, he says that audio isn't necessary with his movie.

"There's dialogue in the film," says Kim. "But even if all we heard was the guitar of the guy next to that guy in the goat mask, we'd still be

---

[57] Next time you're in one of these enormous gas stations in the middle of nowhere, pay a visit to the electronics section. You would be surprised at the quality, variety, and affordability of the second-generation electronic devices. They're sold to long-haul truckers with disposable incomes and few places to spend it, and there are some incredible things there amongst the molded plastic cases.

fine."

I listen to the young man playing guitar, and he's playing in the tune and rhythm of the surrounding music. I hear him singing a strange tune, and though they don't quite sound like words, it blends in well with the growing party's din.

Kim plays the film against a white wall and he's right: the music makes the perfect backdrop to the film, which is a tale about a young man who inadvertently hits a dog in the road and then has to figure out how to bring the animal back to its kindhearted but socially fragile owner. The action on screen blends in with the sounds around, and the characters almost seem to be responding to the musical cues.

"Each medium has a different way of telling a tale," Kim says. "The novel is the medium of thought, of the author's inner monologue. Television comedies have *dialogue* as their currency, of snappy jokes. The plot *drives* the jokes, but the jokes are the ultimate goal."

Kim points to his movie, a scene where the protagonist has a glass of wine with the dog's owner over candlelight, and it's clear that she doesn't know what he's done, and that she's falling for him. The goat-man's guitarist seems to be dictating the music played by Whitecotton and the Gooch, and the music falls into a minor key, just sad enough to portend the dissolution that awaits the on-screen couple.

"But the medium of film is *action*," says Kim. "I don't mean car chases and boxing matches, or rather not *just* those things. I'm talking about *any* action. A man drives his estranged daughter back to her mother's, and the man watches the houses go by, mansions that he can no longer afford. Or a young girl takes a subway for the first time, navigating through a crowd of strangers, each one twice her size, and the movement around the girl frightens both her and the audience."

We come to the scene where the two characters are supposed to kiss, and they don't quite yet. The goat-masked man now sings instead of his guitarist, and I like his voice.

"Sometimes the *absence* of action shows what you're trying to say," says Kim. "A woman prepares coffee for her husband in the first act, he does something to alienate her in the second act, and in the third act, that once-filled pot lays empty and cold."

The guitarist continues to play, and the on-screen couple kiss.

"A perfect film minimizes dialogue, and lets *action* drive it," says Kim. "A wordless script transcends language and culture, and can go straight to any audience's heart."

I look over at Cruz, and he gets it, both the message of the film and Kim's words *about* the message. Cruz gets it all, and I refill his glass before he toasts the film to the party's collective applause.

Clapping the loudest is the goat-masked man, and with a closer look I see that he has only one horn, right in the middle of his head.

/***/

I can't say for sure if the goat-masked man and his friend are real, and I can't trust myself to tell if they are, so I send Cruz. He mingles through the party, and when he comes back he tells me that the guitarist's name is Sami, and that he couldn't quite get the goat-masked man's name. He says he thinks it starts with a *P*.

I leave it at that, and just call them Sami and P. I notice that this pair have stopped their music and are both now looking towards the far wall, which now contains a group of poets having something that the crowd seems to be calling a *slam*. A dark-skinned woman with a tight bun on each side of her head takes the floor, and she has a strange gravitas that causes the crowd to become silent. She starts speaking, and each line holds its own power over the now-rapt audience. The words are bringing a crescendo, and each patch of silence causes titters to travel through the party. The goat-masked man seems to be enjoying the readings quite a bit, and bleats in approval to the girls in his arms after each stanza.

A TALE OF THE HIGHWAY

I soon learn through her words that she's speaking of another poet named Emily Dickinson.[58] The poetess on stage tells us that she wrote this poem with her friend Lateef, who's currently admiring her from beyond the stage. The stage is really just a wooden crate covered with some pads used to move furniture, but still, Lateef looks on approvingly as the poetess speaks the words with fury.

The dark girl claims that she's speaking in Dickinson's style[59] and *about* her, about a shy girl from centuries past who never showed the world her own work, and hid most everything she ever made, to be discovered after her death.[60] The performer speaks of Dickinson's potential fear of fame, and her disdain for the act of publication, how Dickinson called it an *auction of the mind.* The performer alludes to the fear Dickinson may have held, perhaps so terrified of criticism that she kept her brilliance hidden for all but a few closest friends. She asks the crowd what would have happened if Dickinson's poems had stayed in her drawer: Would they have had any value? Is beauty unseen still beautiful?

The audience has no answer for this, and the performer says we don't need one, because one of Dickinson's friends had the foresight to bring the poetess's words to the publishing world posthumously, words that would inject themselves into countless minds, bringing readers out of their darkest times and inspiring them to do things that would in turn

---

[58] The performer looks like Dickinson as well, even though she holds a much larger frame and has skin almost as dark as the creature in my trunk.

[59] Given the dearth of records about Ms. Dickinson's speaking style, let alone audio recordings, this seems impossible. But the performer said things in such a way that it lent an undeniable authenticity to the homage.

[60] There is a certain tragic nobility in artists discovered after their death. Figures like Dickinson and Franz Kafka have influenced millions, and yet they're unaware of this. In fact, they're seemingly the *only ones* unaware of their own impact. And yet, part of this strange phenomenon is admirable. Figures like Dickinson and Kafka are somehow *above* the necessity for adulation, and care only for their work. One could argue that they don't care enough to allow their work a chance at providing value for others, but that is a debate for another time. We have their work, and we should be thankful for this.

inspire others.

Lateef nods approvingly, and the performer continues. She asks us not to remember Dickinson for her shyness, nor dwell on the near disaster of the work being buried forever. Her voice gets low and asks us not to think about how many other Dickinsons must be out there, trapped by their own petty insecurity and depriving both themselves and the world for it, avoiding any judgment but dying as nothing, and inspiring no one.

The performer asks us instead to consider of the *glory* of Dickinson's private endeavors, and while stamping her foot she speaks about how introspection can foster an uncorrupted truth, pure words influenced neither by the public forum nor the vain pursuit of a stranger's approval. The performer then sings words that encourage the audience to go out and *do something*, not for the sake of recognition— but not hiding it from the world either. The performer asks us to do something for its own sake, and then accept the consequences, whatever they may be.[61, 62]

The audience applauses, and after she leaves the stage the din of the party resumes. I hear the goat-faced man has also resumed his

---

[61] They say making art is both a supremely selfish and selfless act at once. Perhaps Dickinson was supremely selfish in her life, and *made* selfless by those who discovered her poetry. But regardless, I still believe if an artist wants to fulfill the selfless part of art's impact, they must do everything they can to get their work out in the public eye.

[62] I've always found a connection between poets and photographers, in the sense that both of their roles often involve finding the beauty that exists all around this world, and then presenting it to us in a way that we can understand. The poetess above captured a big theme, that of making art for its own sake and without an audience, but poets need not discuss such things. Here's an example: Go inside and look at the corner of a ceiling, where two walls meet the roof. Pretty boring for you and me, but give a photographer enough time and they'll find the beauty in that corner, where shadows converge on the clean edges, where straight lines of another's architecture serve to protect us from the elements. Give a poet time to write about it, and they'll show you beauty that you didn't even realize was there in the first place.

singing, and though the sounds coming out of his mouth are strange, I can somehow understand them.

/***/

Howe arrives with his truck shortly thereafter, a big eighteen-wheeler, and opens up the back panel. He pulls down a ramp and then turns on the light inside. We see plastic-wrapped pallets of goods much like the one that started this party off, though there are a lot more of them. Cruz gets up to help and beer-helmeted Danny is there shortly thereafter, still sipping from his helmet but lifting whatever he can.

Howe unloads the rest of his pallets with the help of Danny and Cruz, and they bring everything to a far corner. They unwrap the first pallet, and it's case after case of semi-ruined product, most of it barely-broken drinks once destined for the dumpster. Cruz starts setting them out on a table: dropped cans, dusty bottles and beer just past its expiration date. Most of it isn't top shelf, but it's not bad either, and the party won't notice. I look around and see that everyone's past their first drink, at the point where everything begins to taste better.

One of Clark's friends, a bartender who goes by the name of *Captain Jocko*, has set up a bar in the far corner and takes a few of the bottles. He flips one high in the air before mixing a drink, causing an audible gasp from the partygoers, followed by applause. Another person asks for a drink, and soon there's a gathered line.

Cruz thanks Howe profusely for bringing the drinks and more, but Howe shakes his head.

"I didn't bring you anything," says Howe, taking a sip from his own beverage of choice, a brightly colored nonalcoholic drink with the name

Asskicker that purports to be absolutely packed with caffeine.[63]

I notice that Howe's beverage has a complex aroma—something between berries and a cut-open battery, with the faint undertones of chemicals that might help develop film.

"I left all these goods by the dumpster," says Howe with a conspiratorial wink. "And you guys *chose* to steal them."

Danny and Cruz get the subtext of Howe's words of complicity.

"I didn't mean to call you thieves," says Howe with a laugh. "Let's just say you're *efficient*."

Danny doesn't quite get that reference, and Howe explains that it has to do with the limitations that liability puts on his company's delivery system.

"We're pretty good, but we can't be perfect because of liability," says Howe. "We'd love to sell these barely-damaged goods at a reduced price or even just give them away, but such things can lead to a bad end. A *real* bad end."

Howe points to the first pallet in the corner.

"Let's say instead of delivering it to the dumpster we just donated everything in that stack to charity," says Howe. "Someone drinks a bottle with a cracked neck, swallows a shard of glass, and then there's a lawsuit. And lawsuits take a lot time and a *lot* of money."

Howe takes another sip from his can of Asskicker.

"So *like I have just clearly done*, we throw away such barely-ruined

---

[63] Wine is my drug of choice, but I can't underestimate the value of caffeine. It's the gift to those who choose to follow society's rules. Show up at your desk job every day? You get as much coffee as you can handle. Have a job that involves lifting, or doing something outdoors? Here's an ice-cold can of Asskicker, with a jagged-edged neon tiger on the front.

product," says Howe. "No lawsuit, and a system that's efficient enough. You guys are just *choosing* to proactively raise the efficiency of this system, ensuring that all the effort it took to produce these goods is not in vain."

Danny thinks about Howe's words.

"I don't know, I kind of like the term *thieves*," says Danny. "Thieves throw great parties."

Howe raises his can to this.

"To dumpster thieves," says Howe. "To efficiency, to a good time, and to dumpster thieves."

We all raise our glasses and toast this.

To efficiency, to a good time—and to dumpster thieves.

/***/

The goat-faced man ends a song, a strange tale about how the world has changed, and how his friend Sami and he have changed along with it. They refer to themselves as *gelkins*, and I ask Cruz if he knows what that means. Cruz says he doesn't know. He likes the way they sound as P sings through his snout over Sami's guitar, but he wasn't really listening to the song. I want to speak with these two, but there's another spectacle going on in place of the poetry, a comedian who is apparently warming up the crowd while the stage is being constructed in the distant field for some sort of a wrestling match.

The comedian is absolutely hilarious, and fearless in front of the now-tipsy and somewhat chaotic crowd. The people aren't hostile but are a bit overenthusiastic, and yell their own scattered responses to everything he says. His humor hits on every note and delivers an impact, and soon everyone quiets lest they miss one of the punchlines.

The comedian then tells a long, self-deprecating and somewhat disturbing tale about how badly he disappointed his last girlfriend. The jokes in this tale are manifold, and come at an unexpected times. One joke makes me laugh so hard that boxed red comes out of my nose. Danny laughs at this, and then laughs even more at my appearance, saying that it looks like someone punched me in the face. I think of the Crows waiting for me outside, and I stop laughing. Danny collapses into hysterics though, leaving just Cruz and me to watch the comedian.

Cruz doesn't smile, let alone laugh, but I can tell that he's enjoying the performance.

/***/

The comedian announces that the wrestling stage finally is set up in the distant field, and leaves to thunderous applause. The wrestlers have even brought a few generators to power the lights, and the wrestling match begins, announced by an endlessly charismatic ringleader named *El Macho Gordo.*[64] Gordo is egging the crowd on with personal details about the upcoming villain, a masked aristocrat who calls himself *Owen Elegant*. Elegant is to wrestle an up-and-comer called *Lorenzo*, and the former has apparently called his opponent *an example of the virtuous poor, or at least as virtuous as his kind can be*.

The comedian is now sipping whiskey beside us, and he introduces himself as *Jay*. Cruz is happy to see him, and says he was hilarious. Even though Cruz didn't laugh once, I can tell that he means it.

"Yeah—you got to feel out each crowd before you start your act," says Jay. "These guys are smarter than most. Even though they're drunk and watching wrestling right now, they're smart, and those crowds often want tales. I gave them a tale, and it got a little uncomfortable at times, but that's what humor can do. It can take on things that make us uncomfortable, and beat those things down until we can handle them."

---

[64] This wrestling spectacle is not of the Olympic, grappling variety, but of the pure-entertainment kind, with banter, flying elbows and funny masks.

Cruz asks what Jay means by *uncomfortable* things.

"Job loss, disappointment, just about any kind of failure," says Jay. "The more negative it is in life, the better it is on stage."

Cruz asks if Jay can make a joke about death.

"I could do a whole set on that," says Jay. "Joking's probably the only thing we can do about death."

Owen Elegant[65] jumps up and hits Lorenzo with both feet at once, and then lands on top of his opponent with one elbow on the ground, as if in repose. El Macho Gordo is now announcing the play-by-play of the match and sells the move as *the Man of Leisure*, and this whips the crowd into a semicomical frenzy.

"Wrestling's different," says Jay. "That poet wanted to move us, I wanted to make them laugh, but wrestlers want a reaction, *any* reaction, and the bigger the better."

Lorenzo counters the moves by grabbing ahold of his own bootstraps and kipping-up, and after Owen Elegant falls off he shakes his head in exaggerated shock at his opponent's gumption to deign attempting such a thing.[66]

---

[65] Owen Elegant is an interesting individual. Real name Owen Ellickson, grew up in a tough area of Glasgow, Scotland. Rugby career ended with an injury, then worked as a bouncer, started trying out for the theater, got a few minor roles in plays here and there. Couldn't quite shake his Glaswegian accent enough to get far in the theater, but after trying out for a wrestling league on a whim, he soon found his identity. Ellickson started out as a hero, *Bravehart*, but after a cease-and-desist letter, he decided to become a villain. He soon found that a middle-class British accent counted as upper class to most wrestling fans outside of the UK, and became Owen Elegant to much acclaim. After this event against Lorenzo, Elegant went a little too far with his act, joining a popular but effete team of foppish dandies called *The Oligarchy*. He would eventually leave them, become a good guy, and be publicly accused by his former cadre of being a traitor to his class.

[66] As the crowd cheers on the spectacle of two fighters locked in staged mortal

"In wrestling, it's a little easier to play the bad guy," says Jay. "Bad guys get bigger reactions, and they drive the narrative forward."[67]

Jay's words about *bad guys* and *narratives* make me think of the Crows, though I don't quite buy the analogy. Wrestling is a spectacle, and this is real life (or so I think), and it's different. *Besides, I had my own narrative before Retjar and the Claws flew in. Whatever I'd originally wanted to do, they've done nothing but get in my way.*

/***/

Cruz talks again about the goat-faced man, and says that he looks like a unicorn. I figure it's because the goat mask includes only one horn, obscured by fur, but right in the middle of his head. The masked man begins singing again, and his words refer to him and his friend as gelkins, and I wonder if that's the term for a mono-pronged goat. *Horses are to goats as unicorns are to gelkins.*

Still, there's something more to the man in the mask than just his horn, so I listen in closely to his bleated song. He sings of broad themes: of pride and a fall from grace, of arrogance and limitless potential.

I ask Cruz what he thinks of the song, and he responds that he can't understand it, not a single word.

---

combat, I can't help thinking of Retjar's claim that deep inside, humans are closer to violent chimpanzees than they are to the peace-loving bonobos. I don't entirely buy that they're like the latter, but I don't think the wrestling match suggests that they're like the former either. There's mock violence at this party, but *real* violence is the furthest thing from the audience's minds right now. The crowd isn't partying to relieve stress in between battles. They're living life, forming bonds and exchanging ideas. Whatever they're doing, the people around me are not chimpanzees.

[67] Negative emotions can rile a mob of people a lot easier than positive, productive ones. Most of the time this peculiarity of human psychology ends up as the root of history's various atrocities, but in the world of professional wrestling, it makes for great entertainment.

A TALE OF THE HIGHWAY

/***/

I feel that the goat-faced man is going to set me back on my quest, just as his middle-sized counterpart did in my dreams. So I take one last moment of reprieve and walk with Cruz out away from the party, and well away from the vehicle that awaits me. We have one more drink, from a half-emptied bottle of the sauvignon blanc, and it's chilled to perfection at this point, with a taste that's both round and sharp at once.[68]

Cruz thanks me, and shows me his tattoo of the river of forgetfulness, and I ask him if he could turn it into something else, lest the memories of this night disappear in its waters. He shakes his head, and says he's going to do more than cover it up, he's going to have it removed, even though the prospect scares him.

I ask him why the prospect would scare him, and Cruz tells me that although he's looking forward to remembering his new life, he wishes he didn't have to remember his old one. I tell him that he needs to think about his future instead of dwelling in the past, something that none of us can control.

Cruz thinks about this, and then tells me that my stumbling into his store was the best thing that ever happened to him, possibly the only good thing that ever happened to him.

"I disagree with that last part, at least in a certain sense," I say. "A lot of good things will happen to you, from here on out. You've got tomorrow, and the day after, and the day after that. You've got a tremendous life in front of you, Cruz, you just have to put yourself the right space."

Cruz toasts me, believing it. I can't help wondering if this is *the Last*

---

[68] That's because this sauvignon blanc is blended with one of its most frequent and possibly favorite partners, Sémillon. The blend softens sauvignon blanc's hard edges with the soft, round tones of the Sémillon, and you end up getting the best of both worlds.

Party that I was planning, and if so, what I need to do to make *the First Party* begin.

Still, I've got a task at hand. I brought my value to this place, and this party shows who and what I am. But there's something important in my trunk, and it needs me.

A TALE OF THE HIGHWAY

The Gelkins

Whitecotton and the Gooch have taken a small break to avoid interfering with the wrestling match outside, so when I go back inside I only hear Sami playing his guitar. His song is in a major key, but he plays it with such gravitas that it feels minor. As he plays the goat-masked man sings, and he's now singing in words that those who remained in the back of the gas station can understand. The two women at his side are now wrapped in so close to him that they're enmeshed in his torso, almost a part of him. His rounded lips move in time with the accented words that come out of his prosthetic mouth:

> Oh what a throne
> The seat of humanity
> Ambitions their own
> More than the gods' vanity
>
> But not all gods are vain
> One's different from the rest
> You might think him insane
> But I call him blessed
>
> He's chased by dark ravens
> Who put him in fetters
> They think their prey craven
> But I know him better
>
> The Claws he will snare
> The Beak thinks himself wise
> But while the Claws tear
> The Beak speaks naught else but lies

A TALE OF THE HIGHWAY

From the beginning of time
To the endless abyss
From primordial chyme
To the satyr's last kiss

We may end this Earth
Or we may bring light
But both will have had worth
Because of this night

They will call themselves truth
And threaten the end
But they do not speak sooth
So our hero can't bend

They'll beat him and squawk
Threaten a world become grey
But if they don't let him talk
They must fear what he'll say

The Crows and the Jarkeeper
Demons from deep
They'll claim they are far-seers
But they only want to herd sheep

Can our hero free the Titan?
He can with reflection
The answer will enlighten
And it is perfection

From the beginning of time
To the endless abyss
From primordial chyme
To the satyr's last kiss

We may end this Earth

Or we may bring light
But both will have had worth
Because of this night

It will all have had worth
Because of this night

The remaining crowd erupts in applause and the goat-masked man thanks them profusely, back to his odd words. Cruz tells me that he can no longer understand these words, but I can. I listen closely and it seems the goat-masked man is now talking to me directly.

"Come here, Dion, and talk with us gelkins," he says. *"We have much to discuss, namely progress, potential—and perfection."*

/***/

Sami continues to play guitar as I approach, playing barred chords high up on the neck but leaving the bottom strings open. They reverberate with each strum, resonating with an ethereal, constant pitch that lends an aura of mystery, perhaps even hope. Sami then performs a quick jaunty melody with all five fingers played asynchronously, so that rhythm, bass and the lead guitar come from his one instrument. But as I sit down with them, he resumes his open-ended melodies that go nowhere in particular, filling the room with a sense of wonder and possibility.

I notice Sami is wearing a thick wool cap that conceals a mesh of thick hair, but also a single protrusion in the middle of his head. I wonder if it's a horn like his goat-masked comrade, and I look down to see coarse fur poking out of Sami's pants. He's wearing shoes but they don't look particularly snug around his feet, and his legs appear to have an extra joint in them.

"I'm glad you stopped here, Dion," says the goat-faced man.

"Thank you," I say. "Or should I say *thank you*."

I recognize myself speaking the strange speech of the goat-faced man, and I find that this strange dialect comes more naturally than anything I've said before.

"I don't understand," I say. "I mean, I do understand these words, but I don't understand—"

The goat-masked man interrupts with a long bleat. In another time this would have been strange, but the surrounding party has such momentum that it only elicits a few supportive cheers before everyone around gets back to their drinks, conversations and games.

"*We are speaking in what is now known as ancient Greek,*" says the goat-masked man. "You may speak it freely because no one here understands it. No one on Earth understands it, for that matter."

"Ancient Greek, how do we—"

"*It's your favorite language, Dion,*" says the goat-masked man. "*We all have many languages, but this is our favorite.*"

Sami smiles and opens his mouth to let out a bleat much like his goat-masked friend, though it sounds surprising coming out of Sami's human mouth.

"Sami understands us too," says the goat-masked man. "*Though when the spirit of celebration hits him, he chooses a more carnal tongue.*"

Sami winks at me and then plays a short dancing tune before resuming his arpeggiated chords of mystery.

"*Sami is what we call a satyr, Dion, and I am a faun,*" says the goat-faced man. "*I hate re-introducing myself like this, considering you and I have known each other for millennia, but my name is Pan. Pan the faun.*"

/***/

Sami continues to play his guitar, and the soft strings cover our words. Pan waves his hands over the girls at his side and they fall asleep, nestling into the nook of his arms as if he were a pillow one hour before the sunrise.

"This should do it," says Pan, still speaking ancient Greek. "We can never be too careful in these times, for though the humans are our friends, they can be co-opted, and spies lurk everywhere."

I think of Ari, so in love with me that she abetted my ruin, and then her own.

"Can you please tell me what's going on?" I ask. "No more hints cloaked in a song's stanza, no more allegories. Just tell me what's going on."

"I'll tell you all that I *can*," says Pan. "For you didn't let me know everything, and you didn't allow me to tell you everything."

"I didn't *allow* you to—?"

"I'll tell you all that I can, Dion," says the goat-faced Pan. "And listen closely, for though our bacchanalia here could go on until the end of time, this world may not. We have truth, hope and progress on our side, but time is not our ally."

/***/

Sami the satyr procures an earthen jug from his bag and pours it out into three earthen cups. We drink, and it's so good that I recognize everything I thought of wine before was incomplete. *Whatever is in this jug is so incredible that it makes life worth it by itself. No matter the depravity that came before, it's worth it to have this sip.*

"You made this concoction, Dion," says Pan. "It took quite a bit of experimentation, but you found it. Honey and grapes, ambrosian nectar and the like, all blended under the right conditions. It's good."

"It is," I say.

It's good and I want more, but I don't need more. One sip of this is good enough for a lifetime.

"I've never actually had this before this moment, Dion," says Pan.

"I don't know if I have either," I say. "My memories are gone."

"Perhaps the best way to deal with vanished memories," says Pan, "is to make new ones."

I like Pan's words and it sounds like a toast, so we raise our glasses.

"You began concocting this ambrosian wine when you began planning all the rest of this, which was a long, long time ago. You knew what you were doing, every step of the way."

"I don't know what I was planning," I say.

"I don't quite know either, because you didn't tell me everything," says Pan. "But this is all part of your plan."

Pan laps up another sip of the ambrosian wine through his snouted mouth.

"You used to live for the moment, just like me," he says. "And then you took off the great being's shackles, to the boundless chagrin of your father. You wanted to change the world, and you may do just that."

"Who did I tear from my father?" I ask. "There's a creature in my trunk, and I understand I may have kidnapped—"

Sami stops his music and bleats angrily at me. Pan takes another sip of his wine.

"It's not precise to call it a creature, because the entity in your trunk is more than god and man combined," says Pan. "And you did not *kidnap* it, you *liberated* a divine being, with the hopes of freeing humanity along with it."

Sami is livid, though perhaps a better description would be *upset*. He's not happy with my choice of words, but it's clear that he's still on my side.

"Then tell me," I say. "What's this divine being's name?"

"To be more accurate, this divine being is a Titan," says Pan. "And his name is *Prometheus*."

/***/

Sami begins playing again, this time reverting to a minor key. The name rings a faint bell in my destroyed memory, and Pan fills me in on the rest. *Prometheus stole the fire off of Mount Olympus, and brought it to humanity. He was punished for this by the gods, and was thereafter chained to a rock, with his liver eaten by an eagle. His liver would grow back during the night under the moon, and he'd start his daily persecution again.*

"Much of that story lives as a metaphor," says Pan. "But the basics are all there. If it were not for Prometheus stealing the fire for the first time, humanity would still be in caves, if that."

None of what I see around us would be here. There'd be no gas station, no car, no Howe bringing ruined libations. No philosophy either, not even Shaw's shortsighted High Priest Sargon. None of this would exist.

"I've also heard that if I let Prometheus out, everything will be destroyed," I say. "Not destroyed, but eradicated, completely vanished. Now, I don't believe this, but Retjar did say—"

Sami stops his guitar and bleats at me again. He's so angry that he's frothing at the mouth, and Pan has to stop him from getting up and throttling me.

Or smacking some sense in to me. Devil's advocate or not, I may have inadvertently just taken the side of Retjar.

"I'm sorry," I say.

"It's all right, Dion," says Pan, calming Sami down. "None of us were ever friends of the Crows, but Sami has a particular dislike of them, and even bristles at their names."

"I'm sorry," I say again to Sami. "I really am."

He accepts my apology, sits down and then picks up his guitar again. This time he plays in neither a major nor minor key, but a diminished one, and the sound is quite disturbing.

"Some gods have been echoing that aforementioned mantra since humanity actually *lived* in caves," says Pan. "They said Prometheus was going to destroy everything the first time, that he was going to give fire to humanity only to watch them burn the world to cinders."

Pan takes another sip and looks at the party around him.

"But despite all the wars, depravity and everything, here we are," he says. "Still alive, and living a lot better than when we were mere gods of the cave, represented on Earth by totems at most."

More than just a man.

"Am I—?" I ask. "Are we—?"

"You're a god, Dion," says Pan. "Just like Sami and myself. We three are of the rare type who have learned to take full human form, though none have been able to blend in with this world as you have."

/***/

Sami gradually leaves his diminished key, but doesn't resume a major key just yet. He settles on a minor key, played softly so that I can better hear Pan's words.

"You never told us of your full plan to steal Prometheus," says Pan. "We didn't want you to either. You jokingly called this an act of vandalism, and told us that such things are best done by a single being in the dead of night. You said it was better without a consensus, without a conspiracy that could be found out."

Sami nods his head in approval as he plays.

"Did I plan the rest of this?" I ask. "Ari was somehow tricked into destroying my memory, and I awoke only to be chased by Crows, Crows that torment me into doing precisely the opposite of what I intended. Did I plan it to end up this way?"

Pan shakes his elongated head.

"You didn't plan it this way," says Pan. "But I knew you *accounted* for it. You knew there was going to be trouble. And you made sure that we would help you along the way as best we could."

I take another sip of the wine, and despite the recent revelations, its brilliant taste clarifies the world for a moment. It's so good that I can think of naught else but its flavor.

"I've seen you in my dreams," I say.

"And I've seen you," says Pan. "Well, sort of. I said that *none have been able to blend in with this world as you have*, and that goes for the world of dreams as well. I can act as your guide in the underworld, but it's not the verbal self you see before you."

/***/

Captain Jocko has just prepared a tray of iridescently blue drinks, and in the middle of them he places a cocktail that he promptly sets on fire. The flames shimmer through the blue around them, and it reminds me of the light shared by Pan's dreamt horn, the philosopher's room, and Prometheus's trunk.

"You taught us how to come down here, Dion," says Pan. "You loved humanity so much that you preferred their company to that of your heaven-bound siblings, and you taught yourself to take human form so that you might live amongst them. You taught me how to do this, and then you taught Sami. Since then we've spent more time frolicking in the forest than in our skyward firmament."

Sami bleats again.

"Not that we're missing out on much," says Pan. "I'd rather be down here than on Olympus, listening to our siblings bicker endlessly, and then declare war at every perceived slight."

Sami bleats again and smiles before taking his cap off to reveal a single prong, right in the middle of his head.

"But the war that's occurring *now* is different," says Pan the faun. "After we shed our last pair of horns, only one grew back between them. We began to resemble *gelkins*, unicorned goats, and though we don't quite know the meaning of our single horn, I know that it is significant. Powers are shifting, and perhaps some of it has entered our earthbound bodies. Change is afoot, and whether it's been brought or simply hastened by you, it's coming."

Their single horns don't glow like in my dream, but I sense that they might soon.

"Why doesn't Prometheus just bust out of the trunk?" I ask. "Or we could rush it now, maybe get an axe and hit the back of the car until there's a hole in it?"

Sami bleats in support, and looks like he's ready to lead the charge. Pan calms him down.

"If only it were that easy," says Pan. "But it's not. In this intersection of worlds, there are certain rules that govern us. The Crows would be there, waiting to have their way with all three of us."

Pan stomps his feet, still ready to lead the charge.

"Then what's the code to the trunk?" I ask. "How do I find it out at least?"

"I don't know either of these things," says Pan. "Only you know."

"I don't," I say. "If I did, I would have opened it by—"

"You do," says Pan. "No one else does, because you made the code, and then made it a secret, locked away by Hephaestus."

Pan sees that the name Hephaestus doesn't quite register with me.

"God of the blacksmiths," says Pan. "One of the noncombatants in this struggle, at least for now. He forged the metal around the trunk so that it could contain Prometheus, which is another reason why we couldn't just attack it with an axe. He then constructed a lock so that it could only be opened by your code."[69]

I made the code. Some good it does me now.

"This is about where my knowledge ends," says Pan. "You knew the number but didn't want to reveal it to me, lest I give it away on one of my—*frolics*, and you were right to do that. I probably would have found

---

[69] Some can't get over Hephaestus' physical appearance, but I know that there's an indescribable beauty to him matched by nothing else in this world. He hides under the earth, ashamed of his lame physique, but he sends beautiful things upwards to show his love. Venus may be beautiful herself, but it ends there. Hephaestus makes beauty all around him, and he doesn't stop making it. So next time you see a beautiful construction, be it a small, shiny piece of jewelry or a building that touches the sky, think of club-footed Hephaestus. He probably had some part in the design.

a way to put it in one of my drunken songs."

I understand where he's coming from, though part of me still wishes I'd just told him, however:

> *Oh what a number,*
> *The code of humanity!*
> *It starts with a 6-2,*
> *And ends with a 2-3.*

But I didn't tell him, and I'm sure it's for a good reason.

"Did I give you any hint?" I ask.

"Perfection," says Pan, and he can tell that I've heard it before.

/***/

Pan tells me that though I gave him the clue *perfection*, he unfortunately doesn't know much more about it than I do. So we talk of my story so far, of the Crows who are chasing me. Pan tells me how the Crows have learned to torment my human form, but that's about as far as they can go. I then tell them of a bleeding-eyed woman who tricked Ari into erasing my memory, and Sami bleats angrily in recognition.

"The *Jarkeeper*," says Pan, who snorts to show that he doesn't like her either. "She was sent to punish humanity after Prometheus' first venture, and she's back again. I assume you'll see her soon enough. Her tactics are different from the Crows."

"The Crows," I say. "Speaking of them, who are they? I've listened to Retjar's words, but—"

Sami bleats and gets up, enraged. I hold up my hands in apology, but his jaw clenches and his face takes on a reddish hue. Pan holds him back and I can sense he would never harm me, but he remains livid. I think I can even see a faint glow in his horn.

Pan calms him down, saying soothing, high-pitched words in a language I don't understand.

"He bristles at their true names," says Pan. "But I told him that the times are too tenuous to enrage ourselves fruitlessly."

Pan nods at Sami, who frowns, then reluctantly places his hands over his ears.

"You have been at odds with Retjar the Damned over the centuries, Dion," says Pan. "He's currently tasked with stopping you, but he's enjoying this bit of payback with the help of his friend Ulo. He's enjoying every last moment."

"Ulo?"

"Yes, Ulo," says Pan. "*Ulo the Bludgeon, Ulo the Scraper*. An unthinking, mindless force, the one who does what needs to be done, the one who brings nightmares, even to the gods. Retjar and he are demons from the deep: one with a twisted mind, and the other with a body that holds naught else but anger. And both of them were sent to stop you by any means necessary."

Pan turns his head towards the front of the station and sniffs the air.

"They don't have our ability, to be *here* like we are, let alone your ability to blend in with humanity undetected," continues Pan. "But they can connect quite well with *your* human form, Dion, a human form that you have presently forgotten how to escape. So whatever Retjar threatens, it's not entirely an illusion."

Pan leans back and gestures to Sami that those dastardly names shan't be mentioned again, and that Sami should now open his ears. Sami doesn't though, and appears to be sensing something instead. He looks concerned, and I see that his horn has grown a small crack.

He eventually opens his ears and speaks to Pan in their bleated dialect, and Pan nods grimly.

"Prometheus is in trouble," he says. "They've found a way into the trunk."

The hole in the seat. I left it open.

"They can't kill him, because his kind is beyond death," says Pan. "But they can do all the things to him that they've done to you. Maybe more."

Sami bleats and the tip of his horn snaps off.

"I need to help him," I say.

"You do," says Pan. "You're the only one who can."

Sami the satyr bleats again, angry. He pulls off his cap to reveal his cracking horn and rears up on his bent, cloven legs. He's rather well built, and in a rage now, scaring the girls nestled in Pan's side, though Pan quickly calms them. Pan bleats some forceful words to Sami in their dialect, and then Pan looks at me.

"This is not his fight," says Pan to me after Sami reluctantly stands down. "In another era, on another plane of existence he'd tear Retjar apart, but not this one. *You* must go and solve this – only you can see this through."

"But the Crows want Prometheus destroyed! I can't go out there and do what they want!"

I hear Sami's horn crack under his hat.

"You must, for now," says Pan. "You told me this would happen, and you told me that though your memory would be gone, your self would remain, and this ensures that you won't ultimately do what they want. You should be wary of stopping too much because your *self* can erode under their torments, and you run the risk of fulfilling their objective completely. But your self is still here at this moment, and you told me that you'll figure everything out, just not now."

I know he's right. I have a task, and Prometheus needs me. But I still hesitate, and Pan picks up on it.

"This is the Last Party, Dion," says Pan. "What you see all around you is *who you are*. This is the gift that you give to the world, both the old one and the world that will arrive after the First Party. But there will be no new world to come if you stay here. You must go out and act, even if your actions may seem antithetical to your beliefs at times. You told me this, and you trusted yourself to figure out the code before the end."

/***/

Pan and Sami walk me to the front of the gas station, and the music resumes behind us, though in muffled tones. We see the vehicle by the pump, sitting silently as if nothing happened, as if the Crows had just waited patiently while I threw the Last Party.

Sami bleats again, this time plaintively.

"He wants me to let you know that we'll be with you on your journey, at least remotely," says Pan. "Hermes, the messenger of the gods, is on our side in this struggle, and he'll follow your vehicle. If something happens to you, we'll know, and if you need us, he'll send the message. Just look for his gold helmet."

Sami looks at the vehicle and stamps his cloven foot again.

"This might not be Sami's fight," says Pan, "but if they push you too far, it will be."

I embrace my old friend Pan, and then do the same to Sami, but the latter shirks my outstretched arms. *He may have a human face, but Sami the satyr is more of a goat than Pan.*

A TALE OF THE HIGHWAY

"I know you can do this," says Pan. "You're still the same Dion that you were a few days ago, the same Dion that I've known for centuries. They're doing everything they can to stop you, and they'll do more, but you must continue. Prometheus will do wondrous things, but only *you* can ensure that this Titan is freed. Only *you* can ensure that Prometheus will be able to abet the next level of humanity."

/***/

Sami voices one more irate bleat towards the shadows of Retjar and Ulo, and my two comrades retreat back to the party. I want to leave while nobody's looking,[70] though I can't resist saying goodbye to Cruz first. Luckily, he's thinking the same and comes to meet me in the darkened front of the gas station, in this place between worlds, the quiet area between humanity's Last Party and the Hell that awaits.

I embrace Cruz, and he doesn't shirk away like Sami did. After we separate, he even gets emotional. He doesn't cry, but he gets close, and tells me that this has been the greatest night of his life.

I tell him that I'm happy for him, but that he should see this party not as the apotheosis of his life, but as the *beginning* of it.

"This is the Last Party of the old world," I say. "The last party of the old Cruz as well."

He doesn't quite understand what this means, so I explain the second part of it.

"Sometimes people can't escape their past," I say. "You and I are both struggling with this, for two different reasons. But the next morning will bring a new day, and I'm telling you, Cruz, anything will be possible then. Anything. You just have to open your eyes to see that it is."

---

[70] When you've stayed at the party past the point of collective inebriation, it's okay to leave without saying goodbye to everyone. You can do this even if you started the party. Even if two demons from the deep await you outside.

At this point I can see why Cruz and I have grown so close in such a short amount of time.

We've only known each other for a few hours, but we've truly listened to each other every moment.

Cruz gives me a gift: the waiter's friend corkscrew. It's a perfect one, solid, though not so high-end that I'd be worried about it getting scratched.

We embrace one more time, and Cruz tells me that he's activated my pump and prepaid for a tank. He then asks me where I'm going.

"When I first came in, I told you that *everything I own was taken, and I'm being blackmailed by two very powerful men*. That's the truth, though it's not the complete truth. They took everything that I own and more, but they're not exactly men. They're Crows."

He asks me if he can do anything to help protect me. I say that this is my fight, and he asks me what exactly my fight is at this moment.

"I can't say for sure," I reply. "The Crows are trying to punish me every chance they get, but this is not my concern. My concern is to figure out how to open my fucking trunk, and release Prometheus into this world."

/***/

Before I leave the station I go to an office in the front to check out the video monitor. I don't know what I'm hoping to find, but I soon start scrubbing through the footage. I rewind until I see myself as I first coasted into the gas station, smashed the bottle on the ground and then walked in my scarecrow's rags towards Cruz's store.

Just a short time ago, but also a lifetime. There may be another lifetime to go before all this is over.

I rewind to see myself once more, strangely reassured that I am real.

I can't quite say the same for Retjar and his friend. I see crows on the car, real crows flying up and around like birds in a desolate gas station are wont to do, but I see no clear signs of Retjar and Ulo. I don't expect this, for I know they lurk on the edges of the shadows, but then I see something I can't quite explain. There's a patch of flickering distortion approaching the vehicle, and then the vehicle shakes. I look closer and see that there are actually *two* patches of distortion, moving independently but never quite leaving the screen.

To another observer, the vehicle's shaking could be attributed to the wind, and the distortion would hardly be worthy of a second glance. But it's there, and though I can't be assured that the Crows are real, it appears this way.

Once again I'm stuck between two resolutions: either I've gone completely insane, or absolutely all of this is actually happening.

I can only act on the second conclusion, so I leave the back room and exit the store. I return to the vehicle knowing that, whether or not Retjar and Ulo truly exist, whatever has just happened can't be good.

The Crows' Gethsemane

I walk outside to my vehicle and the world is once again empty, once again completely bereft of sense. The party had an energy and a semblance of direction, but I'm no longer in that world. Whatever awaits me, it's undetermined at best, doomed at worst. I can still hear the music playing in the back of the party, subdued by the steppe winds that have resumed their place around this outpost. I see the distant light of cars coming to the party, oases of life set against the emptiness beyond, but I'm no longer part of their world, nor are they of mine. They'll arrive shortly, one by one, but they'll sneak in the back, away from the blaring lights of the gas pump, and hidden from the twisted destiny that lies ahead.

I fill up the tank and the sound of the pump begins clicking in a rhythm, gradually finding a way to keep a syncopated pace with the muffled beats coming from the station. *The sounds are like a lifeline, the last thing that connects me to the world of Cruz and laughter, to the world of ideas and meaning.*

I think about how much one's *self* is defined by one's environment, how I just went from a celebration to nothingness in a matter of steps. Back there I was part of something, now I'm just a human body with no memory, pumping gas so I can head towards an uncertain fate. The only thing that's changed is that I have a jumpsuit and a solid pair of shoes.

And the vehicle smells a little different too: earthy and faintly sweet. I've got to face what they've done.

The gas tank soon fills up, leaving the muted pulse of the party to go on by itself, to fade into the surrounding wind. I look to the edges of the station's light and there they are, Retjar and Ulo, waiting in the shadows. Retjar looks less furious than I'd expected. He's grinning, not out of anticipation, but out of self-satisfaction. *He looks smug, as if he has won.*

I hear a faint moaning coming from inside the vehicle, and I can feel Retjar laughing at this. I turn around to see him doing just that, and giving me a look that says *go ahead, look inside.*

/***/

It's there in the vehicle, the size of a small boulder and sitting silently in the passenger's seat. Glistening with fluid wherever it can, covered with what was once life. Unmoving and excised, heavy with juice that's neither meant to be smelled nor seen, nor even thought of. *It's difficult to even consider such a thing touching air, but here it is, accusing me with its very presence.*

It wasn't I who removed it, but it sits as if it's all my fault.

Oh no.

I recognize the smell, that bile, unmistakable even without memory of such a thing. *Too large to fit in a regular human, it seems like it would be better fit for a horse.*

It's Prometheus's liver, a pound—*more than a pound*—of flesh clawed out for my misdeeds.

As I watch it gleam within its own crusted blood, I hear the moaning coming again from the trunk. I jump into the back and thrust my hands frantically against the back seat, ripping off the cover that concealed this creature. I take it off and the light is still there, but it now glows a dark, cold red. I call out for Prometheus but the entity doesn't respond, so I thrust my hands into the trunk's hole. I feel nothing, just cold darkness, the kind that I'd experienced in my dream as I was falling down towards Hell. But then I feel something, maybe the creature's fingertips as it reaches out and barely brushes mine, or maybe its body, cold, dead and liverless as it floats through the trunk's ether.

I withdraw my arm, empty and frustrated. *It's as if I tried to save this creature from drowning, only to come up with nothing.* I reach my hand in again, and find even less this time, not even the brush of its hidden body. I withdraw my hand again and look out the window to stare at Retjar. He stares back, even more self-satisfied than before, and then points at me as if to say *you're next*.

Boom! The creature's arm thrusts out of the trunk, wrapping around me with its impossible length, clinging onto my body for dear life, perhaps the only thing keeping it from the abyss. I laugh, too thrilled that Prometheus is still alive to do anything else.

I feel its arm quiver and its grip weakening and know that though Prometheus is still alive, we're still in trouble. Its once smooth, black skin is now crisscrossed with lacerations, gleaming with fluid much like the removed organ in the front seat.

I whisper to my cohort that everything will be okay. Prometheus seems to understand this, and calms down. The creature doesn't let go though: even though its strength shows no signs of returning, it still finds a way to clutch onto me with everything it has left.

I get an idea and I tell it this, gradually peeling its scabbed fingers off my body. Prometheus is still terrified, so I take a wine bottle from the cask—a zinfandel—and wrap its hands around the bottle's neck.

"Hold on to this," I say. "I'll be back in just a few moments."

/***/

I exit the vehicle and then open the front seat. I pick up the enormous liver and take it outside, casting a pointed look at the Crows before walking into the darkness, away from the party and *well away* from the shadows of my tormentors.

I find a spot at the outer edges of the gas station's lights, but still behind the invisible boundary that separates me from the Crows. *I'm outside the lighthouse, on the edge of the rocks as I face the endless ocean, but I'm still on land.* I hold the bilious organ up to the moon as if

I'm offering a sacrifice, or perhaps more accurately, something shown by a child to make his mother proud.

The moon seems to shine in response, and the oversized gland in my outstretched arms takes in the full power of the reflected light's love. I feel the flesh in my hands reverberate with growing strength, and I feel the organ pumping again, producing secretions and doing whatever else a liver is supposed to do.

I let the light bathe the organ for another minute, and it becomes healed. I then stay out here for another minute to be sure of it.

/***/

"I know what they did to you," I say to Prometheus moments later as I hold on to its quivering hand. "I know it all too well, because they've done the same to me."

I take the Titan's hand off the wine bottle's neck and put it on its healed liver, and Prometheus sends out an echoed whimper from the dim light.

"But though their depravity is new to me, I sense they've been doing this to you for centuries," I say. "They take your liver, peck it right out of you, every night."

Prometheus is silent in response.

"But they don't kill you, or rather they *can't*," I say. "Given the choice they'd slaughter both of us in a heartbeat. But they *can't* kill us, they can't do *anything* in this world by themselves."

Prometheus manages a weak thump against my vehicle, and I start to push the creature's liver back in through the hole. Though it's slightly larger than the opening, the organ is somewhat moldable, and it fits through in one piece. The cold glow of the trunk gradually morphs back into a warmer glow, and it seems as if it's headed back to where it once was. Though still in the trunk, the Titan is back in the glowing light, the light of reason that's gradually reclaiming its space, and I know that Prometheus will soon be as whole and strong as before, perhaps even more so.

"The Crows can't do *anything* real on this earth," I say. "Not like I can, and definitely not like you can."

Prometheus thumps in agreement.

"Now I've got to see them once more and try to figure out—"

I'm immediately interrupted by Prometheus's arm shooting back out and grabbing hold of my jumpsuit. I'm relieved to see that the arm is once again whole and strong, its skin almost a pure black, but I don't know if it will let me go.

Prometheus knows it's foolish to jump back into the cold water like this. But I have to go.

"I've got a plan," I say, gently tugging its hand away, but not letting it go. "It involves *listening*."

Prometheus doesn't understand, so I explain further.

"I can't do the brute-force method of finding this code, but I know that Retjar likes to talk," I say. "And every step of the way he's said a little too much for his own good. And from what I gather, he's gotten to know me quite well over the centuries."

I look into the hole, and speak directly to the light of reason.

"I don't think he knows the code, but he knows me," I say, still thinking about the idea of *perfection*. "I had originally set it, and Retjar might reveal something about me that might cue my present self into figuring out what it is."

Prometheus is a bit reluctant to acknowledge my reasoning, and I can't blame my cohort for it. *I'm jumping in the water hoping the sharks can teach me something, and that's not really a plan.* I take a different approach.

"There's truth here, Prometheus," I say. "Somewhere, there's truth. The only way I can find it is to confront it head-on."

Prometheus lets go slowly, reluctantly accepting my words. I begin exiting the vehicle, but turn around to give my passenger another message.

"One more thing," I say, my jaw quivering because sentiments like these don't come naturally to me. "I don't yet know who I am, but I know my destiny is not that of the fighter, of one who seeks revenge. But listen closely: if the Crows even *think* about hurting you again, I'll find a new destiny, one that involves their punishment. I might have been put on this earth to party, but I know what's right. If the Crows or *anyone* messes with you again, Prometheus, I'll find a way to make them wish they hadn't."

/***/

"Glad you could join us," says Retjar moments later, still cloaked in the shadows but clear enough to see. "I really, really am. Though I wish you could have been here for our session with your friend in the trunk. It's remarkable the level of torment one can inflict on a being with a higher consciousness."

I can see Retjar grinning ear to ear, as smug as can be.

"If you had simply gotten your fuel and then departed," he says, savoring every pedantic word. "We wouldn't *have had to do what we did* to the creature in your trunk, nor would we have to do what we are about to do."[71]

---

[71] Don't be persuaded by Retjar's justification for his evil acts here, that he *had to do it,* that he *had no choice.* Evildoers love forcing their own hands like this. *We* had *to do what we did because* you *gave us no other options.* It sounds

Retjar's grin widens, and he's now even more smug than before.

"Those in the underworld forbade us from hurting the creature in your trunk, and forbade us from hurting you so long as you behaved, but you didn't behave, and you didn't just get fuel. You stopped and *threw a party* for those mongrels. This violation of your directives was so brazen that they allowed us to punish the Titan, and rest assured we'll do the same to you, but—"

Retjar's smugness turns into a quizzical look, and I can't tell if it's real or if he's mocking me. He gestures that he's listening to the party in the background, and I take a moment to listen as well. It's still pumping with music and life, a collection of my former friends, all oblivious to the dark interaction that's currently taking place a few footsteps away.

"But first help me understand what you see in them," asks Retjar, shaking his head. "They're animals, and they're beneath us."

I think for moment.

"Well, they're not perfect," I say. "I'll give you that."

The attempt is clumsy, but I don't worry about that too much because he doesn't seem to pick up on it anyway.

"That's an understatement, if there ever was one," says Retjar. "They're flawed. Chimpanzees, all of them. Dirty mongrels."

"They're not," I say, surprised that he's allowing me to talk. "Violence is the furthest thing from their mind right now. They're having fun, and that's it."

"That's it, and that's *all* there is," says Retjar dismissively.

I recognize this tone. He's about to twist my sentiment around until it suits his cynicism. I need to get back to perfection and—

---

logical, but it's false logic at best. There's always an option. There's always a choice.

"Your friends there are actually *less* than chimpanzees, Dion," he says. "Chimpanzee troops do vicious things, and their actions are found within all the armies of the world, making a constant equilibrium of invasion and revenge. But at least those bloodstained cretins have some sort of direction, some semblance of *ambition*."

Retjar points towards the party.

"Your friends have nothing. They won't engage in atrocity, because their lives are too insignificant to do such a thing," he says. "They're not celebrating a vicious battle, they're not celebrating *anything*."

"You don't understand them," I say. "I don't claim they have to code to divine meaning, but you don't understand them."

I couldn't quite get the word perfect *in there this time, but it's OK. Pretend you're arguing with him, and just keep him talking until he gives you some sort of clue, anything.*

"I heard your mongrel conversations in there, and I understand them enough," he says. "The happiness involved in scaling a rock for its own sake. The virtues of writing all your precious little thoughts on a piece of paper and locking it in your desk drawer, too afraid that someone might disapprove of your insignificant meanderings. Waxing heroic about delivering discarded alcohol to an inebriated group of strangers—imagine how *that* will be recorded in the annals of history."

Retjar continues to mock most every aspect of the party that I witnessed, including the wrestling, the comedy and even the hot tub in the back of Clark's truck. *He made no mention of Pan or Sami, however, and he can't hear my thoughts. He's an eavesdropper, but he's far from omniscient.*

"I understand your comrades quite well, Dion," he says.

"No, you don't," I respond.

"If there's some part of their primitive psyches that I don't understand," says Retjar, "then it's because I don't *care* enough to understand. You think their words are so precious, so imbued with meaning, but there's nothing there. You fell in love with that false oracle of yours, but he's just one more of them, one more mortal devoid of meaning."

All right, now we're getting somewhere. I don't know where we're going, but keep egging him on. Keep it vague though, because I don't quite know who he's talking about.

"My oracle is not false," I say. "You have no idea."

"Oh I have an idea, all right," he says. "A small, single mind, wrapping humanity in crafted words until he convinces himself that there's some purpose behind his species' existence."

Dr. Shaw?

I decide to go with it, and add some specifics to be sure.

"He's a unique voice, and he doesn't follow dogma," I say. "He speaks of philosophy and tales of ancient cities, but unlike *your* kind, Retjar, Dr. Shaw doesn't make up his mind and then stop thinking."

"You're comparing me to a *human*—"

"If you'd listen, truly *listen* for once, Retjar," I say. "You'd know why I love these humans as I do, starting with Dr. Shaw. He *listens* to the world around him, and because of this he has so much to offer, more than you could possibly understand."

Retjar, not accustomed to being interrupted, let alone belittled, becomes enraged. His eyes become flooded with hatred and his face contorts into a terrifying look, something that could turn a human to stone. I worry that it might do the same to me.

I think I have him.

"You believe you have it all figured out," I say. "But look at you, unable to do anything on this earth for yourself—*anything*! You can't even lift a grain of sand, so you have no recourse but to terrorize me into doing your simple tasks for you. You think yourself an *almighty god* but here you are, chasing around an amnesiac because you can't drive a car yourself, and then gleefully waiting to punish him whenever he transgresses. You look at the party and see their mortal lives futile, but if you want futility then *look in the mirror, Retjar*. Judging from your shyness around surveillance cameras, you probably can't even do that."

Retjar is too furious to speak. I see the Claws emerging from the shadows with his coal-black eyes, and I know I've got to get to the point before he pounces. Still, there's so much I want to say. *I'm preaching to the unconvertable, but still, I need to say it. There's truth here, and it needs to be said.*

I point up to the moon, and Retjar look upwards too. It's too bright for his eyes, but I still have the last fringes of his attention.

"Humanity's been there before," I say. "They went to the moon and walked on it, and they did this without our help. While you were worrying about whatever trivialities were happening in the heavens, they were down here, coming up with ideas. Trying. Failing. Trying again."

I now point back to the party, and its thump reminds me of Prometheus communicating with me through the trunk's walls.

"And it all starts in *there*," I say. "Within those walls there's freedom, creativity and risk. Plans are started, ideas are germinated. They're not there to celebrate victory in battle, but they *are* celebrating *life*. Everything starts from there, Crow. Everything."

Ulo is preparing to strike, and I know I only have a few moments to plant the seed in Retjar's thoughts. *His mind carries nothing but scorched earth, but I have to plant the seed.*

"Dr. Shaw, like those in the party, are far from perfect, but he's doing everything he can to listen to the world around him," I say. "That's not the case with you. You avoid listening—and thinking—at *every turn*, spewing your arguments like filth, and sewing your opponent's lips shut because you know your words can't stand up to the smallest bit of scrutiny."

Retjar is apoplectic with rage, but Ulo is not. The Claws is as emotionless and as coal-eyed as ever, and I know I'll only get to say one final thought.

"You're not perfect, Crow," I say. "Far from it. In fact, if there's such a thing as the *opposite* of perfection, it's you, standing right here in front of me, devoid of purpose and quivering with futility."

And with that, Retjar's face contorts into the worst thing I've ever seen in my seemingly short life: a demon's rage incarnate. He points at Ulo and I barely see the Claws lunge into the gas station light. My legs are pulled out from me by unseen talons, and I'm yanked into the darkness, well away from any of my former party's prying eyes, too quickly for the camera to notice, and with such force that I don't even have time to scream.

/***/

I'm prostrate again, lying in a dark field. *Twenty footsteps from the gas station or twenty thousand, it doesn't matter, because I'm in the ocean and the sharks have me in their teeth.*

I can no longer speak, so whatever hand I'd put forth is all played out. Ulo begins his assault, exhaling Retjar's rage through his fists. I hear the latter swearing with a terrifying, *angry* energy, saying words so vile they can't be spoken by a human tongue, millennia-old execrations too horrid for even the gods to hear. Retjar shrieks his threats, spewing venom with every sound, and the Claws rains his fists down on me with each abomination spit from his partner's cursed mouth.

But I hear a repeated theme within the menace of Retjar's diatribe: he seems to be talking about Hephaestus, Dr. Shaw, perfection and the *strange ideas I so worship*.

That's it. Hephaestus had a hand in designing this vehicle, and the lock as well. It was by my request though, and there has to be some logic to the code I chose. The code for the trunk has something to do with ideas, something to do with Dr. Shaw.

Ulo strikes me again.

The code is somewhere in Dr. Shaw's lectures.

Ulo strikes me in the midsection, and it brings blood out of my mouth. I cough the blood out, and I think of the square plastic brick of discs in my vehicle.

The code is somewhere in those discs, a tiny clue hiding somewhere in his hours and hours—and hours—of lectures.

/***/

Minutes or hours later, Ulo stops his assault, and Retjar appears to have calmed somewhat. *He's still on an edge, ready to burst into another tempest of anger at the slightest excuse—but I can't speak or move, so I won't have to worry about that.*

"There will be more," says Retjar. "This isn't over, make no mistake about that. Listen to your little earthbound oracle all you want, but we're not going away. We'll be right here, Dion, every time."

I try to respond but my upper body is mostly crushed, and I can't get the words out.[72]

I can still turn my head though, and I notice that a flock of crows

---

[72] For the record, I was hoping to tell Retjar to go fuck himself. In retrospect, I probably should have tried to wring another clue out of him, but at this point I really just wanted him to know that he should go fuck himself.

has now descended around us, forming a circle. I can't quite see them in the darkness, but I can *sense* them, encircling me, Retjar and Ulo. *A flock of winged parishioners descended onto this unlit place to witness Retjar's sermon to come. At least they're here and not pecking at Prometheus' liver.*

Retjar raises his hands and he's backlit faintly by the night sky, itself iridescent with stars uncorrupted by the gas station's lights.

"Do you ever think about how *utterly alone* this planet is?" asks Retjar, calmed from his hysterics but still maintaining his contemptuous tone.

The idea of *being utterly alone* sounds pretty good right now, but I can't speak, so he continues.

"Your oracle seems clever to you, but he's merely *observant* in the crudest sense of the term, like a dog that's figured out how to open its master's bag of treats," says Retjar. "Adroit, perhaps, but ultimately *limited*, forever contained within his owner's house, never to make any impact beyond the walls he sees."

Retjar looks at the stars, then down upon me.

"Even when your oracle speaks of universal things, like your beloved numerology, it's all for naught. He's in a closed system that will perish with a whimper, and no one will know that it has. All his philosophy, all his thought, all his *cleverness* will be erased in a moment, and no one will ever know that it ever existed in the first place."

Oracle, numerology. Keep talking, Retjar.

"But let's not speak of your mortal oracle, let's speak of the absolute *aloneness* that surrounds both him and your beloved humans," says Retjar. "And to truly understand this, we've got to take a step back on this earth, perhaps a century ago."

Retjar raises his hands towards the stars.

"At this time, your humans' alleged powers of innovation invented the radio, and thus they began putting *radio waves* out into the universe," says Retjar. "Just a few at first, errant strands jettisoned from internal communication, but shortly thereafter *deliberate messages* sent out continuously, in all directions."

Retjar spreads his arms out.

"Those radio waves containing humanity's message are out there right now, passing our solar system's closest neighbors and moving forever outward at the maximum speed that the universe will allow. An errant military communiqué, a horse-racing broadcast—both escaped this planet some time ago, and both were given equal importance in the eyes of the cold, surrounding space. The former might meet its fate in absorption by a cold satellite rock, the latter might pass through the entire galaxy unmolested."

Retjar drops one arm, so that only one is pointing outwards.

"And recently, your humans have been even *more* deliberate in these missives, sending out messages that state *very clearly* that their species exists, and that humans are *supremely* interested in knowing if anyone else does. Any sign, no matter how small, would be welcome."

Retjar shakes his head at me.

"No response yet," he says. "Not a single one."

Retjar kneels down and speaks calmly to me.

"But even this complete absence of any response only scratches the surface of how alone this planet truly is," he says. "Humanity's only been around for a short time, and the expanse of radio waves has taken a negligibly small percentage of the universe, *half* of that when you consider that any listening species needs an equivalent amount of time to send a message back."

Retjar whispers into my ear.

"It's not the messages that they've sent *out* that should terrify you," he says. "It's what they've heard during their listening, or rather what they *haven't* heard."

Retjar lets this thought sit for a moment.

"Your humans have set up machines all around the world running day and night, ready to pick up any message, any message at all," he whispers. "And nothing, not a single instance of any extraterrestrial creature saying a *single* thing. Not one coded piece of information, not an errant transmission of an incomprehensible dialect, not even a simple repeated pulse that *might* be of sentient origin. *Nothing.*"

Retjar stands up.

"Why do you think this is?"

I can't speak at the moment, but I have no answer anyway.

Retjar holds up his hands in two tight balls.

"The universe is a big place," he says pedantically. "One hundred billion stars in our galaxy *alone*, and if just a negligible percentage of them holds sentient life, then there's *millions* of planets, each shooting out radio waves of their own, spreading in all directions at the speed of light."

Retjar moves his tight-balled hands around and expands them in different areas.

"Our world should be littered with these spheres of communication," he says, his expanding hands now backlit by the night sky. "The stars get their light here most every night, why can't humanity get one message? One solitary message?"

He kneels on the ground and brushes the earth with his sharp fingernails.

"Why isn't there a single extraplanetary object buried in the earth?" he asks. "Some species should have visited at *some point* in Earth's history, at the very least sent an ill-fated ship or two. But there's no rusted hulk of a ship, not even a fossilized probe."

Retjar shakes his head.

"So tell me, why have we seen no evidence?" asks Retjar. "Is it because humanity is alone, a unique event?"

I don't respond, and Retjar points at the stars.

"Humanity is not alone, and is *not* some sort of unique event, thank the gods," he says. "There's plenty of other intelligent life out there. Don't worry about that."

Retjar then points towards the gas station, and I can still hear the muffled thump of the party coming from beyond the black birds that now encircle us.

"It's because sentience is inherently self-defeating," he says. "An intelligent species will have a few millennia of development, a few centuries of glory, and will *then* become so smart that they'll learn how to destroy themselves, *truly* destroy themselves. And once they've found out how to do that, it's just a matter of time before they succeed in this endeavor. And then no more radio waves, no more ships sent out, just nothing."

Retjar looks up at the night sky.

"Intelligence is a blessing and a curse, but by and large it's a curse," says Retjar. "And this world is fated to join the endless ranks of planets killed by its own children. Humanity will follow this same path, and their destruction won't be just another *extinction event* to augment the one they've already made. It will be an *eradication*, the planet covered in a grey mud, and then erased."

Retjar looks at me, his eyes radiating a furious shade of red. I can't describe the color, exactly, other than saying however Pan's horn glowed in my dreams, this is the opposite.

"Your beloved humans will be abetted in their destruction of Earth by the thing now locked in your trunk," says Retjar. "And that's why we were sent. That's why we're about to do to you what we must."

Retjar signals Ulo to come near, and the crows begin cawing at his approach.

"In the end it will not be war, pollution, overpopulation or even atmospheric destruction that will bring this world's demise," says Retjar. "It will be human innovation, ingenuity, the *spark* that you so cherish during your little parties. Progress will ultimately destroy everything you see, and leave this world as cold and silent as the universe around it."

Retjar listens to the party's muffled music for another moment, and I wonder if some part of the music has been compressed into radio waves and then sent into outer space. If it has, I wonder where its rhythms will go.

"You've been too busy toasting your mortal friends to truly consider the consequences of your actions," says Retjar calmly. "You think you're taking humanity to the next level, but you're only hastening its demolition. Your friend in the trunk will destroy everything, and then scrub the earth clean, leaving nothing but dead rock."

Retjar signals to Ulo that he just wants one more word with me, and the surrounding crows caw in anticipation of this ceremony's upcoming apotheosis.

"You're a *god*, Dion, and it's time you began acting like one," says Retjar. "I just spoke *your* language of reason, hoping that I could reach you. Now it's once again time to hear *our* language, and I warn you, it's not going to be pretty."

Retjar nods at Ulo, and the Claws' eyes find a way to become a shade darker.

"No more words, no more reason," says Retjar. "Let's begin."

The Purple Planet

I'll skip the details, but again know that there are plenty, even more than in the previous session. Ulo the Bludgeon does his work all over my mortal body, and it's worse than I'd thought possible, and I again lose consciousness. I fall, fall and then fall further, the tremors of the beating growing more distant with every moment.

I awake back in Hell, and it's emptier than ever before. Despair has consumed any remaining terror here, and I see that the grey has all but consumed this place in its entirety. I'm in a stagnant pool, unmoving and up to my knees, a flat marsh with nothing to give it any point of reference. Even the body of Cerberus is now fully gone, broken down and turned into the substance that consumed him.

The goat's still here of course. Pan's dreamt form is deep in the sludge but he doesn't seem to notice his dire predicament, let alone worry about it. He comes up to me with his single horn, which I notice has been cracked but is on the mend, still finding a way to glow brighter than ever before.

"I'm assuming you still can't talk while you're down here, Pan," I say. "Can you?"

He bleats to say that he can't. I'm nonetheless thankful that he's still here with me and I reach forward to rub his head, but he shies away, still a goat.

I look in the distance to see that the room with the philosophers is still there, and still glowing with the light of reason. *But it now seems so far away, just a pinprick, shining like a distant star.*

My angry father's chamber is all but abandoned, save for a few defiant sparks crackling through the air. Ari's chamber is empty as well, a large, hollow cave made even larger and hollower by the fact that the walls of the adjacent chambers have collapsed. There's no more burning city, no more blindfolded creature quivering in front of his former captive souls, just the grey substance.

There's no more Ari either, not even a mound where her body would slowly disappear. I fear that she's been consumed completely by the grey mud, but something tells me that she's somewhere else right now. I wonder about where she is, and hope that she's in a better place—somewhere more worthy of her. I hope to see her again as well, not just because I feel for her—I can't explain why, but I do—but because I don't think the end she and I shared was deserved. A bleeding-eyed woman co-opted her into destroying me, and that's not a fitting resolution.

I can't help feeling positively towards her, and I wonder if the feeling is more than just because of what I felt in my past lifetime. *Perhaps it's because of her importance in this tale. She was tricked into betraying me, but that might be a necessary step for a triumphant outcome. Perhaps Ari's inadvertent actions were necessary for a good end.*[73]

But wherever she is, I know she'll live on within me. That's the beautiful part of emotions: that they can remain. My memory was destroyed, but my sentiment for her stayed. Her earthly body vanished and her soul may have done the same, but she still finds a way to remain with me.

/***/

---

[73] Betrayers are loathed throughout history, but there's a theory that they're the real heroes. If it were not for Judas, perhaps Jesus would have just been an ordinary charismatic wanderer. If it were not for Meletus' prosecution of Socrates, perhaps Socrates, too, would have just been an anonymous itinerant thinker. No one knows the real truth of course, but next time you read about a loathed betrayer, think twice before condemning them as history has. Perhaps they inadvertently abetted an incredible amount of good, and without them the world would be in a far worse place.

I reluctantly turn my attention away from Ari's windswept tunnel.

There's one more path remaining, and I've got to go.

I walk towards the purple planet, but hear a spark from my father's chamber that gives me pause.

My destiny, or at least truth, awaits me on that unknown planet. But I'd rather not come down to Hell again, and there are some things that need to be said. Things that just need to be said, even when you're in Hell.

/***/

Pan and I enter my father's chamber to find it all but abandoned, but he's still here. I know it. The grey sludge has claimed this place, but I can hear the residual crackles of some errant discharges. It's closer to static than a thunderbolt, and couldn't even hurt a fly, but it's there. Here.

He's present, or at least some part of him. My father's conceded this chamber to the sludge, but I know there's still enough of him in this place to hear me. He may not listen, but he'll hear my words.

"I don't know you," I say. "But I don't think that has anything to do with my amnesia."

I let my voice hang in the cold air for a moment. There's no volley of lightning in response, nor a yelled retort about what a disappointment I am. There's just a faint spark, and then silence.

"I don't remember you, but I have a pretty good sense of these things, and you were probably much the same before as you are now: distant, enigmatic, absent."

I shake my head.

"You'd break this behavior only when you needed to *threaten*.

You'd come to me in a cloud, yell some directive and outline the punishment should I disobey, but then you'd leave again. Once again, my father: distant, enigmatic, absent."

He doesn't respond, but I know he can hear me.

"I'm your son," I say. "I don't really understand what I did to upset you, but you dealt with this problem by sending two demons to torment me at every turn. You sent two demons after *your own child*."

I shake my head.

"You did do one thing for me though," I say. "You had my memory erased so I'd no longer have to remember you. Perhaps for that I'm grateful."

Pan the goat bleats at my side in support.

"Your demons are making their case, and honestly, I don't know how this is going to end up," I say. "But I know what I'm going to do. I'm going to do the *precise opposite* of whatever it is that you want. Not because I dislike you, because I don't care enough to dislike you. I'm going to oppose you because everything I've seen so far tells me that this will be the right decision."

I smile.

"I don't remember you as my father," I say. "But I know your name. It's *Zeus*, and I want you to know that your son will defy you, every step of the way."

/***/

I leave Zeus's chamber and the goat follows behind me, bleating to let me know that I did the right thing. *It's ok, Pan. This tale may hold its dilemmas, but that was not one of them.*

We walk towards the purple planet and it's still there, floating and impervious to the despair around us. There's a thin veneer of grey sludge leading up to the planet, but it stops right at the edge, refusing to encroach upon the space beyond.

This is not another chamber. It's a window to a place far, far away.

The goat begins heading towards the planet himself, walking over the coat of muck like an oxen trudging through a drained swamp.

The window to the outside gets brighter as I approach it, until I can just see the planet itself. I take one more step and it becomes so bright that I can only see colors, two of them, purple for the most part, touched with shining grey.

I never thought that something could shine *grey, but here it is: currents of light swirling over me, eddies of grey mixed in with iridescent violet.*

I hear a bleat and turn around to see the goat, as unimpressed as ever. I gather from his tone that this journey is mine to take alone. I reach down to pet him and he backs away, but I reach out and grab him with a quick move.

"I'm not letting you get away this easily, Pan," I say with a smile, and he reluctantly accepts my hug. "I don't remember our adventures together, the ones up on Earth, but I've ascertained we've had many. I'd bet a few have been just as bizarre as this, if not more so."

Pan's single horn glows in response.

"A wise friend once told me that the best way to deal with vanished memories is to make new ones," I say. "If I ever survive this thing, that's just what we'll do. We'll have more adventures, and we'll make a lot more memories."

The goat bleats again, and his horn glows even stronger than before. *I know that he understands. I don't yet know if I'll survive this thing, but I know that Pan understands.*

A TALE OF THE HIGHWAY

/***/

I cross the threshold between this world and the one far away, and it's clear that I'm not just entering another chamber of Hell. I'm sucked through the portal, quickly but not instantly, one atom at a time. The transition doesn't exactly hurt—lucid as this dream might be, true pain has no place here—but it does make me question the essence of my very existence. God or mortal, dream or reality, if you can take my pieces and assemble them elsewhere, is that just movement? If I'm experiencing a dissolution of my soul, what happens when I'm rebuilt? Am I still the old me? Or something identical but entirely new?

There's a truth here that I don't yet fully understand, but I see that there's a positive way of looking at this, the tenuous nature of our existence.

We're all fragile, even gods, and all ephemeral when compared to the universe. But this incredible frailty keeps us unique, and gives us tremendous value. We can be so easily destroyed, but after that we can't be brought back. We are the only instance of ourselves, ever.

I disappear for a moment—just disappear. In this dreamt illusion I cease to exist, if only for a blink of an eye. I soon feel the atoms of my body taking shape in some other place, and though I can't quite tell where it is, my location is not my primary concern.

What just happened in the moment between there and here? What happened to me, and who was I in that moment? If we can be remade, in the moments before our remaking, what are we, and where do we go?

/***/

I awake an instant later, fully formed. I still question the nature of my existence, but I've got other things to occupy my mind, because I'm floating in front of the earth. *Not at the purple planet just yet, but this is enough of a spectacle for a lifetime.* The earth is there in front of me, massive and overpowering, and the sight makes me honored to have a part in this universe, even a negligibly small one.

The Last Party on Earth made me proud to live amongst humanity, but this—this gives me hope. The universe may be almost completely cold and uncaring, but it still found a way to make something as beautiful as this.

The earth starts to shrink, and I then realize that I'm being pulled back. I'm not in control of my body's direction, but I can will my body around to face where I'm headed. I pass each planet of our solar system in turn, and my long-term memory kicks in, recalling their names, each one meant to embody my alleged cohorts of the upper world.

I pass by Mars, red and dry. *This represents my nemesis, Ares, who in turn represents the opposite of all that I hold dear.*

I look at the planet closely, and then realize that the representation isn't entirely accurate. The god of war is nothing like the planet that bears his name. This place is cold, dead, but *peaceful*, and except for the occasional mild dust storm I see passing over its surface, it seems like a place for quiet contemplation, not a planet of bloodshed.

I then pass by Jupiter and Saturn, representing my father, Zeus, and *his* father, Cronos. Gas giants both of them, they're terrifying to behold, and scream danger with every ounce of their being. *Nowhere to land, nothing to breathe, and angry storms that can grab you without a moment's warning, and never let you go.* Both planets hold an awe-inspiring beauty, and such terrifying power if you venture too near.

On the cusp of Saturn's rings I see a small, walnut-shaped rock not much bigger than a human city. I recognize it as *Pan*, one of Saturn's moons. I know it's just a name, but I can't help feeling relieved to see this planet quietly shepherding Saturn's rings.[74]

Pan always finds a way to be with me, in some way, shape or form. I'm alone, but there's still something here to remind me of his presence.

Pan the moon fades into the distance, and so do Jupiter and Saturn. The two gas giants are powerful, but like the gods for whom they are named, both planets are harmless when ignored, and I ignore them.

I then see Uranus and Neptune, named for the sky and sea, both as dangerous as the gas giants before them, but both too cold to seem particularly ferocious. They each reflect shades of iridescent blue as they sit at the freezing edge of our system, keeping their night's watch for another century-long orbit.

And then there is Pluto next to its satellite Charon, the former a small rock named after the keeper of the underworld, and the latter a moon named after its ferryman. Pluto, cold and quiet, sits almost as a forgotten afterthought, much like the despair of Hell that I escaped, much like Cruz's gas station in the middle of nowhere.

I think of that comparison, and smile.

I brought life to Cruz's gas station, and I could probably bring life to both Pluto and Charon if given enough time. Maybe even Hell as well.

I move beyond Pluto and its moon, and I understand that these planets are not the purpose of this journey. *I'm not meant to concern*

---

[74] Pan the moon is a *shepherd moon*, one that acts upon a planet's ring system. A shepherd moon orbits within a planet's rings or on its edges, and its gravity allows it to act much like a shepherd. The moon's mass preserves the sharp edges of the rings, or can even maintain a gap within the rings. Material that drifts closely to a shepherd moon is either deflected back towards the ring or ejected out into space. Pan the moon is no exception, and it's fascinating when you think about it. A relatively small, lifeless object can still have an active influence on this universe, quietly employing what little gravity it has to shape the rings around something as massive as Saturn.

myself with Pluto, just as I'm not meant to bring life to Hell.

I'm meant to go beyond anything I've known before, and as I pass the lonely, small rock and its satellite, I pick up speed and realize I'm headed far, far away.

/***/

I pick up more speed, though I don't feel myself moving in the way I'd perceive such a thing on Earth. There's no wind howling in my face, there's no sinking feeling as I begin my acceleration. I just *know* that I'm picking up speed, and everything around me starts to appear flatter than it should. I can't help but think about the radio waves that Retjar described, *that sphere of communication that has been expanding from the earth in all directions for over a century, forever expanding our existence amongst the stars at the maximum speed that the universe will allow.*

I wonder if any entity has listened to our messages already. They may have, and if so I wonder if they understood any of it. At the very least I wonder if *anything* has picked up one of our signals and thought that maybe there is something out there, even for a moment.

I think about this and then everything flattens fully, compressing itself until the entire universe is a two-dimensional disc.

I might be flattened as well, but I can't say for sure. *Everything's lost meaning at this speed, or perhaps gained a new one.* It's like flying above a city, free from all the petty concerns in the lighted rooms below, but more so because I'm headed upwards and outwards, forever outwards, to the stars and beyond.

I'm flying on a grand scale, perhaps the grandest scale imaginable. What's below me—if such an orientation still exists—is not merely a city seen from the clouds. Everything is below me, *every* city, planet, galaxy, *and every god* is in one place.

Retjar and Ulo, Ari and Cruz, Hell and the world above, Pan the goat and Pan the shepherd moon, all compressed into one flat disc.

Even the grey sludge is down there. Everything ultimately obeys the power of the universe, even that which can kill the gods.

/***/

The universe slowly reflates itself and soon envelops me until I am once again floating amidst it. *I'm no longer a spirit traveling apart from its single plane, I am within the cosmos once more.* Whether I'm a deity or still dreaming, I'm once again a *part* of this place, this existence, in all its wonder and danger.

And yet I am *very* far from home. The purple planet spreads out before me, just as enormous and imposing as Earth was, and just as beautiful. I look closer to see that it's not all purple: it seems to have *oceans* that are purple, and they compose the predominant amount of the planet's surface. What seems to be the land is faintly *golden*, and it shimmers beneath me as I float above it.

I soon begin falling towards the planet, and the pull of gravity makes my existence here even more real than it was moments before. I feel a knot in my stomach as I accelerate, and the purple world becomes larger as I approach it. I feel my body hitting the atmosphere of this planet, which first holds light strands of billowy gas, and then more, much more. I feel myself getting hotter, and then realize that I'm on fire. Green flames cross my body as I plummet through the amethyst sky, and I can barely see through their tendrils.

My stomach lurches, the green flames increase their assault and I can see the world coming closer and closer. I'm right on the edge of the purple water and the golden land, and I feel myself being pulled towards the latter. I fall down, down, down, and I brace myself for the impact. The green flames have wrapped themselves around me until I am one with them, and I see naught else but their color.

I hit the ground with a heavy collision, but my body isn't as eviscerated as it should be. This is not the world of the Crows, but it's not the dreamt Hell either, and I pass out from the impact. My mind descends into darkness, but right before I lose consciousness I see a dull color flash before my eyes.

It's grey. The grey has even come out here, all the way to this purple planet.

/***/

I awake amidst gold, shimmering grass. This isn't flaxen grain or the dried stalks of a cornfield, this is grass that shines *golden*, as if it coated in the metal itself.

Its stalks are different as well. *It's not exactly the color of grass, because it isn't grass, not even close.* I notice that it's clearly a sort of plantlike organism, but the material of its body is thicker and heavier than most plants on Earth, two cords of vegetal matter wrapped around each other with a shining yellow hue. I notice there are quite a few different varieties of this substance, each slightly different in size and feel, but each thicker than most grasses I'd seen before, and each with the same golden metallic hue.

Boom! I get hit from my left, and I'm on my back again. I hold up my hands in defense and realize that there's something on me, and it has some weight. It's not as big as Ulo, but it's thrusting into me at several points, and I'm too disoriented to push it off me. I look up to see that it's a creature with a dark, mysterious face and two oversized mandibles that are snapping onto me. When I hold up my arms in defense, it clamps down. I see that the creature is pinning me down with its multiple legs, and they pummel my body as I shift positions. I feel a warm oozing on my arm and I wonder if it's cut my skin, but I then realize the sensation is coming from between the creature's mandibles.

I pull my hand back and the creature immediately clasps its pincers around my head, and I feel the warmth over my cheeks. It reminds me of something. It reminds me of—

Cerberus' tongue in Hell, when he licked me out of the camaraderie of loneliness.

But this creature isn't Cerberus. It could have easily killed me with its mandibles and legs, but it chose not to. I'm not even hurt.

I stop fighting it and push the creature off gently. It jumps back and crouches to the ground. I notice that its face is somewhat unnerving, with features somewhere between an insect's and a mammal's, combined with something else entirely. It has two oversized compounded eyes, and its frame is covered with spikes that each sprout mottled blue fur, as if it had feathers. It has six legs, and two giant mandibles on each side of its mouth.

I notice that the mandibles seem to be dulled, and the creature has some sort of holster on its neck.

"Easy," I hear a voice say in the distance. "Easy."

I look up to see a stocky, shadowed figure of what seems to be a man walking towards me. He's backlit by the sun, but walks with a relaxed gait and doesn't appear to be a threat.

"I apologize for this—my extension gets a little too friendly at times, I'm afraid," says the man, stepping away so that I can see him fully.

"I'm happy to meet you," he continues. "My name is Venelk, and I'm a messenger. I'm also a student with a singular specialty, but by and large, I'm a messenger."

/***/

The humanoid creature isn't as tall as I am, but he's solidly built. He doesn't have the mottled blue fur of the six-legged creature that he calls his *extension*, but he holds some of its features. Venelk has rough, bare skin with a deep magenta hue, but his compounded eyes are just as oversized as his partner's, and he has two mandibles that come from each side of his face, smaller than his creature's, and adorned with jewelry. Venelk's appearance might be frightening if he were aggressive, but he's composed, and he does have a few features that are human-like, though just barely. He has two arms with five fingers on each hand, and a digit besides, making a grand total of twelve. The extra digit comes out of his palm from the opposite side of his fingers, but I can tell that it functions much the same as our thumb. Unlike his creature, Venelk is wearing clearly fabricated clothes, and though their style is foreign to my eyes, he looks quite dignified in them.

"I'm sorry, I don't know your name," he says. "Though I should."

"Dion," I say, wondering why he should know such a thing.

"Again, this is my extension, a sprightly girl at heart just like me, and her name is Venek'll," he—*she*—says, pointing to the blue creature below her, and pronouncing the name *VEH-nuh-KELL* to her own *veh-NELK*.

"Your extension?" I ask, surprised that both creatures would be female.

"Yes, that's what we call these loyal creatures," she says. "Extensions of ourselves, for companionship, service and the like. What do you call them?"

"Pets," I say, though my only reference now is Pan in his full goat form, and that creature is anything but a pet.

"Yes, that sounds familiar," says Venelk. "Again I apologize, I should know both this and your name, but a part of you is *missing*, I believe."

I give Venelk a smile to let her know she's more correct about this than she can possibly understand.

/***/

We walk through the field, and I see that this place isn't well tread. There are no clear footpaths, and I'm forced to follow Venek'll as she bounds forward, plowing through the twined stalks with her six legs moving in a blur. I notice we're walking parallel to a distant forest, and there are tall, unmoving structures that might be their version of trees. The translucent bodies of these giant plants are thicker and smoother than our trees, and their trunks grow much taller as well. They have large fronds that spread out to catch the sun above, and these leaves shimmer a much softer gold than that of the field in which I awoke. *It's as if the trees were made out of honey, and then dipped in amber.*

"The colors of this planet are unique," I say. "I've never seen anything like them before."

"Some of them might be similar to your planet, Dion," says Venelk.

I only have the night in my memory, but I know that this is different. If I return to Earth and survive until the morning, I won't see anything like what's around me.

"I don't think so," I say. "I haven't seen anything like this."

"They might be," says Venelk. "We can send this message to you, but it's hard to see what you see."

I don't understand this, and Venelk picks up on the fact that I don't.

"We know what wavelength of light these leaves reflect," says Venelk. "But after your eyes absorb that reflected radiation, we can't tell how your mind interprets that signal, so we decided to show you how we see our world."

I smile at this harmless but impossible quandary.[75]

---

[75] This is an age-old dilemma, even within the same species. If your brain interpreted my color *red* as *green* and vice versa, neither of us would ever know the difference. Note that I believe Venelk and her kind have at least resolved the dilemma within their species – i.e., through scientific testing

"Would you like me to change this environment to colors similar to your world?" asks Venelk. "I'll just have to keep rotating through colors with each object until you tell me—"

"No, please don't," I say. "Your planet is beautiful, just the way it is."

"Thank you," says Venelk, looking up at the sky.

I follow her line of sight and see a moon. It's not the same as ours but it's similar, and it gazes back down on us in much the same way.

"Our planet was quite beautiful," says Venelk. "And that's part of the reason why we've sent this message."

I find it strange that Venelk used the term *was*, and again, Venelk picks up on this. She clicks her mandibles, and I take the gesture to mean that she's telling the truth. This planet lives only as a memory in my mind. As beautiful as it is, this place is no more.

/***/

We walk on through the thick, golden grass, with Venek'll paving a path for us with her clumsy six-legged strides.

"Other than the possible differences in eyesight, our species our quite similar," says Venelk. "We're both based on the same six-atom element, and I see that we both have similar appendages, and both breathe similar air. Those *kells* you see before you breathe in what we exhale and give it back to us.[76] It would be difficult for you to survive in our world unassisted, and us in yours, but we could both do it. If you were truly here right now, you might be short of breath, but you wouldn't die."

---

they've analyzed how their minds see certain colors, so she could say *this is how we see our world*. Still, I couldn't expect her to resolve this dilemma with a distant, heretofore unknown creature such as myself.

[76] Just to clarify, *kells* are their version of *trees*. Venelk would most likely call them trees were my mind not so addled at this point.

"It's incredible," I say. "That two different planets find a way to produce even *somewhat* similar species."

"It is," says Venelk. "Though perhaps not as much of a coincidence as it sounds. I deliberately sent this message to be interpreted by a similar species, so in a sense you were *selected*."

I understand her logic, though I don't quite understand what she means by having *sent a message*.

"Our convergent evolution is remarkable," says Venelk. "But the universe is a big place, and evolution has to converge somewhere."[77]

/***/

Venelk's extension finds a large white disc in a clearing, and both pet and master step on it. I follow suit, and after Venelk waves her six-digited hand a circular railing rises from the edges, enveloping us. The disc rises until it floats just above the grassline, and then moves forward.

"Where did you come from, Dion?" she asks.

"From Hell."

Venelk has heard of this place but I feel the need to explain my situation further.

"I come from Earth," I say. "But I occasionally dream that I've gone to Hell, and one of the rooms contained your planet. I entered it, and here I am."

---

[77] I've always wondered if there were some general physical prerequisites for intelligent life, something that would make most sentient beings resemble one another—two arms free from the need for locomotion, opposable thumbs, a large brain case and the like. The similarities between Venelk and me can't be ignored, but we're just two specimens. The question of physical prerequisites for intelligent life continues.

Venelk clicks her mandibles as if this all makes perfect sense.

"We sent this message far and wide, and it's not uncommon that someone receives this in a dream," she says. "So I hope you understand that this is indeed somewhat real."

I tell her that I don't understand what she means by this.

"Though this message is coming to you as a dream within a dream, the *message* we've sent is real," she says. "What I'm about to show you really happened, and there is truth here."

"You tell me that it *happened*," I say. "I take it to mean that this planet is no more."

"Sadly, no, in your time everything you see around you is what you would call a ghost, including myself."

I think of the philosophers, their bodies on Earth long vanished, but their message still very much alive.

"I met three men who called themselves *shades*," I say. "Spirits reflecting what they once were in life. They could be called ghosts, and though they no longer live in our earthly plane, they have a profound influence on our world today."

Venelk clicks her mandibles.

"If only we had a fraction of your shade's influence," she says. "Other than this message we've sent in the form of the illusion around you, we don't influence anything. We're gone."

I want to ask her *why* they're gone, but I think I already know the answer. *And I don't want to know for sure, at least not yet.*

Venelk looks below the disc as we hover over the golden stalks. I see creatures scurrying through the field, some insectoid like Venek'll, and some like nothing I've ever seen before. There are heavy creatures with fins on their backs that cut through the flaxen meadow, and tiny, faerie-looking creatures that give them chase. I see creatures with six legs, four legs, and a third with three—more precisely, this creature has two powerful legs and a strong *tail* to help it jump, and it makes extraordinary leaps before disappearing into the foliage below.

I then see a set of miniature bipeds with compounded eyes on each side of their heads, and they appear to be riding the back of an oversized creature with six legs, and a shell that changes color to match its environment.

And this is just one part of this world. Imagine what the rest holds.

"We may have perished eons ago, or we may have been gone for but a few moments," says Venelk. "Before we disappeared, we sent messages like this across the universe in all kinds of ways, and one of them reached you in a dream. But we have no way of telling just how long it has been between our respective existences."

"Perhaps it doesn't matter," I say, still certain that all this happened a long, long time ago.

"Perhaps it doesn't," says Venelk. "We just wanted to send a cautionary tale, and if nothing else, to tell our story."

"It's an honor, believe me," I say. "But you might want to back up your message with a few others. My memory was erased a day ago, and someone might do it again."

"That's it," says Venelk, clicking her mandibles knowingly. "I sensed a part of you was missing, and it's consistent with memory loss. This message is meant to incorporate itself with what you already know: for example, we're currently sharing the same language."

That makes sense. There's no way we'd share an even remotely *similar language, convergent evolution or not.*

"But I don't know all your words," says Venelk. "Part of you is still a bit hazy, so you might need to help me out here and there."

She clicks her mandibles together, and I begin to understand that this is her way of smiling.

/***/

The disc makes its way to a wide vessel that's parked at the foot of a railing, and the craft opens up in the back to allow us in. We fit perfectly inside, the doors close quietly behind us, and we step off after the railing on the disc lowers to the ground. Venelk tells the ship to *take us to the council*, and the vessel moves in response. I look out the window and see it traveling over the terrain for a short time, and it soon slides onto a railing in front of it. Venelk secures herself into a wall-mounted seat and indicates that I do the same. The seats are quite comfortable and my restraints adapt to my form easily, even though I'm built differently than Venelk. I look down and see that Venek'll has put herself in a special container as well, a long translucent tube with padding on the sides.

The vessel thrusts itself along the railing and then slings itself outwards, and I can soon feel we're flying. The flight is so smooth that I can barely tell that we're in the air, but looking out the window, I see that we are. Venelk takes off her restraints and gestures that I do the same, so I take off my belts and stand up to take a closer look out the window. I see the honey-dipped forest below, and I see movement amongst the leaves. I then see pale, squarish heads cut through the foliage, and they're consuming some of the fronds.

These creatures seem to be standing on the ground, yet their heads are at the treetops, trees bigger than anything on Earth. The fauna here is more incredible than anything I could possibly imagine.

"Those creatures are called the *qenelmar*, and they don't have a cap on their own growth," explains Venelk. "Whatever height the kelltops reach, a *qenel* grows to match them. The qenelmar are enormous, but harmless and quite slow. We'd driven them to extinction before we attained our full enlightenment, but we were able to reconstruct them from genetic material, and here they walk again. Still, this gave us a problem. The qenelmar aren't aggressive by any means, but their towering size demands an inordinate amount of land."

I look down at the endless expanse of honeyed forest, and these enormous creatures still look tiny by comparison.

"So we tracked their patterns, and found that they tend to graze in a shape that could be described as a giant oval," says Venelk.

I look down at the qenelmar browsing through these trees—these gigantic *kells*—and try to fathom just how vast their migratory oval must be.

"We found that though a qenel's appetite is enormous, so is its production of waste. Their droppings are the size of the vessel we're in now, but this isn't a bad thing by any means. They end up launching a giant, ringed ecosystem, countless creatures depending on the qenelmar taking matter from the kelltops and depositing it far below."

I look down and see a flock of winged creatures pecking at half-eaten fronds from the kelltops which the qenelmar have partially eaten. The winged creatures then launch themselves upwards, and they have inordinately long bodies floating like strings behind them. One creature flies up to inspect us, and I see that it's got two fierce-looking compounded eyes, both the green color of the flames that enveloped me on my way down here.

"What do those flying creatures look like to you, Dion?" asks Venelk. "I can't find your words right now."

I think for a moment, and let my long-term memory come up with an analogy.

"I'd say those creatures look like something that we call a *squirrel*," I say. "A squirrel combined with a long, spindly dragon."

/***/

We're heading towards the purple ocean, and there's an incredibly thin bridge amidst the waves, which stretches past the horizon. The forest ends, the beach begins, and soon we're slowing down until we're almost floating. We approach the thin structure and I see that it's not a bridge at all, but rather a series of railings, and that the railings split up on the horizon and stretch out in all directions. The ship lands on the balustrade seamlessly and I hear it clasp on. After a moment we speed up again, soundlessly traveling over the supporting structure beneath.

"It takes a lot of energy to fight gravity, so we found that rails are more efficient for travel," says Venelk. "We couldn't put them over the land we were in, because the qenelmar don't like to go under the rail lines, or over them either. So we allow ourselves to fly across their range."

Venelk looks at the water through the rails below as we pass over the ocean at an untold speed.

"We designed these rails well, and they don't disturb the ocean environment," says Venelk. "We save energy by riding them for the bulk of our journeys."

I look down at the violet water below, surely roiling beneath us, but it's so far away that it appears like glass. I look back to see that the land behind us has now disappeared, and it's just us and this rail that stretches towards the horizon. I look ahead and see another vessel coming towards us, which goes by on a parallel track, moving soundlessly as it passes. I catch a glimpse of the creatures inside, and they're roughly like Venelk, but of different sizes and colors. Venek'll has left her special container and clicks her mandibles as she looks out the window. I can't tell because we're moving too quickly, but if the other vessel had any pets aboard, I'd imagine these extensions would be clicking just like Venek'll.

We drive in silence for a few moments, and then I see large, flat clouds at the level of our railing. When I look again I realize they're not clouds, but living things. These floating creatures are incredibly thin-bodied and all but disappear when you see them from their side, but from an angle it's easy to spot them, and they look just like clouds. *Six thin limbs with skin flaps between them, floating in the upper currents, and two large compounded eyes glinting off the sun as they peer down at the ocean below.*

I follow their line of sight downwards and see a pod of large, swimming creatures cutting underneath the surface of the purple water. These swimming creatures are enormous, visible even from our great height, dwarfing even the qenelmar by comparison.

These leviathans are beyond colossal, bigger than anything alive could possibly be.

The oceanic creatures are built like translucent tubes, and they shimmer with colors I've not yet seen. They have spindly tentacles that trail an impossibly long distance behind them, and it looks like they're taking the purple water from in front and pushing it back, propelling themselves forward with a current that moves directly through them.

These creatures that look like flat clouds are staring just as intently as I am at these behemoths below. Maybe the cloud creatures fear predation. Perhaps they're just as amazed as I am that creatures can grow to the size of islands, and are still able to move.

"Those are the *demmelmar*," says Venelk, pointing to the creatures in the ocean. "Juveniles."

"Juveniles?"

"Yes. When they start to grow, they descend to the deep," says Venelk. "We've set up observation stations on the ocean floor, and you can't believe the colors they make when they glow in the darkness."

"I can't even begin to fathom such a thing."

"No one can until they've seen it, because it's beautiful beyond words," says Venelk. "Though there's plenty more creatures down there that are even more extraordinary than even the demmelmar. I wish I could show you."

I wish the same, but I know I'm here for more than just admiring the local fauna. I take one more look at the massive creatures below, and at the cloud-like creatures that gaze upon them. I then look forward as our vessel traverses its rail, and wonder what our destination will be. I also wonder what message Venelk has in store for me when we get there.

/***/

We pass by what I think to be a mountain in the far distance, though I quickly see that it's too tall and straight to be a mountain.

"That's an elevator," explains Venelk. "It was meant for the next phase of our existence."

"It goes to the sky," I say, watching the structure as it stretches upwards into the haze above.

"It goes further than that," says Venelk. "The elevator goes to the furthest reaches of our atmosphere. It was meant to help us get to space whenever we want. It takes a lot of fuel to propel a ship out of a planet's gravity,[78] but with this, it's just a long elevator ride."

"What holds it up?"

"An asteroid, and a few generations of consistent effort," says Venelk. "In any case, we took the asteroid from space, moved it here

---

[78] Gravity seems to be a prerequisite for life. It keeps a protective atmosphere around a planet, and does countless other things to allow the living to remain alive, but it's also extremely difficult to escape its grasp. Perhaps when a planet finds a way to nurture life into existence, she hugs her children closely so they can't leave. Precious analogies aside, this space elevator bypasses what's often the hardest step of space travel: the first one.

and outfitted it with our own equipment. It's in geosynchronous orbit with our planet, so the elevator stays still."[79]

"It takes farsighted thinkers to work on things that won't be completed in their lifetime," I say.

I then realize I'm not entirely sure what the word *lifetime* means to this species. I don't know how long they live, but it goes beyond that. From what I've seen, I wouldn't put it past them to have found a cure for mortality.

"When you think beyond your own generation, there's no limit to what you can accomplish," says Venelk. "And though we've managed pretty well down here, we've seen but a fraction of what lies beyond the edges of our own planet. We hoped to change this with our elevator."

I look more closely at the structure: an enormous design undoubtedly filled with countless ingenuities, but based on an idea that's so straightforward it can be described in a few sentences.

"You're not breaking the laws of physics," I say. "But you are finding ways *around* them."

Venelk clicks her mandibles in agreement.

"That's exactly right," she says, pointing towards the top of the elevator. "There are some laws that we'll never be able to break up there either. But maybe we'll get around them as well."

I wouldn't be a scholar even if I'd had my memory, but I believe Venelk when she says this. *The universe is a big place, but they would*

---

[79] We primarily think of asteroids as destructive entities, but consider the importance of asteroids in Earth's history: an asteroid may have ended the reign of the dinosaurs, but that destruction made way for the mammals. Imagine if humanity ever constructed a space elevator like the one I see here— one asteroid would have opened the door for humanity on this earth, and another would allow us to leave it.

have find a way to explore it. They might never have been able to break the speed of light, but they would have found a way around it.

"But you never got to work around those laws," I say. "You never got to explore the universe."

"We did not," says Venelk.

"What happened?"

Venelk thinks about this for a moment, then clicks her mandibles.

"I'm trying to find the right word from your consciousness, but it's hard to find," she says. "What happens when a living thing no longer exists?"

"That creature goes extinct," I say. "The word is *extinct*."

"That's not quite it," says Venelk. "That's part of it, but not the exact word."

"I'm sorry," I say. "My memory was erased."

"That's the word," says Venelk. "We were *erased*."

/***/

Even though she probably knows this, I tell Venelk my story up until now. I tell her of the Crows, and how Retjar claims that our Earth will not only go extinct, but be erased. I then tell her of Prometheus, and how the Titan might either bring humanity to the next level of existence, or abet this erasure.

While I talk, I look at the space elevator, and wonder if Prometheus could do both.

Venelk listens to my words patiently, with her five fingers and thumb on her jaw. She then clicks her mandibles, and looks up at her planet's moon.

"We have our own version of your Prometheus on this planet," she says. "We call her *Dabron*, and she brought us out of the dirt so many generations ago. She returned, and helped bring about all you will see in this journey."

I think about the space elevator, and the vessel I'm in, moving so effortlessly along the rails beneath. I also think about the natural world I'd just left, and how these creatures and their advanced technology manage to coexist so well within it.

"But Dabron eventually brought about your demise," I say. "Your *erasure*."

Venelk takes her attention away from the moon above and stares at me, her mandibles quivering. If I had to guess, I'd say that she was upset.

"It's not that straightforward, Dion," says Venelk. "If a fire levels an entire city a thousand years after Prometheus first brought the flame to humanity, is your Titan to blame?"

Her words sound like an assertion that I would make, and I realize that I need to put forth the viewpoint of the Crows if I hope to get a counterpoint to Retjar's words.

I then steel myself to put forth an argument that he might say, and hope that Venelk understands that I'm playing devil's advocate. I figure she must, because she's in my head.

"What happened to you, and might potentially happen to us, is different than a fire in a single city," I say. "A city can be rebuilt, even if flame levels it to the ground. We're talking about *erasure*, on your planet and mine, a fire that consumes everything in the world, and allows nothing to regrow, ever."

Venelk's pincers slow their quivering, and finally relax completely.

"I understand that there's a difference, believe me," she says. "And

I have no counterargument to your words. But I will say that I'm still grateful to Dabron because though our planet is no more, I shudder to think of what our existence would be like if she'd never come."

At that moment, I realize that not all truths arise from argument and the clash of ideas. Some truths are born of *understanding*.

"Could you describe what your world would have been like if Dabron never returned?" I ask.

Venelk reaches down and pets Venek'll.

"It might still be here," says Venelk. "The planet at least. For our species, we'd probably have vanished. We'd have had progress, but there would have been an end. Over the generations we would have fallen into an equilibrium of growth and contraction, peace and war. We'd have existed, but not much more than that. And eventually, something would have brought about our extinction."

"Extinction," I say. "But not erasure."

"Yes," says Venelk. "Our species might have perished, but we wouldn't have taken the rest of our planet with us. Those demmelmar would have hidden amongst our ocean's depths, and reemerged after we'd disappeared. The sky and landbound creatures would also have slowly reclaimed the rest of the world, flying and treading through our emptied, decaying cities."

I consider this hypothetical fate, and realize that though it's better than erasure, it still doesn't seem like a satisfactory alternative to the grey substance.

"So you believe Dabron's progress was worth the risk?" I ask. "Even now, after you've lost everything, was she worth the risk?"

"Yes," says Venelk. "Again, I have no argument to support this sentiment. But yes, Dabron's progress was worth the risk, and I tell you this after we've lost everything."

I look forward and see that we're approaching land.

"But all this conjecture doesn't do us any favors," says Venelk, eyeing what looks to be a city on the horizon. "Now it's time for us to show you our fate."

/***/

We approach the city, nestled densely within the crook of a seaside mountain range. The buildings are magnificently built, and each structure is constructed beautifully in its own unique way. Some have soft rounded edges, some are cut like diamonds, and some shimmer just as beautifully as the island-sized creatures I saw in the ocean. Some are built *below* ground, and have clear ceilings and floors so one can see all its inhabitants as they traverse beneath.

Our ship slows and docks onto a platform, and after it comes to a stop Venelk opens the rear doors. She beckons me to get back on the circular disc and I do, and after Venek'll joins us the railing comes up again. The disc floats into the air and moves forward past the platform, and the view is breathtaking. This city glows vibrant and clean, filled with translucent structures so that I can see everyone moving at once.

"We found that maximum productivity occurs with a certain threshold of population density," says Venelk. "The *right* kind of population density. Not the kind that comes with crushing poverty, pollution, and unending competition, mind you, but the *productive* kind of collective proximity, the one that allows for the rapid exchange of ideas and enables denizens to gather easily and bring those ideas into reality. We've also found that once we abet certain conditions, the population density optimizes itself and then stays there.[80]

---

[80] There are two kinds of population control: the forceful kind and the kind that relies on choice. The former can come in a variety of unpleasant ways, but the latter only comes about with the right conditions. Give your citizens an environment of security, education and quality of life, and they'll often choose to limit their offspring by themselves.

I try to follow one of the creatures as it moves through this city, but it's difficult because everyone is moving too quickly. Each individual is moving on their own unique path, some on their own power and others in various devices that improve their short-term movement. Some creatures move with hovering discs like our own, some are on wheeled mechanisms that attach to small railings and a few have sturdy leg extensions that help them take longer strides.

The road below interacts with each denizen as they move forward, and seems to be absorbing their movement's energy. The crystalline path subtly changes hues, and the colors of the entire city form a beautiful rhythm, as if it's breathing in and out with every step. I can even see the creatures walking underground in the transparent structures, and though it should make me feel disoriented, it doesn't. *Everything's moving so fast, but everything is still so visible. It makes me feel connected.*

"Each one of these denizens is given a place to live here if they so choose it," says Venelk. "But they're also allowed a place within the natural world you've just seen. A few prefer to stay in one or the other, but most like living in both."

"I didn't see any homes out where we were," I say. "Were they hidden?"

"Yes, though more accurately they were built to hide within the natural environment. Our bucolic residences have little to no impact on the migrating creatures around, and they're of course completely safe from any errant contact," says Venelk. "And these secondary dwellings can be *anywhere*. A few of our more intrepid denizens choose to live in the bottom of the ocean where a *demm* might grow into her massive, glowing form."

I take in the city in front of me, and though the creatures are moving rather quickly, they don't seem to be in a hurry.

"A home in the city when you need to converse, and a home in the country when you need to think," I say.

"Or *homes*, plural," says Venelk. "A few opt to hold places in various locales, though no one tries to claim more territory than they need, like we've done so much throughout our history."

One group claiming more territory than they need. Is history anything but this?

"Ideal conditions lead to ideal conditions," says Venelk. "Show someone a life of peace and productivity, and they won't want anything else."

I notice a streak of crystalline yellow beneath us, and I see another creature pass us by, treading with quick steps. *This one isn't just moving quickly, but hurriedly.* Three denizens watching a projected screen notice the yellow beneath — they step aside to let this creature pass, and she[81] soon walks by them and disappears around a corner.

Venelk is following the hurried creature, but before I turn around the corner I look at the projected screen. The three creatures are watching what seems to be a news report showing footage of a grey patch floating in the purple ocean. The watching denizens seem to be amused by the sight of this more than anything else. One of the creatures points at the screen and starts clicking her mandibles, and the others follow suit.

"Sometimes ideal conditions aren't enough," says Venelk as she beckons me forward. "Even the most perfect worlds can be erased."

/***/

We follow the rushing creature around the corner, and up close I

---

[81] I believe there are males on this planet, but since I haven't seen a clear dimorphic pattern between the sexes, at this point I have no recourse but to assume they're all female.

see that she's bigger than Venelk and fiercer-looking, and has a rounded belly. She doesn't seem to notice us even after we draw near, and together we enter a large building. The building's interior feels rather comfortable, but there's quite a bit of security here. Soft-cornered robots with black and gold hues fly around all the creatures entering the building, and scan their six-digit hands with a laser before allowing entry. Venelk leads me around the line walking in, and none of the robots seems to notice our presence.

We walk in front of what appears to be an elevator, and we're now with the fierce-looking creature and several other important-looking individuals. Our surroundings are no longer crystalline, ephemeral and translucent, but rather opaque, and set in dull, secretive colors. The round-bellied denizen scans the six digits on her hand, one by one, and then pushes her fierce-looking face forward, and a set of lasers scans her mandibles. The doors open up, and we all enter the elevator. She then presses a button and enters a code onto a circular keypad on the wall, and we begin to descend downwards, downwards and downwards some more. The elevator comes to a stop, and I feel a jolt as we begin moving forward at significant speed. I sense us stopping and turning left, then right again.

The door opens and there's five more black-and-gold robots that scan our fellow riders. One even pricks a sample from each creature's arm, which they allow willingly. Thankfully, they ignore Venelk, Venek'll and me. Two more creatures enter the room wearing full bodysuits, and they bid the group to remove their garments. The fellow travelers all do so quickly, though Venelk holds me back and says that this is not necessary for us.

Once disrobed, the two bodysuited men spray the creatures with some sort of substance, seemingly meant to disinfect. The creatures click their mandibles in response to the mist, and a few expectorate some liquid onto the ground. After the spraying is over, they are led into another room where there is a pool that shimmers blue. It's not the blue that I remember from Earth, but a disquietingly *artificial* blue, and the creatures click their mandibles again in shock at its biting scent. They go in willingly though, expectorating some more and laughing convivially with every cough.

They creatures swim through the substance.[82] Venelk and I follow along with Venek'll, getting in with our clothes still on. The path is long but these creatures appear to be proficient swimmers, and their large hands paddle the water backwards with quite a bit of momentum.

We get through to the other side, and meet another set of creatures in full bodysuits. They spray those coming out again, and then point to distant showers. The showers are putting out water, clear and clean in this form, and not purple like the ocean. Venelk, Venek'll and I are dry, and after our compatriots rinse themselves off with the water, they quickly become the same by walking through an adjacent tunnel that blows air over them. After they exit the tunnel they find a table covered with pure white garments, and begin to clothe themselves.

I hear sounds of a meeting in progress in front of us, and the tone is that of worry and anxiety. I look at the big, fierce-looking creature as she puts on her garment, and take another look at her prodigious belly. I see the faint outline of a mandibled face pressing against her skin.

She's a female all right, though I wonder if this planet gave her enough time to become a mother.

Whatever the case, she's not worried about the fate of her unborn child, only the meeting in front of us. She and all her compatriots are now quiet, and they are no longer laughing.

/***/

All told there are more than thirty of these creatures in the room, two-thirds of which are present. The remainder exist as holograms

---

[82] This is yet another step in the disinfecting process, in which participants have to submerse themselves in some substance that is meant to rid their skin of pathogens.

projected within particulated air above small floating plates, discs similar in shape to the ones that had transported us to Venelk's vessel. The denizens are sitting in a rather egalitarian arrangement, though there's one creature in the middle who welcomes the newcomers. She introduces herself as *Counselor Meem*.

Meem beckons the group to sit and they do, taking position around her. The big fierce-looking one walks to the back of the room and chooses to sit next to a hologram of a smaller creature. The two embrace as much as they can, but neither show much joy in this reunion.

Meem strikes a two-pronged tine against a square on a podium in front of her, and it lets off a resonating pitch that cuts through the din of the assembly. She then presses a button on the lectern and a three-dimensional projection of the purple planet shows up in the center of the group. The hologram holds remarkable clarity and is in full color, save for the small patches of grey that now spot its surface.

Perhaps the perception of color isn't entirely arbitrary. Venelk's colors or mine, grey is still grey.

"As many of you already know, seven cycles ago these spots were found in two locations," says Counselor Meem. "As of today, the locations have increased by a factor of ten.[83]

The planet spins and we see that it's riddled with these patches, all of them still small, but strongly entrenched.

"Is there any more understanding about what this substance is?" asks the hologram next to the fierce-looking creature.

"No," replies Meem. "But we are getting a sense of where it may

---

[83] Note that I can't say precisely what Meem meant by this. The creatures have twelve total digits, so I assume they count in base 12. But I figure it doesn't really matter if there are now twenty or twenty-four patches at this point on the purple planet. The grey is growing just the same.

have come from."

Meem presses another button and the face of another creature appears, along with indecipherable markings next to her, markings that I assume to be this society's script.[84]

"It appears to come from this individual, who I assume you all know," says Meem. "Our esteemed, and much-beloved *Gereg*."

A din of surprise goes through the crowd, and a creature in front stands up.

"I have known Gereg for half of my life," says the creature, somewhat irate. "In addition to what she's already done for us, I can assure you her intentions are completely benevolent, even *sacrosanct*, and—"

"Her intentions are *beyond* benevolent," interrupts Meem. "For those of you who don't know, Gereg's previously invented processes have cured countless diseases, and she's dedicated *every last bit* of her being to improving our society, and our conditions, on all levels."

Meem pushes another button and we see a building in the forest by Gereg's likeness.

"She'd started working independently after her last success, and we of course allowed this," says Meem. "All we know is that she was attempting to explore the origins of life, possibly by recreating them."

Meem presses the button again and Gereg's face makes way for a grainy projection of what appears to be small, moving cells. It's difficult to see them because the projection is filled with distortion and runs

---

[84] It's a bit incongruous that Venelk didn't translate this script into my thoughts. It might be because I received it in a dream—and you can't normally read in a dream, so it might even be gibberish. But I've sensed so many other things that one can't sense in a dream, so that explanation isn't certain. I don't overworry about this little discrepancy of lettering though, because the message from Meem that follows holds little ambiguity.

only on a short, repeating loop.

"We don't know what she'd found, but Gereg had sent us a message that there'd been a disaster before we lost contact with her laboratory," says Meem, pointing to a grey spot on the map, one larger than most. "That's her laboratory now: gone, completely gone, just like Gereg."

"So it's some sort of biological agent," says a creature in front. "And it's already spread to various locales around the world."

"We believe you're correct in both regards, unfortunately," says Meem. "All indications suggest that this wasn't made purposefully, let alone with malevolent intent. But this grey substance is here, and it's growing. The cells you see before you are what we believe to make up the grey substance. We don't know much more."

Meem presses another button and the distorted loop fades into more of their script. I still can't understand it, but I sense that it had been written erratically.

"She did send what appears to be a final message though," says Meem.

The other creatures read the script, and the room becomes somber.

"She says that we shouldn't try to fight the grey substance," reads Meem. "She says that doing so will just make things worse."

The room erupts: concern, skepticism and anger all at once. Meem yells at the room to be quiet before striking her tine again, and after it quiets she points to the fierce-looking creature to give her the floor.

"We shouldn't *fight it*?" asks the fierce-looking creature in disbelief. "With all due respect to Gereg and her strange substance, we've got a whole arsenal of antibiotics, much of them from Gereg's own discoveries!"

"I second that," says the holographic creature beside her. "We've even saved some mixtures for situations such as these, including the *verdant bullet*. It's only to be used in emergencies, but this is an emergency and—"

"We've used all the antibiotics, including the verdant bullet," says Meem. "To absolutely no effect."

Meem points to a grey spot in the ocean.

"The team that went to investigate sprayed everything we have on Gereg's compound," says Meem. "Nothing happened. We requested their immediate return, asking them to bypass the railing and just fly here. Their vessel crashed into the sea, and from there the grey started to grow in this spot you see here."

Meem walks over to the projection and swipes her hand to move the planet. It rotates at her touch, and she taps the grey areas to light them up.

"Some of these spots came from follow-up missions," says Meem. "Some have come from an unknown path."

"An unknown path?" asks a hologram sitting in front, incredulous. "We have satellites that can track even the smallest—"

"Our primary control center for the surveillance satellites has been evacuated," says Meem. "The grey substance started to grow near it, and those inside were asked to flee."

The room has no response to this, and lies silent.

"So this grey substance, these *rudimentary cells*, are growing," says one creature in the back. "And there is nothing we can do about it."

"We're doing everything in our power to act on this crisis," says Meem. "But nothing has worked so far, and in fact every action has made things worse, just as Gereg warned."

"So there's nothing we can do about it," repeats the creature in the back.

"As it stands, that appears to be the case," says Meem.

There is silence, and then the fierce-looking creature speaks up.

"Tell us what you're doing, then, at least," she says. "Tell us everything."

Meem clicks her mandibles at the question.

"We're studying it from a distance," says Meem. "We can't get too close because every time we do, those we send die, and then spread this grey substance further."

Meem swipes the planet away with her hand and it's replaced by an image of two creatures in protective suits, and what appears to be a small town surrounded by a dome.

"We're going to alert the public of this, and instruct them to stay home, and in various underground locations," says Meem. "We also have several settlements we'd placed in extreme weather environments, and they have various barriers to protect them from the elements. We're hoping to settle as many as we can in this manner, though we know there won't be enough space for everyone."

"I've been to most all of these settlements, because I helped design them," says the holographic creature. "Almost nothing can live outside the domes, so they should be safe! And I'm speaking to you now from *my* home in the ocean, at the bottom of the *Burkol Trench* where there's no light, the temperature is almost freezing, and the pressure can quash even the hardiest life out of existence—"

"You're safe for the moment, but that may change," says Meem. "There is currently a patch of grey on the surface above you, and if it doesn't grow downwards to reach your home, it will grow until you'll be unable to find a place to surface. As far as the domes in our extreme areas, these might not be successful either. This substance is quite hardy, and can live anywhere. The *rudimentary* biology of these cells allows it to be quite adaptable when it comes to survival, and again, if they can't find a way to penetrate the domes they'll keep the inhabitants inside until our planet is consumed."

The holographic creature has no response to this. She looks up at her ceiling, and I think she's wondering if she'll ever escape her home at the bottom of the Burkol Trench.

"There's got to be some safe zone," says the fierce-looking creature, clearly worried about her friend underneath the purple ocean. "There has to be some place we can go—"

"Gereg did suggest one place," says Meem. "It may be protected from the grey substance, but it's not a fully realized solution."

Meem swipes away the images, and there's more indecipherable writing next to an image of a long rod, and I soon recognize it as the space elevator.

"The moon?" asks a creature in the front. "Our station there isn't yet independent. There's nothing up there but dust, and there's no way a society of *untrained* inhabitants would be able to live—"

"It's not a fully realized solution," Meem repeats. "We've been developing hydroponic agriculture up there, and its inhabitants would have to develop it further to ensure survival. They'd have to overcome a myriad of other problems as well, and there would be no safety net. There may soon be no one to help them back on Earth, and no place for them to ever return home."

Meem shakes her head.

"But the denizens up there are quite innovative," she says. "And as long as we don't allow the grey substance to reach the moon, they should be safe. No help and nowhere to go, but safe."

The audience is not yet sold on the idea, and Meem seems like she doesn't expect them to be.

"We'll do everything we can," she says. "We'll observe and fight this substance from a distance, and we'll send denizens to the protected domes. We'll send as many as we can up to the moon. None of these are guaranteed to work, but they're options. And in the face of this threat we need every option available, and we need to act on them now."

/***/

Venelk snaps her fingers and we're in a different room, this one much quieter than the last. I look around and see Venek'll sleeping on the floor next to her, and above Venek'll is a giant window. I look outside the window and see grey, but not the grey of the substance consuming the purple planet. *It's grey dust, lifeless and inert, too indifferent to its surroundings to either support life or take it away.*

"We're on your moon," I say. "In a station."

Venelk clicks her mandibles, then kneels in front of her sleeping extension. She pets Venek'll's mottled blue fur and looks out the window alongside me. She's looking up, and I follow her compounded eyes to see her former home, or rather what's left of it. The grey has all but covered the once-purple planet. I can't see it completely due to the shadows of space, but I can tell the planet has been consumed thoroughly, even the poles.

"What *is* that substance?" I ask. "The grey."

Venelk hangs her head, and her mandibles quiver faintly.

"We don't know," she says. "It arrived quite quickly, and we all had to hurry. I was able to come here, and even got to sneak Venek'll and another passenger on the last trip before the elevator stopped working."

Venelk points out the window along the surface to another set of mandibled creatures in an adjacent window bay, talking amongst themselves quietly and occasionally pointing towards the now-monotone planet.

"We studied the substance from here," she says. "But there's only so much we could understand. From this vantage point, the grey substance was nothing more than a color."

That makes sense. They came here to quarantine the last bit of life on the planet, and couldn't bring even the smallest bit of the grey mud, even to study.

"And this is where you died, the rest of you," I say. "You became stranded on your moon, and you all died in this station."

"I believe so," says Venelk. "I can't tell for sure because I wasn't the last to perish, but all signs pointed towards that fate."

I take a moment to listen to this place and it's rather silent, even for a station on the moon. Venelk reaches down and gives Venek'll a pat to tell her that we're about to go somewhere, and my guide's extension gets up and stretches her mottled blue frame, extending her spikes as she does so.

"You spent the remainder of your life finding a way to send this message," I say. "The one that I'm experiencing now."

"Yes," says Venelk. "I told you when we first met that I'm a messenger, and that's what I did here. I found a way to send this message in a variety of forms. I have no special insight into what the grey substance was, let alone how it can be stopped. But I could take what I saw and share it widely, and I'm fortunate that part of it found its way to your kind."[85]

---

[85] Venelk never shared the specifics of *how* this message was so lucidly shared, nor did I think to ask at the time. Technical details aren't my strong suit, and

"*I'm* the fortunate one," I say. "To glimpse the beauty of your planet is beyond any human's wildest dreams—"

"I said *your kind*, Dion," says Venelk.

I don't know what Venelk means by this.

"If you recall, I originally told you that I was both a messenger and a student," says Venelk. "And I also told you that I had a singular specialty."

"What was your specialty?" I ask.

"I studied *your kind*, Dion," she says. "Gods."

/***/

We leave our window and walk through the hallways, and the occupants of the station don't seem to notice us, though it's a different feeling than the sense of invisibility we experienced in Meem's council.

They don't seem to notice us, but they don't seem to notice much else either. Whether I'm a ghost or fully visible to them, at this moment I'm just another denizen here in this dreamt illusion.

Some inhabitants of the space station are halfheartedly attending to one blinking device or another, but most seem to be just staring at the windows. They're waiting out their time here, shielded from the grey sludge that eviscerated their home, but I can see that they've paid a dear price for their safety. The sterile atmosphere doesn't quite hold the despair that I found amidst the grey mud of Hell, but there's no spirit of *reason* here either, the one that I found in the philosopher's room. I just feel the dull sense of resignation, and nothing more.

---

perhaps subconsciously I didn't ask because of this. What I still wonder to this day is how many other places, and how many other entities, this message reached. Venelk broadcast it in all directions, and I can't be the only one who has glimpsed the purple planet.

A TALE OF THE HIGHWAY

We turn a corner and there's a hallway filled with a projection of a natural scene from the purple planet. I see the golden, corded stalks waving in the wind, and I see the outline of the qenelmar grazing on the kelltops in the far distance. There are sounds, smells and even a touch of humidity[86] in the hallway, and the whole experience works to great effect.

Unfortunately, we exit the hallway at the end and come to another wing of the station much like the one that preceded it: clean, quiet and filled with despondent inhabitants, staring forlornly out the windows.

"Do you ever wonder why gods exist, Dion?" asks Venelk as we walk unnoticed through the silence.

"Not recently," I say. "But I'm sure I wondered it quite a bit before my memory was erased, if I hadn't figured it out already."

Venelk clicks her mandibles as we reach a door. She sticks out her hand to press a large, purple circle with her thumb, and the door in front of us slides open.

"Before our eradication began, I spent much of my life trying to figure out the same thing," says Venelk. "I believed you existed, even though the majority of my fellow denizens refused to believe in any higher power whatsoever. Still, I was allowed to study gods in earnest, because it's accepted in our society to study such strange things. Even the most skeptical of our kind knew that every once in a while an impractical theory turned out to be truth, or at the very least revealed some *secondary* truth, so I was able to explore mythology as a *scientist*.

"I began my study by looking at our own history, and I'd ascertain the path of *your kind's* existences mirrored that of our gods of old. In our past there were a few deities in primeval societies, and they grew in

---

[86] Again, this may be a dreamt illusion taking place only in my head, so I can't say for sure that I actually *felt* the humidity and *caught* the wondrous scent of this planet's nature. But I did dream that I sensed them, and the hallway relaxed me just the same.

number as societies progressed, perhaps into too many. These gods bickered endlessly, were lascivious, petty and violent, a reflection of those that worshipped them. And then as our societal consciousness evolved, the gods began to lose their place."

Venelk takes another right and then presses another button to open a door, this one heavier than the last. There's another hallway, this one completely empty and even quieter than anything that came before.

"Does this history seem familiar to you, Dion?"

"Again, I have no memory," I say. "But yes, it does seem familiar. I'd say the overarching path of our planets' gods are quite similar."

The windows in this hallway are bigger than those I'd seen previously, and I have an unobstructed view of this moon's endless expanse. I can see its surface with perfect clarity, all the way until its lifeless dust curves past the horizon.

But I can't quite see that far. There's a sharp edge of darkness where the purple planet's sun is unable to reach.

Venelk opens up another set of heavy doors at the end of the hallway to reveal another large vessel on rails, similar in shape to the one that traversed the purple ocean. We get inside and the rear doors close tighter than they had previously, and I see that another door shuts behind us, and another panel comes down over it, thick and windowless, made to reinforce.

The door in front of us opens into the moon's thin atmosphere, and we move forward. We pick up speed, but not too much: there's no need to rush anywhere on this place, I suppose. It still seems fast, as our track doesn't elevate us like we did over the ocean. We go through craters and over small hills, but we're never more than a few body lengths above the cold, quiet ground. The dust passes beneath us uncomplaining, and I look forward to see that we're approaching that sharp edge of darkness, where day becomes night on this moon in a single moment.

"There's an underlying commonality between the gods of my planet and yours, perhaps the gods of all planets," says Venelk. "The fact that you're here now listening to me supports this notion."

I don't fully understand what she means by this, and Venelk knows it.

"I told you I was a messenger," she says. "And I was a messenger before our destruction. I knew that I couldn't *find* our gods, but I did study ways of sending them messages, speaking to them on *their* plane of existence. Was I successful? I can't say for sure, but I did develop certain techniques, and once I got to this moon I had little else to do but practice them."

"And when your planet died, it took most of its gods with them," I say. "So you started sending these messages outwards."

"More or less," says Venelk. "I hope I was successful in this regard."

"You were," I say. "You've reached me now, and reached me completely."

"I have no way of knowing that because I sent this message *one way*," she says. "But I know that I would have been thrilled to find you."

I consider Venelk's past awareness, that her entire existence is now an illusion, a recording, an existence that means something to others but not to her or any of her vanished kind. I then think of the philosophers, and how their messages made such an impact after their bodies had disappeared from the earthly plane.

"Before this eradication, in all your time of sending messages, did you get any proof of the gods?" I ask. "Did anyone or anything contact you back?"

Venelk clicks her mandibles.

"One did," says Venelk. "I think the grey substance caught her by surprise as well."

"One god?"

"Yes, I'll show you her right now," says Venelk, pointing to a building on the horizon. "Her name is Dabron."

/***/

The building is straddling this moon's border between day and night, and it's topped with a translucent dome. The clear structure has countless sharp-edged shapes glinting in the sun, and its form reminds me of Venelk's compounded eyes. *It's as if Venelk had given the moon her sight, so that this quiet satellite could better keep its watch over the purple planet.*

Our vessel slows and then enters a door, and then the door closes behind us. Another panel shuts over that one, and the room begins to pressurize itself.[87] After it's filled, the door opens in front of us, and the vehicle moves forward and then comes to a halt. Venelk opens our vessel, and we step out onto a platform.

She and Venek'll walk down the steps that rise to meet us, but I choose to stay on the platform for another moment, because the view is absolutely breathtaking.

/***/

The room's enormity is more evident when viewed from the inside. It's made even bigger by the shining dome above us, and it's filled with countless objects. I can see them quite clearly even from a distance, and

---

[87] Since this is a dreamt illusion Venelk doesn't need to pressurize the area, and could very well have us walking directly on the moon. But I suppose she's keeping the experience as she saw it, so I wait patiently alongside her.

A TALE OF THE HIGHWAY

I'm sure Venelk made this strange clarity possible. *She may have wanted the universe to remember the purple planet, but I sense that she really wanted this, a menagerie of most everything her kind had brought into being.*

There's a fire burning in one part, and a copy of the space elevator in miniature on the opposite end. There's a long shelf of tomes that I assume to be their greatest works of literature, and a small crystalline cube next to it that might hold all the rest. There's a stone object that appears to tell time with the sun, and a tiny metal object that looks like it's meant to help navigate by the stars.

There's a bevy of mathematical symbols, some etched into stone, some written out of molded metal and some as projections within a crystal. Though I don't understand most of them, I can feel their significance, and their immutability.[88] I see architectural models, sheets of music, engineering diagrams and paintings of what appear to be courtrooms. I see agricultural equipment and canals in miniature, inventions and computers, vehicles for exploring the land, the sea, air and space.

And at the end of the shelf is another crystalline cube, which I'm sure stores the plans for everything I see and more.

These objects are these creatures' history, but not history as it's normally seen: a compendium of land lost, won, and then lost again. This is the history of achievements, the history of ideas, perhaps the only thing that really matters in the end.

"This was just supposed to be a museum," says Venelk. "But it's turned into something of a vault."

---

[88] Plato loved the immutable nature of numbers, and he'd find no exceptions here. Prime numbers would still be prime numbers to Venelk's kind, and though *Pi* would be slightly different—her twelve-digit species may count in *base twelve*—the number still holds a universal value. They might count Pi differently, but *Pi in base twelve* is the same number on both their planet and ours, and our *Pi in base ten* is the same number on both our world and theirs.

"Perhaps there's no difference between the two," I say.

"Perhaps," says Venelk, pointing to the far center of the dome. "But whatever the case, she prefers to spend her time here."

Venelk's fingers point to a dark figure, mostly black and tinged with gold, staring out at the dust forlornly, much like those I'd seen in the hallway. The creature is similar in shape to Venelk with six digits on each hand and oversized mandibles, but she's much larger than my guide. The creature turns to look at us with two sad, compounded eyes, defeated and empty, as if she's let us down.

"If you recall, I told you that I got to sneak *Venek'll and another passenger* aboard the space elevator's last journey," says Venelk. "I tricked Dabron into coming up here I'm afraid, otherwise she would have stayed down on the surface. I can't help feeling bad about that."

"You shouldn't feel bad," I say with a smile. "Sometimes you have to trick a divine being if it's for the right reasons, sometimes you even have to kidnap one."

Venelk gets the reference immediately, and clicks her mandibles in agreement.

"It might be," she says. "If *right and wrong* still hold value in this time."

I look at Dabron staring out the window, and then I think of my own Titan stuck in the trunk, and wonder how Prometheus relates to Dabron. Do they have similar origins, and do they ultimately share the same purpose? They're alike in form and temperament at least: their oversized bodies both seem to hold the same sense of stoic sorrow, the same quiet strength that takes on the weight of a world's troubles by itself.

Their respective melancholies are different though. Prometheus's distress comes from a stymied potential, but Dabron's heartbreak comes from a lost one. Prometheus is trapped, and Dabron is free but irrelevant, a god that failed, a deity with no more place in this universe.

I feel myself being pulled upwards, just a few errant atoms, but I know that I only have a few moments left in this place.

"Was it worth it?" I ask. "The time your kind had with her?"

Venelk looks towards Dabron and the Titan is lit brilliantly in this moon's undiffused twilight, yet clearly despondent amongst her denizen's ideas and accomplishments.

"I can't help but say yes," says Venelk. "We're gone, vanished, but I'm still compelled to say yes. Nothing remains of us, perhaps not even this trophy room. But I feel our time was worth it, though I don't have a reason how I can say such a thing."

"Perhaps some answers don't need reasoning," I say.

"Everything can use a little reasoning," says Venelk. "But I still say yes. If Dabron hadn't come …"

Venelk's words trail off, and my atoms are pulled up faster and faster, abandoning this dusty moon at an exponential rate. I'm pulled through the translucent dome and up through the thin atmosphere. I take one more look at the purple planet, now smothered in grey, and then look back at the dome, now fallen into disrepair.

Venelk is no longer there, nor is her extension Venek'll, but I do see Dabron. She's standing where she had always been, right in the middle of the cracked edifice. She looks at me with her sad, compounded eyes, pleading with me to do the right thing. I don't know what that is, but her look implores me to do the right thing.

The Jarkeeper

I wake up back on Earth, not on the road but amongst the thorny wilderness, and I'm feeling slightly broken down but not completely demolished. The moon is there peeking out behind a cloud, *our moon*, and I wonder if she knows that I'd just visited her cousin, hovering around a once-purple planet, in a place and time so very far from here.

I also wonder if she understands that no matter how kind she might be, and no matter how constant, it will be all for naught if she shines on an empty Earth.

But the earth's not empty now. In fact, it's precisely the opposite.

I want to get up and heal my body, and I want another bottle of wine, but I don't stand up just yet. I take a moment to listen to the sounds coming from the surrounding shrubs: countless creatures shouting out to find a mate, to find a meal, or to avoid becoming one.

Life and death, the persistent song of the night.

I think of all the creatures nearby, and how they've been chased by terror every moment of their lives. One momentary lapse in awareness, one misstep and then *snap*, they're gone, a unique existence extinguished forever. Even the fiercest predators have their foe: starvation itself. Death is always there, behind you, waiting for just the slightest opportunity.

Every living creature is chased by their own personal pair of Crows. Every one.

Mother Nature's strength is terrifying—and yet, I can't help but feel grateful as I lie amongst her thorny shrubs, very much alive, and looking forward to the next bottle of wine. *She can wring the sweetest grapes from cold dirt, and she can sprout an entire forest with nothing but a handful of dry seeds.*

I then realize that perhaps Mother Nature isn't cruel—she just keeps an ordered house, and does so with brutal, unforgiving efficiency.

Her world is filled with undeniable beauty, but everything pays the cost for that beauty when its time is up. I'm sure it was the same way on the purple planet, countless creatures consumed to yield something as beautiful as the island-sized demmelmar. *There could be a planet somewhere that acquires its growth from something else besides competition and incredible efficiency, but I can't think of how it might exist.* If you're not fit to survive in *this* plane of existence, nature recycles you with perfect efficiency, joylessly sending her recycling agents in the form of a predator, disease, or just bad luck.

Maybe the Crows are just Mother Nature's agents, sent here to recycle me and keep the system pristine. Maybe they're her faithful stewards, and nothing more.

I then figure it can't be the case. Nature is terrifyingly efficient, but she doesn't enjoy doing what she has to do when one of her children's time is up. The Crows enjoy their role, and that makes them wrong.

/***/

I shake myself out of my doubt. The purple planet was a dream, and our moon is here *now*, and has just healed me. I should be grateful.

I am grateful, and I'm ready to resume this journey, or at least return to Prometheus. My body is largely whole, though I see that the ground still glistens with my blood. I figure the moon healed me while I rolled around in my stupor, shining her light through this wilderness and salving my wounds whenever she got the chance.

Whatever the case, my body is healed, save for a few cuts from the surrounding rocks and thorns.

I stand up and see that I am very far from my vehicle. I can barely see the light of the station, and can't hear the music beyond a persistent, muffled thump. I can see the faint blur of small lights traveling towards the station, however, and they're coming from both sides. *At least the party went well in my absence. I hope it continues to do so, and I hope that Cruz is having a good time.*

/***/

The journey back to the vehicle is slow going because I don't have my shoes, and the ground is rough. *The moon healed my body, but she also took away any sort of callouses I might have had beneath my feet. I guess soft skin is the price of a healed body.*

I eventually find my shoes strewn across the ground, most likely pulled off as the Crows dragged me through the grass. I put the shoes on and pick up my pace until I'm back at the station. The party has doubled in size, maybe even more, and I peek around the back to see that El Macho Gordo's wrestling friends have shown up. There's an oversized Jeep filled with masked men, not the terrifying kind of masked, mind you, but a group of *entertainers*. One of them is now perched atop the plastic Jacuzzi cover in the bed of Clark's truck, and the wrestler is preparing to do some sort of back flip. He jumps, lands on his feet, and there's applause from the crowd as he bows.

I see Cruz there, and he's laughing—legitimately *laughing*. The wrestler beckons Cruz to come forward and he does: the host of the evening. Every person applauds, and Cruz is appreciative in return. He continues to laugh while shedding tears of gratitude.

/***/

I can't join the party, though every part of my being wants to.

I guess that's me: I just got beaten for straying from the path, and all I want to do is stray once again.

I want to go inside and hear their tales, I want to see who else has come, and I want to drink more. I want to drink a lot more.

I know I can't stay though. I remember Pan's words—that the Crows will punish me if I stop, eroding my *self* until I risk fulfilling their objective. I'm the only one looking after Prometheus now, and I can't give the Crows another chance to destroy what's left of me.

I knock on the trunk, and Prometheus thumps back. I take another look at the keypad, and hear a *caw* as I do. I turn around to see Retjar and Ulo still on the edge of the shadows, warning me to stay away from my cargo and to get back on the road.

Something looks different about Retjar, though. He still holds his familiar scowl, but he looks perturbed. He doesn't look so much angry as *nettled*, and his vacant eyes suggest he's been embittered by something beyond me.

/***/

I drive forward nonetheless, and tell Prometheus everything about the purple planet. I explain about its perfect society and the death of its beings, and about the eradication of everything else there. I tell my cohort about Dabron, and the incredible sadness I saw in her eyes. Prometheus listens and thumps in understanding.

I then tell Prometheus that I'm going to start calling it a *he* to make a delineation between him and his feminine counterpart, and he doesn't seem to have any objection[89].

I admit that I still don't understand what the grey sludge is, and how a creature such as Dabron could abet any kind of destruction, and Prometheus doesn't appear to understand this either. I ask if he thinks he could do such a thing, and he has no response to this.

"I understand that's a tough question," I say. "It undercuts your whole being, everything you *are*. It labels you as the ultimate

---

[89] The Gelkins actually first referred to Prometheus as a he, but I ask Prometheus anyway. You can't always assume these things when it comes to an entity like my fellow passenger.

destructor, when you're anything but that."

Prometheus thumps in response, letting me know that he's OK.

"And I guess I should bring up one more thing while we're at it, something I should have brought up a long time ago," I say.

Prometheus thumps to allow my thoughts.

"I'm bringing you towards your purported destruction," I say. "I don't want that of course, but that's where we're headed."

Prometheus thumps, albeit reluctantly.

"Am I headed in the right direction?"

Prometheus thumps, and I consider our situation.

"I assume this was part of my plan," I say. "*Our* plan."

Prometheus thumps in agreement.

"I'll figure out the code before your destruction," I say.

Prometheus thumps his walls.

You might be the savior of humanity, or you might destroy it, Prometheus, but right now I only wish you could talk.

/***/

I'm going to need a drink to start figuring this out, so I reach back for a bottle, any bottle. *There's no right wine for a time such as this. There's nothing to savor, nothing to smooth over.* There's just a mystery and decisions yet to come, and a clock somewhere that's most likely running out of time. Any wine will do.

I bring out a bottle, a Riesling. As I'm examining the label, I notice there's something beside me in the front passenger seat: a jar. The container is ornately decorated — it's bejeweled and has carvings of arcane symbols, strange creatures and scenes of copulation.

Whatever this jar is, I can't take my eyes off it, and my hand is drawn to its lid.

"I wouldn't open it if I were you," says a soft voice from the back.

I look in the review mirror and see a figure cloaked in the shadows, a woman.

"I bring the jar wherever I go just to remind those I'm with of what I once did," she says. "But that's the old me, and I've come to visit you for a different purpose. So don't open my jar. If you do, bad things will happen all around, and *no one* will be happy, neither man nor god."

I look back at the woman and I recognize her, at least from Ari's words: *pale skin, and eyes that were rimmed with blood. She was also carrying a strange jar—*

This is the spirit who visited Ari in her dreams and tricked her into destroying my memory. This is the woman who started this whole tale off.

"Good evening, Dion," says the woman. "My name is Pandora."

/***/

In addition to her pale skin and blood-rimmed eyes, Pandora is wearing tall leather boots beneath a short skirt. Her jet-black hair is short in some areas and long in others, as if she decided to cut it herself, and then changed her mind halfway through. She's covered with tattoos, inked images that reflect what's on her jar. She has one tattoo that stands out from the rest though: a drawing of a scaled tail that works its way up her thigh, passes through her skirt and comes out on the other leg as the head of a snake, holding an apple between its jaws.

She's still beautiful though, even as she looks at me with eyes rimmed with blood.

"I brought that jar to the world long ago," she says. "It was sent as punishment *the first time* Prometheus stole the fire for the humans."

I take a sip from the bottle, and the Riesling is warm, but it's still a solid white: light and dry.

"Looking back, I don't think opening the jar was a punishment to this world," she says. "In fact, I think it was a good thing in the long run."

Seeing the jar, I'm not convinced it was a good thing, though I wouldn't blame anyone if they decided to actually open it. Its designs tempt me now, despite Pandora's warning, and despite the fact that I'm the only one who can deliver Prometheus to safety.

"Your father sent me to punish humanity when Prometheus escaped, but did I really do that?" she asks. "My jar contained all the alleged evils in this world: doubt and slander, envy and aggression and so on. But I don't think it *truly* stained the world, and not just because it contained hope at the bottom."

Pandora looks wistfully at the seat cushion that holds Prometheus in.

"Your companion Prometheus stole the fire that brought humanity out of the caves," she says. "But my jar did everything else."

She smiles softly.

"Doubt makes a person work twice as hard to survive," she says. "Slander makes them improve their skills of rhetoric to rebut the false words against them. Envy makes them buy things they can't possibly afford, bringing out the impossible from this world. And aggression brings endless war—"

She scratches a tattoo on her arm, one of a sword set against an ornately decorated shield.

"Half the world's technology came from war," she says. "Probably more. Do you agree, Dion?"

I consider this and then shake my head *no*. She's framing the argument in her own terms, placing it within her own context, trying to get me to indirectly agree with her justifications of destruction and violence.

Pandora senses that I'm resisting her argument, and then points to the waiter's friend corkscrew that Cruz gave me.

"Stainless steel came from the *Great War*, you know," she says sweetly, as if she were talking about planting pumpkins. "They needed better gun barrels, better engines for their machinery. Millions of people died, but now the survivors don't have to worry about getting their silverware wet."

I'm still not convinced by her logic, but Pandora is undeterred, and appears to be enjoying the challenge.

"There was a great philosopher named Plato once," she continues. "He was a big fan of unchanging *ideas*. Millions died in the Great War, but they would have died anyway. But your beloved humanity now has the *idea* of stainless steel, of an elegant corkscrew, *for all time*. Perhaps the war, and the root aggression that came from my jar, was worth it."

Pandora walks her long, chipped fingernails like a spider over the snake tattoo on her thigh.

"Even the monotheists have their own version of this tale," says Pandora. "They rue the day that Eve, that dastardly *rib-born* woman, first tasted the apple in the soft, green Garden of Eden."

Pandora looks up through the skylight at the moon.

"But I say Eve knew what she was doing," says Pandora. "Eve made humanity's first *choice*, and everything they've accomplished has come from the resultant strife. You don't feel compelled to fly, build buildings or explore space if all you need to do is sit in a garden."

Pandora shakes her head.

"But jar or garden, triumph or fall from grace, that's all in the past," she says. "Our dear Prometheus already stole the fire, and the humans have already raised themselves out of the mud. I was raised from that same mud to punish them, and I already gave them my jar filled with a thousand shades of death. That's the past, and right or wrong, the world is as it is now because of it."

Pandora pats the cushion that contains Prometheus. I can't tell if her ghostly hands are actually touching anything, but she still pats it gently, like a girl bidding her doll good night.

"And now we are in a different situation entirely," she says. "Prometheus has returned, and he's brought another set of problems, one that can't be contained by a single jar. Do you understand this?"

I shake my head that I don't.

"Do you understand the gravity of this situation then, Dion?"

"Up to a certain point," I say. "I apparently freed him to bring humanity to the next level. He'll either do this or eradicate all life from this world."

"He'll do both, and we'll get to that later, the grey included," says Pandora. "But I feel that deep inside you do understand the gravity of the situation, so we can continue. But first, I need something from you."

I want to ask her more about *the grey* as she calls it, and how a creature as noble as Dabron could leave her planet as a lifeless swamp that will soon become dust. I want to ask her how a divine being as virtuous as Prometheus could do the same. But her tone is quick, and I find it difficult to interject a counterargument. In her own way she's just as forceful as Retjar the Damned.

"To begin, I need a location," she says. "Any place will do."

I consider this for a moment, and can't come up with anything.

"Your memory's gone, of course," says Pandora, realizing. "The fact that *I* didn't remember this fact holds so many levels of irony."

I laugh at this, though I don't know why.[90]

"Just try to *describe* a place," she says. "We'll make do with what you have."

I look around at the endless night surrounding us, and then think of the grey sludge that lies in wait. I think of the purple planet, and of the Garden of Eden, and wonder if leaving it was worth the cost.

"Somewhere *green*," I say. "A green land. An island, maybe."

She thinks for a moment.

"That will do," she says sweetly. "Now we can begin."

/***/

"I'd like to tell you about myself—my *new* self," says Pandora. "But first, I have a question. What do you think of the Crows?"

"I try not to," I say.

"I don't blame you," says Pandora. "Retjar and Ulo are demons."

Pandora shakes her head.

"Demons' powers are not suited to deal with the likes of you," she

---

[90] I now understand that she purposefully showed just enough fallibility to make me like her. Speakers, comedians and lawyers do this all the time. They'll make fun of themselves first thing, and that makes their audiences and juries connect with them. I laugh here at Pandora's alleged fallibility even though she's referencing the time she stole my entire past and then orchestrated the destruction of the one thing in my life that I ever strived for.

says. "And they're not suited for this task. So they sent me."

She looks out the window behind us and I wonder how many birds are trailing us in the night, cawing bitterly at their recent exile.

"The Crows do dreadful things, but terror is a *vastly* overrated method of coercion," she says. "I'm sure you understand."[91]

I look in the rearview mirror and can see her staring at me with her blood-rimmed eyes.

"And terror does not work on you, Dion," she says. "They thought it would, because you've never faced pressure before, or done anything of consequence. Previous to this event you took no sides and made no choices, choosing instead to sit on the sidelines, cloaking yourself in human comrades and chalking up every one of your misadventures to inebriation."

She says the words flatly, without judgment.

"But you were more than they bargained for, Dion," she says. "The ne'er-do-well adolescent ran away from home to party with his wastrel friends, and he returned while no one was looking to let the dog loose. They thought a simple spanking would push you back in line, but you're no longer that adolescent anymore, are you?"

I don't reply, but the words hold truth. *I'm no teenager, that's for sure. My memory might be less than a day old, but I feel like I've walked this earth for a thousand years.*

"So they sent me to clean up this mess, again," she says. "The first

---

[91] Pandora actually makes a pretty good point here: terror has its limits. Put a hot poker to a man's neck and he'll give you his secrets, plus ten falsehoods mixed in—if only you'll leave him alone. Terrorize a nation and they'll pay you tribute—up until the day of their revolt, when they bring the terror back to your soldiers ten times over.

time I was meant to smite with my jar, but the times are different now. Humanity's different and *you're* different, so I'll do no such thing."

She looks out the window again.

"I'm not here to punish you as the Crows did, and they want so desperately to do again," says Pandora. "I am here to *coerce*."

/***/

"You have changed since our time in Athens, Dion, and I admire this, your recent catastrophic actions notwithstanding," says Pandora. "But I've changed since our time in Athens as well, after I began to spend my time with the Muses, Polyhymnia and Calliope in particular.[92] But what really changed me was studying your humans' so-called *liberal arts*.

"The liberal arts still hold a vast and deceptive power over the world nowadays," says Pandora. "But never was their strength so apparent than back in Athens, where there were two levels of education, the liberal and the vocational. The former was only for the free, and was thus called the *liberal* arts. The latter could be taught to anyone, including slaves. Teach a slave to smith, and he'll make you a sword. Teach that slave the liberal arts—history, logic and rhetoric—and he'll convince his indentured comrades that they should revolt, and they will.

"It was during my time with the Muses that I started coming of age, and realized the true power of these free arts. I'd not learned to walk this earthly plane like you, and still haven't mastered it, but I did learn *coercion*, and I soon realized that this gave me more power than our mightiest gods.

"Case in point: Ares once bestowed one of his favored armies with power, and on the other side Boreas planned to bring the north wind

---

[92] These are the Muses of rhetoric and eloquence, among other things.

that would freeze them in their tracks. Who do you think won this skirmish, Dion?"

I have no answer for this.[93]

"I visited the invading general in a dream that night," she says. "And I convinced him that the fight wasn't worth it. His army stayed home, and ten thousand soldiers got to keep their lives."

She smiles again.

"I'll give you a more specific example, one from the modern era," she says. "There was a certain chemical plant that the gods found necessary for their plans, and it had recently shut down. There was a strike, due to the low wages paid to the janitorial staff. Garbage piled up, the conditions stopped passing inspections, and the plant had to close its doors.

"The strike went on for a week, and then other workers joined for their own self-interest, and the strike went on for *months*. The gods were upset at this, because their plans in this regard balanced on the head of the pin, a pin whose base was now bent in the wrong direction."

Pandora presses one of her fingers against the apple on her thigh, and keeps pressing it until it contorts into an impossible direction. It looks painful to me, but she doesn't seem to mind.

"Ares said he could handle it," says Pandora. "He said he would bring *anger* to the police, and he did. Boreas said he would work from the other end and bring *the cold* to make sure the workers needed to pay extra for heating."

Pandora shakes her head dismissively.

---

[93] Masters of rhetoric, quite fittingly, fill their arguments with rhetorical questions. This engages their opponent while still allowing them to control the dialogue.

"Both plans failed thoroughly," she says. "Ares and Boreas—all the gods, really—they thought that they were about to engage in some cultivated legend from antiquity, where the gods speak and humanity follows. But this was real life, and a world long-accustomed to ignoring our kind."

Pandora smiles.

"That was when the gods first sent for *me*," she says. "And I solved their problem with the *liberal arts*—coercion through a single idea."

My ears perk up at the word, and she notices this.

"Ideas are powerful, Dion," she says. "The Muses taught me of their power, and they taught me well."

I think back to Plato and his love of these powerful, immutable *ideas*. I look in Pandora's bleeding eyes and come to the realization that though Plato's beloved ideas can be powerful, they're not always good. Some can be quite destructive.

"Since I could never quite walk this earthly plane like you, Dion," she says, "I figured that to break this strike, I needed to share an idea with one who did: a real human. And I needed the right human, a master of the liberal arts in their own right."

She releases the bent finger from her thigh, and snaps it straight again.

"A lawyer," she says. "I needed to share my idea with a lawyer."

I squint my eyes at the thought.

"Lawyers run the world through their liberal arts, Dion," she says. "They argue, they convince, they negotiate. They launch businesses and end wars, act as leaders or choose them, and of course *make* the laws that govern the world. And in the case with the strike at hand, *one* idea in *one* lawyer was going to *break it completely* so that the chemical plant could resume its operation, the one plant on Earth that produced the substance that could destroy *your* memory if dropped into a glass of wine."

I think of Ari, and how completely I now forgive her for whatever it is that she'd done. *When you placed your heart in front of this bleeding-eyed woman, Ari, you never stood a chance.*

"Ideas can be quite powerful, Dion," says Pandora. "More than even *you* realize."

/***/

We drive on in silence for a few moments. I find myself upset at her, and she lets me be. I wonder if she has some reason for this, or if perhaps she just wants me to drive further towards her ultimate goal.

I eventually calm down, and ask her to continue.

"I found my perfect lawyer from the firm hired by the plant," she says. "She was a junior attorney, young enough to take a risk, and hungry enough to do something odious. I whispered my words into her ears while she slept, and the next day she presented our plan to her superiors, one so elegant in its simplicity that she was able to present it in under two minutes."

Breaking a strike with a few sentences. Ideas are powerful indeed.

"She told her colleagues to concentrate on the *immigration status* of the local workforce," continues Pandora. "As I'd warned her, her superiors promptly countered that all the workers had legal status, and she responded that she knew this to be true. She then told her superiors of the notion that virtually all the striking employees had relatives living with them who were *not* legally allowed to be in the country."

Pandora seems to be proud of her gambit.

"Her superiors promptly hired a firm of private detectives," says Pandora. "These detectives were able to do their job quickly, and in under two weeks returned with a complete list of names of undocumented individuals who were living with the striking individuals. The law firm then couriered a tailored list of these names to each striking employee, and told them that if they did not report back to work within five days, these names and addresses would be shared with the appropriate authorities."

Pandora smiles.

"The workers' union promptly dissolved, and three days later all employees agreed to an unconditional forfeiture of their demands. The plant was back to full production within a week, and it once again began producing that rare substance that was needed to erase the memory of your earthly body, which in turn was so important to keep this world from obliteration."

I don't particularly care for the story, and Pandora senses my disapproval.

"It was a conniving, loathsome act, Dion, I'm aware of this," says Pandora. "I didn't enjoy it, nor did I enjoy convincing Ariadne to poison your earthly body. But this all *had to be done*, do you understand this?"

I think about Ari's full name, and how I like the way it sounds. Still, I don't quite believe Pandora's words that it *had* to be done.

"You may have *wanted* it to be done," I say. "But you didn't *have* to break the strike, or give Ariadne the chemicals. You chose this, and no one forced your hand."

"I had to do what I did to protect this earth," says Pandora. "Like your humans, you might think this world is secure, but I see it for what it really is: a rock protected from the cold universe by nothing but a thin layer of gas. Existence here balances on the head of a pin, and we sometimes need to do strange things to keep it from falling over."

I think back to my journey through our solar system, where I saw each planet in turn. They each seemed as powerful and eternal as the gods they represented, but I do see her point. Even mighty Jupiter is just a rock clutching its surrounding gases tightly, a relative pinprick of mass set against the empty canvas of space.

But I still don't believe that her hand was forced, and Pandora recognizes that I don't. She laughs and then shakes her head.

"Here I am, speaking in threats and omens like the Crows I've supplanted," says Pandora. "I'm here to convince *you* to destroy Prometheus of your own accord. May I present my argument *why* you should drive this vehicle until the road ends, and then drive some more? I'll present my argument and then leave. The ultimate decision will be yours, and yours alone."

I nod that she may.

"Good," says Pandora. "Because the events that are about to transpire have far more consequences than the relative welfare of a few chemical-plant janitors, the soul of a lovestruck mortal, or even your shortsighted plans, Dion. In any case, I'll begin now."

A TALE OF THE HIGHWAY

The Jarkeeper's Coercions

"I'm going to lay out my argument for you in three parts," says Pandora. "The abstract, the personal, and the truth. First the abstract. Please turn on the radio, I believe we'll get a signal here."

I turn on the radio to static, and reluctantly hit *seek*. The station number goes up around the bend until it's small again, and then stops. I hear a voice, still interspersed with static, but I can hear a woman speaking.

It soon becomes clear that she's reading the news, talking about sports scores, local crimes and so on. Pandora sits patiently, and there's a sound cue to indicate the woman's about to talk about global current events. Pandora smiles again, and we both listen:

"In a strange bit of weather phenomenon," says the news reader, *"a cold-weather hurricane has hit the south coast of Greenland. For more on this, we turn to our meteorologist. Weston?"*

"Thank you," says Weston the meteorologist. *"This is a rare phenomenon indeed, because hurricanes don't form in cold weather, at least not before this. We're still trying to figure out what's causing this anomaly, but in the meantime we're tracking its progress. We had originally expected this hurricane to go inland, which is largely uninhabited, but the storm has changed directions and appears to be mirroring the coast. We don't have word on any casualties, but this doesn't bear well for those who live in Greenland, because they aren't accustomed to hurricanes, and they tend to live in isolated communities with no roads between them."*

The newscast fades to static, and I turn off the radio.

"Do you understand the significance of that, Dion?" asks Pandora.

I think I do, and I'm too upset to speak.

"Earlier I'd asked you to *describe* a place, and you said *a green land, an island*," says Pandora.

"Greenland," I say.

The name still holds enough of my long-term memory to tell me the significance of what she's done.

"You gave us a green land, and an island," she says. "*Greenland*. We did what we could."

I feel angry, but Pandora cuts me off before I can act on it.

"No one died, Dion," she says. "And no one will. Poseidon and Boreas made sure of it. We just wanted to show you what we *can* do if you do not continue to comply with our demands."

If this is the first part of her argument, she sure knows how to get my attention.

"A warning shot," I say. "I disobey, and you'll place the punishment somewhere else. Innocent victims, to be specific."[94]

"We have no recourse, Dion," says Pandora. "Because if you stray from this path they will all be punished in the end, *erased*, if you recall."

"Right," I say. "But for now, if I get off this path, innocent people

---

[94] The punishment of the innocent can be a remarkably powerful device when it comes to *coercion*. Roman soldiers were often subject to *decimation*: If a single soldier in a troop fled a single battle, the others would be punished collectively. One in ten soldiers would be picked at random to be beaten to death by the other nine who got to live, their former brothers, those that they'd fought beside, those whose lives they had probably saved at one point or another. The practice of decimation has thankfully faded into obscurity, but punishment of the innocent to coerce has not. I believe its effectiveness is due to cognitive dissonance in those coerced, those who presumably hold at least a basic level of morality. They're thrust into an atrociously unfair situation, and they recognize the only acceptable situation is to follow the rules and avoid the fate that places culpability upon them.

die. And they die at random."

"Not at random," says Pandora. "You've been doing some talking, and I've been listening. We'll take *your* words, *your* actions, and turn them into a place, or a punishment. For example, you taught Cruz about the wine's *legs*, so maybe we'll trace that wine back to the vigneron and give him a malady that affects his legs."

I put my bottle of Riesling back in its holder.

"Or maybe we'll forgo the vigneron's legs and just destroy the whole region," says Pandora. "Put something in ground so nothing can grow, that kind of thing. No one will die, but countless traditions will. So you're right to put that Riesling away—it could be the last of its kind."

I'm not taking this, not now.

"You purport yourself to be better than Retjar," I say. "And you talk like this."

"I never claimed to be *better* than anyone, least of all the Crows," she says. "I'm just more effective."

"They harm *me* if I disobey, you harm others," I say. "You might be more effective, but you're cut from the same cloth as Retjar the Damned, and Ulo the Scraper, for that matter."

Pandora considers my words very carefully. *She's listening to me, as closely as a child listens when her best friend says blue is her favorite color.*

"Perhaps my words haven't been as effective as I would have liked," says Pandora. "That part of the argument was the *abstract*, a promise from the gods to obliterate those you don't know. We will act upon this promise if you disobey, make no mistake about it. You will not be harmed, but others will, on a scale you can't even imagine."

Pandora shakes her head.

"But the abstract only goes so far with you," she says. "Now it's my time to explain the *personal* part of my argument. If you stray from this path, I am going to personally hurt someone you know, for whom you care very deeply. And I'm going to do it very, very precisely, Dion."

Perhaps I'm wrong to compare Pandora to Retjar the Damned. She might be worse.

/***/

I take another sip of the Riesling, no longer concerned with her vague threats to punish its anonymous vigneron or its region, because I'm too worried about who she's talking about *now*.

Could she be talking about Ariadne? Probably not: Pandora's already put Ari on the path to Hell. Pan looks like he can hold his own, especially with Sami by his side. *Prometheus?* No, she wouldn't punish him. She's different than Retjar, and less direct. Prometheus is quite vulnerable right now, but that's not her style—besides, she wants *me* to destroy Prometheus for her.

"You really changed Cruz's life," says Pandora. "You opened up his whole world tonight, you really did."

Cruz. She's going for Cruz.

I take another look at her jar in the front seat, and my hand once again draws near it. *I want to take off its lid, but not because its decorations are enticing. I want to open her jar to end this. I want them all gone: Retjar, Ulo, and now Pandora. I just want to take off its lid and end this tale, and have all these demons leave me alone.*

I think of my duty to Prometheus, and then take my hand away. *But Cruz? She's going after Cruz?* I muffle my consternation, lest I betray the feelings I have for him, but Pandora sees right through this and continues.

"You bond so well with human friends, and you bonded really well with this one," she says. "You only knew him an hour or so, but that's all a god like yourself needs. You are his *friend*, Dion! And he'll never forget the night you stumbled into his gas station, half naked and helpless. He's going to start living from this point forward, and he owes it all to you."

Pandora shakes her head.

"But you fall in love with your human friends so quickly that you never bother to see their whole story," she says. "You see them when they're laughing, you see them when they're drinking and dancing, but that's about it. You like to leave right before the dawn comes, right before real life creeps back in."

I don't like where this is headed, but Pandora continues regardless.

"And you don't really know Cruz," she says. "This is not to say you wouldn't do anything for him. You threw him a great party, and maybe if you ever return you'd set him up with a girl, the potential love of his life?"

I nod that I'd do that, and she has me.

"Like I said, you don't know Cruz," says Pandora, belaboring her point. "He wasn't in the mood for girls this evening, and he'll never be in the mood. Unbeknownst to you, your best friend prefers the other gender."

Of course.

"Don't worry if you missed the signs," she says. "Cruz barely knows it himself. Before you he's not had a single friend, let alone a relationship."

I think of Cruz, and realize that he's even more alone than I'd previously thought.

"You remember that half-completed tattoo on his chest?" asks

A TALE OF THE HIGHWAY

Pandora.

I do remember it. The river of forgetfulness.

"We called it *Lethe* in our day,[95] says Pandora, "but the story of that tattoo began when he left his home. His brothers were growing more psychotic by the day, so it was a good thing he left. Regardless, he sought acceptance elsewhere, or at the very least *safety*, though whatever he found came with a price."

Pandora shakes her head in an overt display of forced disgust.

"That set of his wasn't just a bunch of kids playing hoodlums, it was a real street gang. They called themselves the *Cholos Norte*. They promised him protection, acceptance and more,[96] and even gave him the river Lethe on his chest. The Cholos Norte give that half to all their initiates, but the other half is to be earned."

I look in the rearview mirror and see that Pandora's eyes are a little heavier with blood than usual. She looks like she's tearing up, or at least pretending to do so.

"Cruz's initiation was straightforward," says Pandora. "He simply had to beat up another child in his school, one whom they targeted for being—*different* than most."

---

[95] Lethe was a river in Hades that the shades of the dead would drink so that they'd forget their lives back on Earth. Some say that there was a river, Mnemosyne, that would help the dead not only remember everything, but obtain omniscience. Who knows what was really there—everyone has their mythos, even gods.

[96] Gangs often lure their recruits in with more than just the promise of protection: they can make for a surrogate family. There was a tale of an inmate who refused to join his prison's chapter of the Aryan Nation. They told him he was all but a dead man without them there to protect him from the other gangs, but he still refused. You know what eventually got him to join? Birthday cards. His family on the outside had forgotten him, and he got forty-two signed birthday cards from his soon-to-be Aryan brothers. He joined the next day, and quickly adhered to their depraved agenda, all because of a few birthday cards.

Pandora wipes her eyes, and if she's just pretending to cry, she's doing a very convincing job.

"The child they targeted was quite like Cruz himself: no real family, and no friends for that matter," says Pandora. "And like Cruz, this child was also a homosexual."

The blood wells up in her eyes, and she starts to shake.

"The Cholos Norte attacked the child as he was walking through an alley," she says. "They softened him up with a few punches and threw him against the dumpster. They then formed a circle and allowed Cruz inside, and then told your friend that if he truly loved the Cholos Norte, he would beat this boy."

Pandora shakes her head.

"And Cruz did as he was told, make no mistake about that, Dion," she says. "What the Crows did to you, Cruz did to this child. The only difference was that Cruz's victim didn't have your godlike powers of indifference."

Pandora simulates strikes in the backseat. I think of the Crows' beatings and wonder how much worse it would have been if I couldn't just dismiss them out of hand. *The Crows hurt me, but only my body.*

"Fortunately, the child lost consciousness quickly," says Pandora. "And Cruz walked away, ready to join his new family. But they pushed him back, because he wasn't yet done."

Pandora's eyes well up with blood again, and I see a coagulated drop growing on her lower eyelid, threatening to burst open at any moment.

"They told Cruz he needed to keep beating this boy, *this friendless, effeminate boy* lying unconscious, lying helpless. They wanted Cruz to kill the child, Dion. Kill him, right there by the dumpster."

The coagulated drop is about to break open, but she catches it with one of her long, chipped fingernails.

"Blood in, blood out," she says, wiping the drop away. "Some human families demand nothing less."

Pandora stretches her arm out.

"Your friend Cruz didn't kill the child, Dion," she says, changing her tone slightly. "He's not a sociopath, not a killer, and the full reality of *what he was not* hit him at that very moment. At that moment Cruz knew the truth: that it was better to walk the world alone, to do nothing, to *be* nothing, than to ever do anything like that again."

I know that Cruz made the right choice. The cost was a life of loneliness, but still: better to live in Purgatory than to become a demon and rule Hell.

"As expected, his once-promised family turned on him immediately," says Pandora. "They each took their turn beating him, punching him into unconsciousness, and then kicking him some more. They eventually left him there next to his former victim, broken and bruised, with a half-tattoo and the solitude that he had chosen."

Pandora looks at me through the rearview mirror, and her eyes begin welling up with blood again.

"They both lived, Cruz and the boy," she says. "Do you think this a noble ending to this tale?"

I think for a moment, and then shake my head.

"No," I say. "Though perhaps given the circumstances, it's an acceptable one."

"If that were the end, it would be acceptable indeed," says Pandora. "But it didn't end up like that. They both recovered, but the victim killed himself six months later."

Pandora rubs one of her cracked fingernails over the rim of her left eye and then touches her cheek. The blood leaves a stain in the shape of a teardrop.

The Cholos Norte still got their murder in the end. Blood in, blood out. All for one, and none for all.

/***/

"Cruz was OK, actually, until *you* walked through his door," she says. "He was living like a ghost, doing nothing and being nothing, and it actually served him well. You deliberately brought him in close to yourself, and now he's a part of your tale, and here we are."

Here we are, all right. And now, the threat that will tie this personal coercion together.

"You need to keep driving this vehicle forward until this road ends, and then drive some more," she says. "If you stray off this path, even slightly, I am going to visit Cruz in his dreams. I'll first show myself an unremembered shadow of his victim, and gradually as a full-on likeness of the boy that he killed. I will make sure that Cruz revisits his past *every single night*, Dion. Each time Cruz closes his eyes he'll see *this boy*: battered and bruised, humiliated, sent on a path to his grave, alone and unloved."

Pandora laughs dryly and without pleasure.

"You came into Cruz's life this evening, and opened his heart to a world of emotion," says Pandora. "If you stray from this path, I will make sure these emotions will be to his unending torment."

Pandora looks ahead.

"Two monsters will be waiting for us when this road ends: *Scylla* and *Charybdis*," says Pandora. "Poseidon bent the rules to allow his creatures to appear, but they will be there, and they will take this entire vehicle and dispose of Prometheus accordingly. Do you understand this?"

I reluctantly nod that I do. I won't necessarily follow her directives, but I understand her words.

"And do you understand that if you stray from this path, even slightly, I will haunt Cruz's dreams?" she asks. "And that I will do this consistently, for the entire four decades he has left on this earth?"

I nod that I understand,[97] though my understanding turns to anger when I think of her hurting Cruz.

She notices this, and remains quiet while I drive on in a silent fury.

/***/

I finally settle down, and Pandora speaks at the precise moment when I become calm.

"I don't enjoy threatening your mortal friend any more than I enjoyed breaking that strike," says Pandora. "But we are stewards of this world, and must act accordingly."

"Stewards?"

"Yes, stewards of the world we've inherited," says Pandora. "We—gods. We were sent to guide this world, to guide these humans. These volatile, violent and wondrous humans, whose base nature you've seen in the Yanomami and the Moriori,[98] whose full nature you'll see if you

---

[97] Pandora's employing the technique of clarity here, one often mocked by those who don't understand its purpose. A lawyer might ask a coroner: *When the deceased victim got to you, did he have a pulse?* Self-evident questions like these are often ridiculed out of context, but these statements lay the foundation to prove one's case beyond *a shadow of a doubt*. I believe Pandora is repeating these words primarily to control the argument, but she is also ensuring her threats are clear, and letting me know—beyond a shadow of a doubt—that she will act upon them.

[98] In speaking of the Moriori, Pandora was referring to a failed experiment of the gods on the Chatham Islands of New Zealand. I didn't include this in the

walk through any city."

Pandora smiles, a genuine smile, free of any cautionary undertones.

"And I truly mean it when I call them wondrous," says Pandora. "We all marvel at their power, all of us."

"It doesn't seem like that," I say. "At the very least, Retjar doesn't seem too fond of humanity."

"Retjar's the exception," she says. "The Crows are demons, and demons aren't too fond of anyone. But I promise you, Dion, the gods who sent the Crows know what humankind can do. We *all* know the potential humanity wields, and that it's a potential far greater than our own. So we are their stewards—overlords at times, but ultimately their stewards."

Pandora looks back at the place holding Prometheus.

"He stole the fire so long ago," says Pandora. "And now he's returned to bring more than just fire. He's bringing *power*, enough to coat the entire world in the grey substance."

---

main narrative due to the fact that I'd already mentioned the Amazon's Yanomami, and didn't want to appear as if I was condemning indigenous peoples as a whole. But in short, the Moriori were a group of pre-Māori people who migrated to a cold and incredibly inhospitable set of islands in New Zealand. The inhospitable conditions of these isles were actually due to the workings of Poseidon, who felt that if he sent the right currents around these islands, they would prove unsuitable for crops, and this would lead to a precivilization culture of cooperation and peace amongst its inhabitants. It worked at first: the Moriori developed a pacifist culture that avoided warfare and any kind of intratribal violence. Poseidon's experiment in cultivated pacifism failed soon after the European invasion, however. In 1835 a group of displaced Taranaki Māori hijacked a European ship and invaded the islands, and promptly began killing, enslaving and cannibalizing the peaceful inhabitants until the Moriori were all but exterminated. Today, there are no pureblooded Moriori in existence. Fascinating story, and it shows that gods like Poseidon did try to cultivate a different slant of humanity.

Here we are, the grey sludge.

"Will Prometheus bring this—substance?" I ask.

"He won't, at least not directly," says Pandora. "But he will bring humanity the power that will allow them to make it themselves."

I don't understand this, and Pandora takes a deep breath before continuing.

"I have presented the abstract and the personal," she says, "and I will now present *the truth*."

"The truth."

"Yes, the truth," says Pandora. "The truth of what's to come if you release Prometheus."

"The erasure," I say. "You're going to tell me about how this will happen. The grey sludge, the eradication."

"I am going to tell you everything," says Pandora. "I am going to tell you precisely what the grey substance is, the substance that Prometheus will unleash. And I am going to tell you how this grey substance will coat the earth, and extinguish every living thing in its wake."

/***/

"It will most likely be made in a lab, perhaps a century from now, or five centuries from now, or more," says Pandora. "This lab will be in one of the perfect cities that Prometheus' gift will bring about, made by technology that even the most skeptical scientist today might think of as magic."

Pandora stretches out her pale, thin fingers.

"The grey substance will come from an elegant fate, deadly in its simplicity, really," she says. "And it starts with something called *chirality*. Have you heard about this, Dion?"

I haven't, or at least I don't remember that I have. Pandora brings up her hands in front of her face.

"Organic molecules can twist one of two ways: left or right," she says, putting down her right hand. "Every living being on this earth has genetic material that twists *left*. No one knows why this is the case, and there might not be a reason. My own guess is that the first blocks of life *just happened* to turn left, and nothing has changed ever since. But whatever the circumstances, every living being, from plants to humans, from fleas to dinosaurs, have left-handed molecules as their blueprint. This is the way it is."

Pandora holds up her right hand again.

"Prometheus will enable humanity to move towards perfection, and he will do this by removing their limitations," she says. "He'll bring a world where anything and everything is possible. Poverty, war, disease and such things will become relics of the past. And *technology*? If someone can dream it, they'll be able to do it."

I think of the purple planet, right before its dissolution. *Dabron brought her denizens so close to perfection. So close.*

"One day a scientist will dream about the origins of life, and then want to recreate them," says Pandora. "And in Prometheus' unlimited world, this scientist will be successful."

Pandora puts down her hands and looks at the seat cover containing Prometheus.

"It may be *this* scientist that does it, or it may be someone else centuries hence," she says. "But after that inevitable moment, the world's days will be numbered, because someone *will* make the grey substance that you've seen in your dreams."

Pandora brings up her hands once more.

"It comes back to chirality, and again, quite elegantly so," says Pandora. "For on this fated day in Prometheus' unlimited world, the scientist will make a single-celled organism that is *right*-handed, and to give it a food source, will engineer this organism so that it can consume *left*-handed organic matter."

Pandora takes her right hand and places it over her left hand.

"Once consumed, this left-handed matter will be broken down and then reassembled as right-handed bacteria," she says, twisting her left hand around to match her right.

"A substance that turns its prey into itself," I say. "It will make more of itself, and then there will be more of it to search for more prey, which will in turn make even more of itself."

"Precisely," says Pandora. "It will take the right conditions of course: the right engineered organism, the right accidental contamination of the external world. But it will happen eventually, and this substance will consume the world."

I shake my head.

"Humanity will be able to contain it," I say. "We're talking about Prometheus' future, whereas *you* clearly stated, *anything and everything* will be possible. They'll be able to contain this substance."

Pandora listens to my words, and then grimaces.

"We've foreseen that humanity will not be able to contain this substance," says Pandora, taking no joy in her response. "This bacteria will move too fast, contaminate too quickly. No creature will be able to consume it, for its tissue will be a foreign substance. In fact, the bacteria will begin consuming whatever tries to consume it, even turning its predators into more of itself. No antibiotics will be able to stop it of course, and no wall will be able to keep it out. Any quarantined room will become a prison, and its inhabitants will starve."

I shake my head again in disbelief. *There's got to be a way.*

"They'll figure out something," I say. "They'll sterilize it. If it's contaminated a building, they'll burn the whole thing down."

"Then they'll have a burnt building, and colonies of the substance growing in the adjacent structures," says Pandora. "And what happens when it contaminates the ocean? Will they be able to burn that down as well?"

I think of the grey substance taking over Venelk's purple oceans, falling deeper and deeper into the Burkol Trench.

"Sometimes simple organisms can be quite hardy, and can live in a variety of environments," says Pandora. "This bacteria will work its way into the world's ecosystems, isolate them, take them over one by one. Like humans, but more so. Humans mold many of the world's ecosystems to their own liking, building cities, exploring the ocean in a submarine and so on. But this substance will creep into *every* area, take it over and grow unabated. It will grow until—"

Pandora spreads her hands apart and drops them neatly by her side.

"Erasure, eradication, nothingness," says Pandora. "At best a biological reset, where life starts anew with simple organisms, this time right-handed. But we have to take into account that this substance isn't photosynthetic, and might have no way of sustaining itself. It may subsist for quite a while consuming the remaining scraps of this world, and then cannibalizing its neighbors, but it too might die, leaving this world completely empty, just a rock, as barren as the moon above."

I take another look at the moon, so calm, so present—*so lifeless.* She's the salver of my wounds, my constant companion, but her white complexion belies an empty surface, and I imagine our satellite watching helplessly as her blue sibling slowly joins her ranks. *The earth becomes irreversibly sterile just like the moon, just like most every other place in this universe.*

"I don't buy it," I say, forcing myself to be skeptical. "What's your evidence?"

"Apollo," says Pandora.

"Apollo?"

"Apollo, god of the sun and so many other things, including oracles," says Pandora. "And just as he's always done when it came to foretelling the world's future, he spoke with all his oracles."

"He spoke with all his oracles," I say, still skeptical. "You want to destroy Prometheus because Apollo spoke with oracles."

"Apollo's oracles have been correct in predicting over 25,000 developments in human history," says Pandora. "And they all see this coming."

I shake my head, exaggerating my skepticism.

"You're making humanity pay a heavy price for a single prophecy," I say.

"A handful of oracles saw other things happening," says Pandora. "Twenty other fates in all, each with identical results: subatomic experiments gone awry, weather control mishaps, even occurrences born of time travel. None of these fates will be deliberate or malicious— acts of greed, war and so on—but they'll all have an equally *and completely* catastrophic end."

Pandora looks at the trunk.

"This is what we have foreseen," she says. "If you release Prometheus, humanity will light itself up for a few centuries, and then burn itself down, taking the whole planet with them. That is why you need to keep driving, Dion. Keep driving until you get close enough for

Scylla and Charybdis to take this vehicle, and Poseidon will take care of the rest."

/***/

I drive on, thinking of her arguments, and doing so logically. I first think of her abstract threat that began with the cold-weather hurricane in Greenland. Could this warning portend something real? I figure that there's one of two answers: that it was just a trick of the radio, or it's very real, and if I veer from this path a lot of innocent people will die. *If it's the former, there's no problem. If it's the latter there is one, so I can only think about that.*

Could I sacrifice a thousand innocent people to free Prometheus? A million or more? Won't those people be dead anyway a hundred years from now? Even if she punishes half the world, might it be worth it? *Millions died in the Great War, but now we have stainless steel corkscrews forevermore.* If I free Prometheus, humanity will get a lot more than a better wine key.

I think about this, and realize the foundation of my quandary doesn't make sense: I asked *myself* if I could sacrifice the innocent to free Prometheus, and *I* am sacrificing no one.

It's Pandora who placed the burden of these anonymous lives on my decisions, and she did so in order to force my hand. *It's she who will be sacrificing these lives, it's she who bears the responsibility.*

But that counterargument doesn't quite hold true with me either. If I was a vigneron unable to grow grapes due to corrupted soil, it wouldn't matter if it was I or Pandora who decided that this was his fate.

To an innocent murdered by another's decision, reasoned culpability counts for nothing.

I move on to think of the next argument, that of the personal. I did play a bigger part in this, and I do shoulder much of the responsibility. *I was the one who actively walked into Cruz's life, and showed him a glimpse of a god's power.*

This one is on me, though I figure that since it is, the response is on me as well. *Pandora first levied the threat, but I can make the first move. Vengeance is not in my nature, but if Pandora or anyone comes near him, it will be. I might need Sami on my side, but they'll leave Cruz alone.*

Hmmmm. We're getting somewhere, but we're not there yet. The abstract threat is an unresolved quandary, and the personal attack on Cruz is one that I can handle at least. But the third one, the *truth*? This will take some thought. It's a lot bigger than a single event, Cruz or myself. It could be everything.

/***/

"You're not certain of this future," I say, a few minutes later.

"Oh we are, Dion," says Pandora. "If we weren't, I'd be the first to tell you to turn this vehicle around."

"No you wouldn't," I say. "And you're not certain."

Pandora contemplates my words.

"All right," she says. "Tell me why I'm not."

"Because your oracles saw other fates," I say. "The *subatomic experiments gone awry, weather control mishaps, the occurrences born of time travel.*"

"That should strengthen my argument," says Pandora. "If humanity somehow manages to escape the grey fate, there's more catastrophic endings awaiting them. Eradication will happen one way or another."

"No it won't," I say. "If an idiosyncrasy of chirality is to be the world's end, every other fate would be moot. Every oracle would only see the grey substance, and nothing else. The oracles seeing other fates means that there's a chance that humanity will escape the grey substance, and that means there's a chance that humanity will escape *all* apocalyptic fates. You can't ignore this reality."

Pandora shakes her head dismissively.

"If Cruz were to jump in the ocean—"

"Don't bring up Cruz," I say. "Mention his name again and I'm stopping the car. Do whatever you want after that."

Pandora takes my threat in stride.

"If *your friend* were to jump in the ocean," says Pandora, "a part of the ocean filled with sharks, you'd tell him *Don't jump in the ocean, because of the sharks*. Now, by some miracle he might escape being eaten by the sharks, but he could drown, die of the cold, be stung to death by jellyfish, or countless other things. But you'd tell him *Don't jump in the ocean, because of the sharks*. That's the fate you worry about first and foremost, that's the fate that will happen. Your friend could spontaneously grow gills, and thrive in the water, but you don't take that into account. You tell him not to jump, because you *know* what is going to happen."

I think about these words for a moment.

"If I saw a cold ocean filled with sharks, I'd tell my friend not to jump," I say. "And I'd probably tell him not to jump *because* of the sharks."

"Then you see my point?"

"I see it," I say. "But it's incomplete."

"How so?"

"Because *I* would have to observe the ocean first," I say. "If all I knew about this ocean was from an oracle, an oracle who'd not even seen the water, *not even once*, I wouldn't know what to say to my friend."

"But it would give you pause," she says. "If every oracle you met prophesied destruction, it would give you pause."

"No it wouldn't, because I shouldn't be listening to oracles in the first place," I say. "Look around you, Pandora. Look at everything humanity has brought to this world. It all came from thought, from observation, from trial and error. None of it came from oracles. Maybe Prometheus' fire was but a single truth: *That humanity should stop listening to oracles and start listening to the universe. At the very least, they should start listening to themselves.*"

The Perfect Code

I drive on in silence and Pandora allows this, and soon disappears completely, leaving only her jar. *She's left me alone with my thoughts and humanity's problems, each moment getting her closer to their goal and no closer to mine, whatever either might be.* I think of the Crows and their bodily assaults, and Pandora with her words aimed at my sense of reason.

Could they be right? I know their means are nefarious, but that doesn't necessarily correlate to an unjust end. If Cruz was indeed dead-set on jumping into the ocean with sharks, I'd consider tripping him, drugging him, tricking him or anything else, just so he won't take that leap. I'd probably do the same if a set of oracles warned me of this, even if I hadn't seen the water in the first place.

But Pandora's resolution can't be it. My previous self must have known what he was doing.

And my previous self didn't seem to be overly concerned with rebutting Pandora's arguments, nor the Crows' for that matter. All my previous self seemed to care about is me finding the code to open the trunk.

I think back to Retjar's words before my last beating, how he mocked my *little earthbound oracle* who spoke of my *beloved numerology*.

It was a high price to pay for a little hint, but it's a start at least, something to get me away from Pandora's unresolvable arguments. It's something, and I've got to give it a shot. I take up the brick of CDs, rifle through the titles, and halfway through, there it is: *Numerology: Mysticism and Reality*.

Well, Pandora, maybe there is one oracle that's worthy of my attention after all.

/***/

I put in the CD, and queue it up. Dr. Shaw begins speaking immediately:

Numerology: Mysticism and Reality

Numerology is an ancient concept, and at its heart it's a belief in the divine and mystical relationship between numbers and our own world. A numerologist might try to glean meaning in the numerical equivalent of letters in a name, while another numerologist might study the very real phenomenon of prime numbers.

But ultimately, whether you're studying the coincidental or the practical, the raw materials of numerology are unchanging and inherently quantifiable *numbers*, and this separates the concept from most other forms of mysticism.

Let's take High Priest Sargon as an example, who found his truth in the form of a talking lion, and found it while under the influence of strange herbs. Let's compare Sargon to a numerologist who finds strange anomalies surrounding the number *1729*, and argues that these happenings are due to more than just coincidence.

We can most likely attribute Sargon's lion to a hallucination from the herbs he'd taken previously, and we could argue that the sleep deprivation probably didn't detract from the illusion. Could the talking lion have been real? It's unlikely, but whatever the case, Sargon's experience isn't replicable. Like most branches of mysticism, the only evidence is the mystic's word, take it or leave it.

Now let's consider the numerologist. The anomalies she finds surrounding the number 1729 have an observable, replicable basis, and whether you believe her words or not, she can show you precisely what she has seen.

Numerology is not science, and the numerologist's gleanings from 1729 might hold no more value than the words coming from Sargon's lion. But still, we can *observe* her reasoning just as she saw it, and this gives numerology a place in this world, or at least deserves it a second look.

Plato's Unchanging Ideal

Let's first take a look at the reality beneath numbers, and instead of exploring the arcane nature of the number 1729, let's start with the more approachable fact that *2 + 2 = 4*.

St. Augustine called numbers a *universal language*, "offered by the deity to humans as confirmation of the truth," and though their origins are unknown, we can definitely argue that they are something of a universal language.

Take any culture around the world, from any point in history, and they should all ultimately agree that *2 + 2 = 4*.

Take an intelligent species *from another planet*, and they should understand that *2 + 2 = 4*.

Numbers are indeed a universal language, and an unchanging one. There are no number dialects, no archaic expressions. They're numbers, and like Plato, Pythagoras argued that mathematical concepts were *more* classifiable and immutable than the world around us.

This, in a sense, gives numbers a super-reality. You cannot touch *2 + 2 = 4* like you would a stone pillar, but if the world's empires grow and fall one hundred times over, *2 + 2* will still equal *4*.

/***/

Shaw goes on to speak of numerology as a whole, and talks of the somewhat apocryphal relationship between numbers and letters, and the unchanging truth of Pi. He speaks of quantum mechanics and geometry, of alchemy and the kabbalah.

He then mentions *perfect numbers*, and I feel an extra sense of importance in his words.

Perfection. Here we go.

Dr. Shaw talks about how perfect numbers are those that are equal to the sum of their divisors, like *six* being the sum of *three*, *two* and *one*. He then talks of Philo of Alexandria, who attempted to fuse Greek and Jewish philosophies and claimed that perfect numbers were related to the beginning of this earth, because the earth was made in six days, and the moon's cycle is twenty-eight days, also a perfect number.

Dr. Shaw warns his listeners that they shouldn't necessarily take the mysticism surrounding perfect numbers as fact, and I don't. *But there's something very real here: a message my old self sent to my current self. I knew my memory was going to be erased, so I sent a message deep in Dr. Shaw's words. Numerology might not contain facts, but there's a truth here, a truth that might forever change this world.*

DION

/***/

I drive on, calculating numbers in my head. I quickly come to the realization that my mathematical skills aren't exactly divine, but I know that the answer is somewhere in my long-term memory, and I keep at it.

While I'm contemplating this, the land around me flattens out, emptying itself with every moment. The farmland is gone, as are the interspersed forests, but I don't feel like I'm in a desert either. *There's life here, quite a bit of it, it's just not apparent.*

I look forward and see a flash of gold: Hermes' winged helmet as he flies about in this earthly plane. *Pan told me the messenger of the gods would be here, and here he is.*

I don't have the message yet, though I'm getting there. I open the moonroof to take another look at my constant companion, and wonder if the perfection in the number twenty-eight is in any way related to her cycles. *It might be, it might not be, but whatever the case, it doesn't matter. Twenty-eight won't help me open the trunk, because I need four digits and—*

I get a glimmer of my long-term memory, just a flash, and I understand the message I sent to myself. I don't know the code, but I know where it lies.

I smile and take in the air around me, which is humid and salty. I think about where I am, and think about my first command: *Drive until this road ends, and then drive some more.*

I'm driving towards the ocean. This whole time they've wanted me to drive this car into the ocean, where Poseidon's monsters Scylla and Charybdis will wait to extinguish Prometheus' fire once and for all.

/***/

For the first time in my journey, time is not on my side. *I know what I'm supposed to find, I just need more time to think about it.*

I think of my original self, so sure of what I was doing when I initially freed Prometheus. I then think about my tormentors, Pandora and the Crows, so devious in their methods but just as sure of what they want.

I need time, that's all. Time to allow my semidivine mind and its less-than-mortal mathematical abilities to think about a few numbers.

I can't stop the car, because the Crows will catch me and send me back to Hell until I forget about the numbers, and Pandora will surely argue with me until I once again forget my identity.

I acted when I first freed Prometheus, and it's time I act again. The gods have resorted to drastic measures to stop me. It might be time for some drastic measures myself.

/***/

"Hold tight," I tell Prometheus.

I don't know how he'll *hold tight* in the ether of the trunk, but he sends back an affirmative thump in response. He knows I'm doing the right thing.

I look at my front seat and remember that though Pandora may have disappeared, she left her jar.

"It's going to be a little bumpy, and this is a little off-topic," I say. "But if we break her little box of sin wide open, can you handle it?"

Prometheus gives a confident knock. *With his guidance, we'll be able to handle anything.*

I take the jar and place it down on the gas pedal. I then take a bottle of wine, possibly my last. I don't really care what type it is, because *all wine is a gift from the gods*, and I more than anyone should know that. I take the corkscrew, and its stainless steel born of millions of dead souls embeds itself easily in the top. I open it with one hand still on the wheel, and then stand up through the moonroof's opening. I toast the night sky, and toast the moon, dead and lifeless on her surface, but giving so much life to me and to this world. I then look at Hermes, a glittering speck flying in the distance.

"Tell Pan to come!" I yell through the howling night air. "And tell him to bring everyone, and I mean *everyone*!"

Hermes understands this, and moves so quickly back towards the station that he seems to disappear instantly. I take one more drink of the wine, and it's good. I then push the wheel hard to the right, and the vehicle veers off the road, bumpy at first, and then shaking with the force of a small earthquake. There's another bump, and then a big one, and then the car is airborne, twisting in all the ways a car should not. I see the ground coming near me and I think of all those I've met on my journey, the good ones at least. I think of Plato, Socrates and Aristotle. I think of the Pan in my dreams, an intrepid little goat. I think of the Pan on this earthly plane, an old friend unremembered, and I think of his friend Sami. I think of Ari, whom I love as *Ariadne*—who was sent to Hell by her own indomitable feelings of love, by emotions so powerful that if allowed to start over again, she might end up in the same place. I think of Venelk, and the bond we shared thousands, if not millions or even *billions* of years after she stopped existing. I then think of Cruz, living his life for the first time this evening. I realize with my banished memory that he and I are the same age. In a sense, Cruz and I have grown up together, and we're childhood friends.

I think of all these people, spirits and gods and how much I'd like to see them again—in this world or the next.

A TALE OF THE HIGHWAY

The Garden

My consciousness is pulled back with the impact, but it's not dragged down to Hell as it was before, nor is it flung out towards the purple planet. My soul is pulled back through *time*, and I find myself surrounded by the entire world moving in reverse. I can sense everything all at once, the entirety of human history regressing to where it once was, with paintings melting back into their component colors, and stone carvings gathering marble around them until they're amorphous boulders. I then see the painted colors fade back into their original form as minerals, clay and plants, and I see the statues' boulders go back into the quarry where they'd been born.

It's disquieting to see beauty deconstructed and decomposed like this, but not everything I see is bad. Ruined cities become unsacked before turning back into dirt, and though pyramids fall brick by brick, the slaves that assembled these monuments are freed, and one by one they leave their chains in the sand.

Warriors disengage from each other, put down their weapons and then revert to a childlike existence.

I notice that nature too is reverting, rapidly becoming wild and unruly. I feel vines growing over me, and more than anything else I want to rest. I'm in an unconscious dream, but I still want to rest. To stay in this moment before the world's troubles began, but not before the world began itself. To stay here now, to close my eyes under these vines and dream further still, to contemplate history before me, wonders and terrors, incredible joy and unimaginable grief, and all of it filled with limitless potential.

/***/

I wake up in soft grass, with the vines now underneath me to form a soft bed. It's day, and I see the sun through the swaying trees above. I stand up and the vines retreat beneath me, waiting until I choose to rest again, for now making way so that I might walk unimpeded. I see green in all directions, but not the unruly overgrowth that conceals thorns or poisonous insects. *I'm surrounded by life, but not the kind of life born of competition, the life that wants to take something from me, or warns me to leave it alone.* There's nothing here that will bite, nothing here that will sting in self-defense, nothing that will take something from me so that it might further its own position. This is the kind of green that I can tread on with bare feet.

I feel a presence behind me and wonder if it's Pan in his goat form. I turn around to see an oversized wolf, and it looks familiar. It's much bigger than a wolf should be, but it exudes no sense of danger. In fact, it projects just the opposite. Its fur is soft, its eyes are kind, and though its gleaming white fangs are sharp, the canine shows them for beauty and not predation.

The wolf turns its massive head to its left and grabs onto one of the vines growing up a tree. The canine bites onto a dangling cluster of glowing fruits, and the clutch falls off the vine quite easily. The wolf presents them to me, and I notice that the fruits are glowing with an iridescent gold that expands from its center outwards, as if each piece has been kissed by its very own star.

I take one of these translucent grapes, and it fills me with joy. Perhaps not taste, because I may still be dreaming, but joy nonetheless. I look back at the tree to see that the vine has already regrown its fruit, waiting patiently to be taken once more.

/***/

The wolf leaves the area and beckons me to follow. I do, and see other animals in this place, from giraffes eating the leaves at the top of tall trees, to shiny dragonflies perched lazily on their backs. I see predators too: hyenas and jackals nestled amongst cattle, and stinging wasps sipping nectar from a group of flowers.

I even see animals that I don't recognize from my long-term memory: big, furred creatures that paw at trees with long nails, and small, shy creatures lurking under them that resemble horses. I also see the shadows of dinosaurs looming on the horizon, their enormous forms casting a gentle silhouette against the sun.

I walk with the wolf for several moments, or perhaps days, and we soon come to a covered garden, its shape made by a canopy of trees. There's light inside, so much light, but it's not overpowering. It invites me in, and I walk into the garden side by side with the wolf, which I now recognize.

The creature beside me is Cerberus, the once three-headed hound of Hell.

This benign animal might be a previous incarnation of the monster, or some small part of it shorn off and then cleansed by the light. I can't explain how a creature so mild could turn into something so ferocious and unforgiving, but the connection to the terrifying behemoth that met its end in the grey sludge is undeniable.

Perhaps nothing is pure evil—not even demons.

/***/

I see Pan in his goat form chewing grass on a mound in the distance, and beside him is a thick brown-skinned man, with eyes shining like jewels. The man notices me, and beckons me forth. I approach, and Pan the goat bleats at my arrival. The wolf lies down beside me, and I feel compelled to sit down as well. I do, but before I reach the ground vines grow beneath me and take the shape of something like a chair.

"I'm so glad you could make it, Dion," says the man. "It's rare that someone gets to see this."

"It's a shame that they don't," I say. "Where are we?"

"We're nowhere, really," says the man. "This garden doesn't really exist. Well, it does and it doesn't, much like the other places you've seen. Do you understand what I mean by this?"

I do. I think of the sludge-covered Hell, real in the moment but visited only through nightmares, and I think of the purple planet, perhaps as real as it once had been, but now a lifeless rock, dead for countless generations.

I then think of the real world above, existing and in grave danger while I sit here amongst the dreamt grass.

"Can you tell me the code?" I ask. "I'm sure you know my problem."

"I know your problem, Dion," says the brown-skinned man. "And it is not the code."

"I don't understand."

"Your code, your perfect code, you already know this," says the man. "It's buried deep within your subconscious, so deep that they couldn't erase it along with your memory. Now that you know its trail, your subconscious is retrieving it, even as we speak."

The man points upwards, and I see flashes of lightning set against the canopy above us. It's not the lightning of my father, and not meant to intimidate or harm.

"Those are your neuronal connections at work," says the brown-skinned man. "Your mortal mind finding those four digits while you sleep, and I assure you that you'll have them when you awake."

"That's good," I say. "But you say you *know my problem*. What's my problem?"

"The question of whether or not to release Prometheus," says the brown-skinned man. "Whether to listen to yourself, or the impassioned and rather substantiated arguments of those who torment you."

"All right," I say. "Which path should I take, then?"

"I said I know your problem, but I can't answer it," says the man. "The question of releasing Prometheus is for you to decide, and you alone."

All right. Well, that makes sense but—

"Why am I here?" I ask.

The man smiles.

"The question should be *Why are we here*, Dion."

"*We?*"

"I have brought you to this garden to tell you why *we* have come to this earth, to this universe," says the man. "And by *we* I mean *gods*. I am going to tell you why the gods are here."

/***/

The man raises his hands and vines travel up through the ground to make a hole in the canopy above. Rather than see the sun, however, we see the endless night sky: stars in greater clarity than I'd ever seen before, even when I had left for the purple planet.

"The universe is a vast, cold place," he says. "And inconceivably inhospitable. Every ounce of it wants to crush life into oblivion, and it will do that given a moment's chance.

"Life is like a small fish living in a water droplet," he says. "A water droplet dangling from a stick suspended above an endless desert. So fragile, so easily assaulted. So much could destroy it, from a sandstorm to a faint breeze."

"Earth is just a rock coated with a thin shell of gas," I say. "Not much more protected than the fish, in the grand scheme of things."

"You understand," says the man. "But I'm not speaking negatively here, of life's weakness and fragility. I'm speaking of life's incredible *value*. Think of the fish in the droplet of water. It's surrounded by lifeless sand, and that makes the fish incredibly important. For though the desert is overpowering, there's a lot of it, and it's not that rare. And in the universe there's a lot of cold space, but only a few pinpricks of life."

"A few small diamonds suspended in a sea of burning coal."

"Yes," says the man. "But back to the fish in the water droplet. Imagine that once every million years, for just one day, that fish can think, and that fish can speak."

I consider this for a moment.

"What value would that fish hold to the universe?" asks the brown-skinned man.

"The fish's value would be quite high," I say. "Even though it lives for a single day."

"Now imagine that fish is so clever that it figures out how to extend its day," says the brown-skinned man. "It even figures out how to leave its droplet and explore the surrounding sand, and maybe one day see what's beyond the desert. What is its value then?"

"Beyond measure," I say. "Without the fish, the desert may as well not even exist. You might say the same for what lies beyond it."

The brown-skinned man smiles, and something about him now looks familiar.

"As rare as that hypothetical fish might be, humanity is rarer still," he says. "It took this earth hundreds of million years to abet life, and then another three *billion* years to make the leap to complex, multicellular life. Another half billion years or so, and then for one day in the grand scheme of this universe, *humanity exists*, a species with unlimited potential, a species that might not just see what's beyond the desert, but might one day go there."

I think of the universe as an incredibly large circle scattered with tiny specks representing its stars. I visualize how many of those stars hold planets that can support life, and the majority of them fade away. I think of the remainder, and consider how many hold beings that are self-aware, and most all of those fade away in turn.

"There are others out there, but their scarcity underscores just how exceptional humankind is," I say. "Set against the backdrop of a cold, lifeless universe, humanity's value is immeasurable."

The brown-skinned man looks to the heavens, and I see a ball of light coming down towards us. The ball splinters into countless pieces, and each of those splinter into countless more as they approach the ground, fading into spirits as they reach every corner of the earth.

"We were sent to this world when humanity arose," says the brown-skinned man. "We don't know who sent us, but we know that we were meant to guide humanity."

"You're speaking of gods," I say.

"In a loose term, yes, I speak of gods," says the brown-skinned man. "We reached the peak of our influence a few thousand years ago, when humanity called us that: *gods*."

Pan the goat bleats, and I shake my head in disbelief.

"If we were sent to guide humanity," I say, "why all the infighting?"

The brown-skinned man nods his head at the question, and his eyes gleam in the starlight. *Something about him is rather familiar, but I can't quite think of it.*

"We were sent to guide humanity," he says, "but we couldn't agree on the end to which they should be guided. Some believe this discordance is part of the plan of those who sent us. In any case, our disagreements led to a mythology filled with pettiness and bickering. As our influence waned amongst the humans, the frequency of our fighting did not, but we did clarify our squabbles by picking sides."

"A civil war," I say. "Fought between dying gods."

"It's a civil war, all right, but we're not dying," says the brown-skinned man. "We still exist, and will continue to do so as long as humanity does the same. It's just that humanity doesn't *listen* to us like they used to, so we simply have to be a bit more clever in our points of influence. We might act through a phenomenon of weather, or might appear as a ghost. Pandora, as I'm sure you're aware, visits just the right person and says just the right thing, all in a dream."

"She visits the people she wants and says what she wants," I say, thinking of Cruz. "But I wouldn't say that she visits *dreams*. Everything she touches turns into a nightmare."

"Yes, unfortunately, you're correct in that regard," says the brown-skinned man, his eyes downcast. "Fear is an incredible method of influence, and she employs it just as well as any of the monsters."

"Monsters?"

The man laughs gently at my naïveté.

"Monsters used to be gods, or rather beings just like us, sent to guide humanity," says the man. "They've chosen to guide through fear, lurking in the night and showing themselves as haunted spirits, bogeymen, vampires and the like."

"If Pandora's not a monster," I say, thinking of her terrifying threats and her eyes rimmed with blood, "she's pretty close."

"Indeed," says the man. "But I'm here to speak of humanity, and the choices of gods such as yourself, not monsters, dreams or nightmares."

Gods and monsters, dreams and nightmares. That's it. This brown-skinned man is in a dream now, but I saw his monstrous self in a nightmare.

"So if there's a civil war, the gods must have two sides," I purport. "I've seen plenty from the one side: those who rule through fear, and themselves fear Prometheus. But what about the other side? Who are they?"

Pan the goat bleats.

"You've already seen a few," says the brown-skinned man, looking at Pan. "But know that there are others who are hoping you succeed in your task. The side of fear has more, but you're not alone."

There are demons roaming this earth, but there are gods who will help. There are monsters terrorizing humanity, but there must also be guardian angels who love humankind unconditionally. Socrates said wherever there is reason, there is light, but I can take his words further: there is always hope. It may come from truth, or it may have come from Pandora's jar, but there is always hope.

/***/

The brown-skinned man raises his right hand and vines pop up on the far wall of the forest and gently pull a set of trees aside to show another hidden garden, a small place. Inside are a woman and a man, both naked, and they are sitting underneath a tree filled with doves. They are listening to another being standing beside them, a being much like the brown-skinned man in front of me. This man is thinner and lighter-skinned than my companion, but his eyes still shine like jewels as he speaks to the humans beneath him.

I recognize him, and my dreamt heart skips a beat, and then sinks.

Crows and doves, demons and angels. It can't be—it just can't.

"That's—"

"Don't mention the name of his earthbound counterpart," interrupts the brown-skinned man. "And don't mention mine. It will sully what we have down here."

I nod my head that I understand.

"But you may call us by the name we hold down here," says the brown-skinned man. "The man you see giving wisdom to humanity is Rajter, *Rajter the Blessed*."

I look at this being sharing his wisdom, and I try to connect him with Retjar on the earthly plane above. I can't connect the two, even though they're clearly cut from the same cloth. This being is the polar opposite of Retjar the Damned—no one is further from my earthly tormentor than Rajter the Blessed now before me.

/***/

I think about the Crows' two selves for a moment, or perhaps years, and about how they came to be. Are these two before me reflections? Souls split in two?

Perhaps such things have no meaning here, and perhaps they don't require one.

"I want to tell you about this place," says the brown-skinned man. "This garden. If you recall, I said that it both *exists* and *doesn't*. Does this make sense to you?"

I nod that I do, and think of the purple planet, its past so real to me but now empty, eradicated for countless generations. My guide considers my dreamt thoughts, and shakes his head.

"It's not quite like that," says the brown-skinned man. "The purple planet existed, but this place never did. This garden is what we gods imagined the world to be like before we arrived, when we were just beams of energy pulsing towards this earth, waiting to fade into spirits."

"A perfect place," I say. "Perfection in a garden."

"Perfection and naïveté," he responds. "For if the world had been like this, perhaps we would not need to be sent."

I take another look at Rajter lending the humans his truth, and I can't help but wonder why this world never came into being—or rather, into *fruition*.

"Perhaps our naïve fantasies served a purpose," I say. "Perhaps this garden represents an ideal to strive for."

"Perhaps," he says. "Some might say this is just an illusion, a fairy tale that can never be achieved. Some might say that humanity can far surpass this ideal."

I think about the purple planet, once containing splendor that the two humans sitting in the garden most likely can't even imagine.

"Those who sent us gave us choices, Dion," says the brown-skinned man. "Choices have defined what has happened, from our arrival to the earthly plane of the present that you see above."

"So I must make my own choice," I say. "Whatever choice I make will be the correct one, and will be truth."

He nods in agreement.

"My name is Olu," he says. "*Olu the Enlightened*. And I have shared all that I can. Now it's your time to return, for your world needs you more than this place."

I feel myself being pulled back, or rather *forward* through time. Great triumphs and incredible sorrow both resume their place in this world, and both hit me with equal measure. Colors join each other and become beautiful paintings, boulders shed themselves of stone until they become statues. Dirt becomes cities, cities that become sacked and then rebuilt again. Pyramids grow on the backs of slaves, and children grow up to hone their physiques and become warriors. They then meet on a battlefield and hack each other to bits.

I cast my eyes upwards into the cold universe from whence the gods inexplicably came. I know it's a desert, sand stretching to the horizon with every grain holding the potential to end us forevermore. *But both humanity and the gods can feel, and the sand cannot. An entire galaxy devoid of life can't feel a fraction of what a single child experiences in a single moment. Our experiences give us value, and that makes us worth it.*

The First Party

I wake up alive and surprisingly unbroken, my body thrown from the vehicle into a small dune. It may have been a soft landing, or it may have been the moonlight healing me while I slept—but I am whole, and I stand up without difficulty. I turn around to see that the vehicle's roof is crumpled but it's upright, and more or less whole as well. I figure after it threw me it rolled, but landed on its wheels.

I approach the vehicle cautiously, and see Pandora's jar in front of it, broken in two pieces and completely empty save for a single glittering jewel lying in its base. I pick up the gem, and it fills me with courage. I hear thunder coming from my right, and turn to see an incoming storm.

Pandora's broken jar is not my concern now.

I look away from the storm and see the ocean behind me, its water roiling, and tendrils flailing about on the shore. I look closer and see that they're not tendrils, but Scylla's six necks, each one waiting to clamp Prometheus in her jaws before throwing him into Charybdis's whirlpool beside her.

Poseidon's monsters are powerful, but they're still powerless without me. Scylla can't reach far enough to grab the vehicle, so she just flails about.

I turn away from Poseidon's monsters and turn to face the lightning, the storm of my father approaching me. The wind alone nearly knocks me over.

He can knock me down, but I owe him nothing. My father Zeus birthed me, and then vanished. I owe him nothing.

I walk behind the vehicle and the trunk is still there, waiting to be opened. The keypad is still there as well, without a single scratch.

Hephaestus might hide himself from the world, but the things he makes are incredible.

I give the trunk a thump, and Prometheus thumps back in return. I ask him if he's ready, and he thumps back that he is.

He was ready ever since he first glimpsed the garden I just saw. It gave him the idea to bring about something just as perfect, perhaps even better.

Speaking of perfect—

I enter an *eight*, and then a *one*, and then a *two*. I'm about to enter the last number but I can't help but pause, to savor the moment right before the world changes. *The final shiver in a cold cave before Prometheus brought the first fire. The thinker right before he realizes that the earth revolves around the sun. An explorer in our future, the moment before she makes contact with a species not from our Earth.*

I savor this time for a moment too long, and it's a mistake. I'm distracted by the caw of a crow above, and when I look up my legs are pulled from under me. I'm dragged away from the vehicle, towards the storm brought by my father Zeus.

/***/

"You still won't listen, Dion," says Retjar, lightning breaking through the night behind him. "You still won't listen."

I can't move, but I can see Retjar and Ulo, the Beak and the Claws, the Damned and the Bludgeon, standing over me. The former's eyes are angry, the latter's are dead and cold. I try to think back to their counterparts with eyes shining like jewels, but I can't.

I don't know if there's a connection to those in the garden at all. The two above me are different entities entirely, demons born unto themselves.

"Pandora's tricks are great to settle trivial things," says Retjar. "Union strikes, the occasional battle and the like—events of no consequence. But when it really matters like it does now, they send us. We'll work on you and work on you and work on you until we *know* you'll do what's right. We might not get it the first time, or the second time, or the next session after that, but we'll keep at you until you see the truth. And now—"

Lightning flashes behind Retjar, and right as it does he snaps his fingers. The lightning freezes behind him, though I can still see it pulsing with energy.

"We just made a deal with Chronos," he says. "God of time. He doesn't normally take sides in these things, but we explained our plight and he made an exception, just for you."

The lightning pulses more behind him, spikes of the energy splintering off the main arm and forming their own branches. Ulo approaches, and Retjar kneels down to whisper in my ear.

"Chronos slowed the time around us until it's all but stopped," says Retjar. "So please understand that there will be no end to what we do until you see things our way. We'll not stop when you beg for mercy, and if you pass out and enter one of your belovedly lucid dreamworlds, we'll be here when you awake."

Ulo stretches his fingers, talons unfurling into outstretched claws.

"This is not a transgression, and we are beyond punishment," says Retjar. "This is your *world* now, your existence, your *entire universe*. We'll only stop when we *know* that you'll do the right thing, when we *know* you'll push that car into the ocean, so that Poseidon's monsters can do the rest."

Retjar shakes his head in disgust.

"You think you've visited Hell, but you've seen nothing of the sort," he says. "You've had mere dreams, and now it's time for a nightmare. No lessons, no avatars guiding you along your way. Just us, and the torment that we bring. And our torment—this will be the real Hell to its fullest extent, and it won't end until you see the truth."

Retjar smiles, and he points to Ulo, whose dead eyes are focused beyond me.

"Now, for what will be the last time, Dion," says Retjar. "Let's begin."

/***/

Nothing happens after this, and Retjar doesn't seem to understand why. He bides Ulo to begin striking me, but Ulo remains still. Retjar becomes livid at this and begins shrieking his indecipherable curses, but the Claws doesn't hear them. I muster my energy to look up, and then realize that my body is now free to move. I stand up to see Ulo still staring beyond me, and he's looking at the ocean. His eyes are open wide, and they hold an expression that I'd not thought possible from his kind. I've seen him as a Crow and demon both, but I've not seen him like this. His eyes are no longer cold, nor dead. They're quivering, and filled with emotion.

What I see in Ulo the Scraper's eyes is fear. Unadulterated, abject *fear*.

/***/

I turn around to see people, a crowd of people, their faces indistinguishable and blurred due to the time shift. They're all around us, and I see Retjar's time discrepancy weakening. It soon fades altogether, and I see them, all of them.

Pan got Hermes' message all right, and he brought everyone.

We're surrounded by humans—both familiar faces and quite a few that aren't. I see beer-helmeted Danny, Dany with one *n* and Will, Clark and Captain Jocko. Next to them are Lorenzo, Owen Elegant, El Macho Gordo and his masked friends. I see Whitecotton and the Gooch, Lateef and his poetess queen. I see Jay and Kim, and Howe next to his delivery truck, an ice-cold can of Asskicker in his hand.

Everyone seems to have brought friends as well, because it's a crowd, a full-on crowd.

Pan is there as well, and Sami the satyr is more furious than I've ever seen him, and about to charge. There are other gods amongst the crowd too, manifested as strange creatures: fauns, faeries and various forest sprites.

Olu the Enlightened said that there are deities on our side. The side of fear has more, but we're not alone.

In front of the crowd, gods and humans both, I see Cruz. He's standing proudly, unafraid to take the first hit should the Crows try to attack. He's not there to prove himself, or to fit in with some gang. He's there because he's alive, and he wants to do what's right.

I hear a shrieking sound, and I look to the far horizon and see a strange, ominous mist lurking in the distance: the spirits freed from Pandora's jar. I hold the gem I found at the base of her jar tightly, and their shrieking gets a little quieter.

The spirits of Pandora's jar are for another day. Still, if she decides to fulfill her threat of haunting Cruz's dreams, I'll be there to stop her.

I hear a bellowing from the ocean, and I turn to see that more spirits have joined our side. I see a herd of centaurs and what appears to be a griffin, and they're fighting Scylla, driving her flailing heads back into the ocean. One hulking creature the size of a building is roaring particularly loudly, and when it moves its head I can see the moonlight glinting off of its single eye.

I'll be there to stop Pandora, the Crows, and anyone else, and I won't be alone. Whatever happens from this day forward, I won't be alone.

/***/

Zeus's lightning continues crashing behind me, and the storm continues to grow. Sami stomps his cloven feet and bleats defiantly, and then Pan joins in. Their single horns glow brilliantly, and they start beckoning the crowd to start yelling in support. The crowd does just that, and I look around to see lights on the highway: a seemingly endless train of cars are coming to our side.

Retjar scowls and Ulo shirks backwards, but I know there's one more thing yet to accomplish. I can't afford to savor the moment again, so I walk to the vehicle's trunk and quickly enter the code: 8128.

A perfect number, a number that is equal to the sum of its divisors.

The number 8128 has no apparent value in and of itself, but it does represent one of Plato's immutable *ideas*. Unchanging, eternal, indestructible. Empires might rise and fall, the gods might engage in a civil war, but *8128* will still be a perfect number. Nothing can change that, and that's why I picked this message. I knew they were going to erase my memory, so I picked an idea that they couldn't figure out, and more importantly, that they could never destroy.

They couldn't erase this idea. They couldn't erase this truth.

The trunk opens and light fills the sky, just as strong as my father Zeus' lightning. It might even be stronger, because it's persistent. Everyone around stops and takes notice, and from this trunk emerges Prometheus, thrice my height, with skin pure black, darker than the night above.

He is here, released from this strange prison, and he gazes upon the flock of humans that he so adores. Though I can't see the features of his face due to the light, I think he might be smiling.

I situate myself perpendicular to the ocean so that Poseidon, the Crows and Zeus might all hear me, with no room for misinterpretation.

"These are my people," I say, pointing to the crowd. "They are not my *worshippers*, because in this new age such a concept will become unnecessary. They are mine, and I am theirs, and this is the First Party of the new world."

The lightning crashes again, and I can hear Scylla hissing from the ocean, flailing her heads in anger onto the beach. The one-eyed creature the size of a building responds by roaring and beating her backwards until she retreats. I locate Hermes' gold, winged helmet in the sky and address him, though I speak so that everyone present can hear me.

"Send a message to every god, spirit, angel and demon on this earth," I say. "That the true era of humanity has begun. From this point forward, this world will have no limitations."

I walk over to the car, open the back door and pull out a bottle of wine. I don't pay attention to the vintage, because that's of little importance at a time such as this. Wine is an idea in and of itself, and I am going to partake in it. I see that Pan is doing the same, and is passing out the ambrosian wine to all assembled.

I wait for everyone to fill their cup, and then uncork my bottle and raise it to the sky. Sami bleats again, and the crowd raises their glasses. Even the creatures on the beach take a break from fighting Scylla, turn around and begin bellowing in support.

I stand beside the Titan I freed, Dabron's counterpart. I look at him and know that we'll get it right this time. *Whatever the outcome, it's worth the cost. But we'll get it right. I know this.*

I raise my bottle and prepare to toast all those around, the first toast of the new world.

"My name is Dionysus, god of the grape, god of wine and freer of Prometheus," I say. "And this is *our* party now."

A TALE OF THE HIGHWAY

Partial Bibliography

Here is a partial list of the works that have influenced this book in one way or another, either for factual basis, thoughts, or style.

- Alighieri, Dante, and Sean O'Brien. Inferno. London: Picador, 2006.
- Ballingrud, Nathan. North American Lake Monsters: Stories.
- Clarke, Arthur C., and Stanley Kubrick. 2001: A Space Odyssey. New York: New American Library, 1968.
- Dorst, Doug, and JJ Abrams. S. Canongate, 2013.
- Finlayson, Clive. The Humans Who Went Extinct: Why Neanderthals Died out and We Survived. Oxford: Oxford University Press, 2009.
- Gaarder, Jostein. Sophie's World: A Novel about the History of Philosophy. New York: Farrar, Straus and Giroux, 1994.
- Hawkins, Paula. The Girl on the Train.
- Ligotti, Thomas. Teatro Grottesco. London: Virgin Books, 2008.
- Neff, Douglas. Dante's Inferno In Modern English. Cork: BookBaby, 2011.
- Wade, Nicholas. Before the dawn: recovering the lost history of our ancestors. New York: Penguin Press, 2006.
- The movie *Locke*
- The TV Series *True Detective*
- The Wine Writings of Ed McCarthy and Mary Ewing-Mulligan
- The band *A Pale Horse Named Death*, in particular their songs *Dead of Winter* and *When the Crows Descend Upon You*
- The band Steel Panther

It's always a partial bibliography with these things. I am sure I forgot something or someone. If I forgot a work, I hope to add it to further editions.

A TALE OF THE HIGHWAY

ABOUT THE AUTHOR

Jonathan Maas is a writer living in Los Angeles. He writes during his bus ride to and from work, and owes much of this novel to the traffic on the 405. He is a fan of all types of literature, with his favorite writers being Cormac McCarthy, Sherman Alexie, Bernard Malamud, Tom Wolfe, and Stephen King.

Photo courtesy of Dustin Hamano

Other works by Jonathan Maas:

The Dog That Laid Eggs
Flare
Spanners – *The Fountain of Youth*
City of Gods – *Hellenica*

This book was edited by the inimitable Patty Smith. You can find her at www.foolproofcopyedit.com.

The cover art is by Manthos Lappas.

Cover design is by Danny Rapaport.

A TALE OF THE HIGHWAY

"The Crows' Gethsemane"

by Jonathan Maas

Made in the USA
San Bernardino, CA
13 April 2017